To John, of course.

Acknowledgments

Sincere thanks to Aileen Wright for creating the painting for the book's cover, the original of which is displayed proudly in my house. Special thanks to Andy Johnson for the map of Blackman's Moor.

Many thanks to my husband John for reading so many versions of this novel and for his unfailing enthusiasm and constructive criticism. Thank you very much to John Cupper, Janet Rose and Aileen Wright for reading the novel and for their suggestions (all of which were taken). Sincerest thanks to Andy and Karen Johnson who proof-read and copy-edited the whole manuscript – any mistakes are solely my responsibility and are due to my inveterate text-fiddling.

Author's Note

Please note that the characters in my novel 'Set You Free' are entirely imaginary and not based on any person, living or dead. No similarity is intended either in speech, appearance, personality, deed/profession or lifestyle. Any similarities that exist are entirely coincidental and inadvertent.

The locations in the book are also imaginary. For example, I know there are a number of places in the UK called Stourton but the Stourton in this book is fictitious.

However, Blackman's Moor does bear a fair resemblance to a place I knew in the past although it was never under threat in the way that I suggest in this novel. Indeed, I am happy to report it is a protected site and much loved.

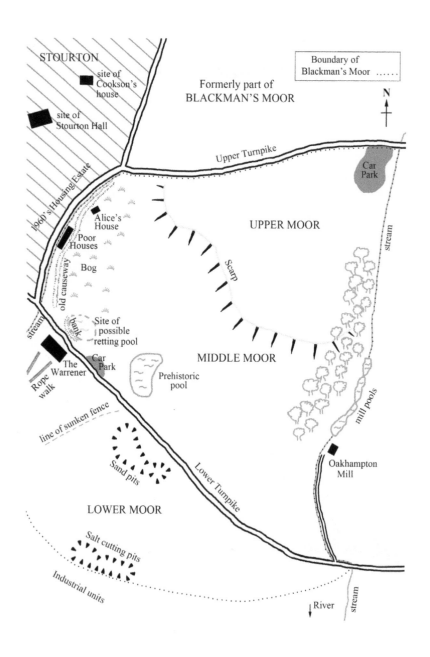

STOURTON

■ site of
Cookson's
house

■ site of
Stourton Hall

Formerly part of
BLACKMAN'S MOOR

Boundary of
Blackman's Moor ......

N

Upper Turnpike

Car
Park

1960's Housing Estate

■ Alice's
House

■ Poor
Houses

Bog

UPPER MOOR

Scarp

old causeway

bank

Site of
possible
retting pool

stream

stream

■ The
Warrener

Car
Park

Prehistoric
pool

MIDDLE MOOR

mill pools

Rope
walk

line of sunken fence

Sand pits

Lower Turnpike

■ Oakhampton
Mill

LOWER MOOR

Salt cutting pits

Industrial units

↓ River

stream

Chapter One

'Blackman's Moor is a waste of 500 acres, 10 roods and 20 perches in total that lieth in the manor of Stourton. On its western side are moorish grounds and to its east and middle ground it is but dry and barren land. Only to its northern extent doth it have any promise of tillage'.
Surveyor's Report of September 1778

This strange tale began thirty-five years ago in late October 1985. I was newly qualified with a degree from a local university and no prospects of a permanent job in my specialised field, as some acquaintances liked to point out. It was in the middle of one of the all too familiar economic recessions. I read, decades later, of a 'mid-1980s boom in western economies'. A boom? Really? Not if you were an inhabitant of a Midlands industrial town. The 'forgotten land' we liked to call it, where industries and small business ℰↃ collapsed like plague victims, and the government created endless job schemes under the Manpower Service Commission and its ilk. Which is why I was about to start a placement at the County Council with the only other Manpower employee on this particular scheme, one Hugh Winfield.

Mr. Winfield. The name suggested a stout, ageing man, possibly a retired bank official, with a balding head and spectacles. Thus, when I opened the door into a windowless office which was not much bigger than a box room, I was surprised to see a man in his mid-thirties sitting hunched over a computer, stabbing at the keyboard.

I fought the urge to say 'Mr Winfield, I presume?' But I did ask 'Are you Hugh Winfield?'

'Do you know how to work these damn things?' he demanded, looking straight at me.

'What do you want to do?' I set my coat on the only empty chair.

'I want to open a program to write something. What's wrong with paper and pen?' he snorted. 'They've served mankind for thousands of years, so I'm told.'

I moved towards the keyboard. 'May I?' I pointed to the chair.

He moved out of the seat. I sat and, after a few clicks, brought up a text file.

I heard a short '*Humm!*' behind me.

'I'm Charlotte, by the way.' I said, extending my hand. 'The Manpower placement.'

For a moment he frowned, then shook my hand. 'I'm Hugh Winfield, the other one.'

Winfield was a striking-looking man – the word 'well-formed' came into my mind. A symmetrical profile, handsome in its conventionality, stared at the screen – he was slim, clean-shaven and had straight light brown hair which was rather dishevelled, as though he had been raking his hands through it in exasperation. He was dressed in a hooded sweatshirt, faded jeans and scuffed trainers. Certainly no bank official. Turning, he scanned me briefly, and with little interest.

'We have funding for a year and, if we play our cards right, Kiddo, we might get another year's.'

Kiddo?

I smiled in reply.

'Look, I don't know about the niceties of office-life,' he said. 'So I'm going to be upfront with you. I took this job (a) because I need the money, (b) I want to keep Blackman's Moor as it is, and (c) I want to stop that developer blitzing yet another site. So you and I need to get researching and find every damn reason to knock these...um...*people* back.' He stopped, waiting for a response.

'I'm totally with you on that one. Blackman's Moor is an extraordinary place.'

He leaned back in his chair. 'Good. Give me your background.'

'I recently graduated with an ecology and land-use degree, and my dissertation was on the land-use history of another site, which is why I applied for this. And I'm married and--'

'Bit young aren't you?' he interrupted.

I shrugged.

'Any reason?'

'Probably the same reason you married,' I said, surprised.

He smiled to himself.

'Right then, we seem to be on the same side,' he said. 'And call me Hugh. Can't stand this Mr Winfield stuff.'

The door banged open and a thin man in a suit walked in. 'I'm Smith,' he announced. 'From Planning.'

Hugh looked suitably unimpressed.

'Just come to see what we tax payers are funding,' Smith said.

'We're looking into the history and natural history-' I began.

Smith wheeled round and stared at me as though he had only just noticed me. He had receding black hair, large ears and a noticeable over-bite.

'Oh are you *really?*' he said, and, as suddenly as he arrived, walked out again. '*Amazing* what this council spends our money on!' were the words that floated back to us.

Hugh mumbled something under his breath.

'I take it that's a definite vote of non-approval,' I said, leaning against the desk as Hugh thumped away at the keyboard.

'Oh Mr Smith!' he said, then stopped short, and his expression closed in.

Over the next few days we drove around in Hugh's ailing estate car, visiting the County Council's handful of nature reserves. It was sunny and felt almost like high summer, except the shadows were long and the sun rested low in the sky, as though it was a late July evening.

We were jolting up a rough sandy track to the side of Blackman's Moor when I asked. 'So what about your background?'

Hugh shot me a look which bade me be quiet.

'Well, you asked me about mine.'

'I don't have to answer your questions,' he said, looking straight ahead as he fought with the steering wheel.

'That's not very fair, is it?' I heard the spoilt child's tone in my voice and winced.

He slowed the car, seemed to think for a moment, then said. 'We used to run a bookshop on Stourton High Street, which we had to shut because the trade fell off, so now my partner, Craig Lyle, sends out book catalogues drawn up on an Amstrad. That enough for you?'

Alice Heath heard the crunch of twigs behind her. She always liked this part of the day: the early morning chores were done and she had a moment to think about other things than merely surviving. She tucked a loose hank of black hair behind her ear and strained to see who was coming around the fat hazel coppice. A strangely-clad figure emerged. For a moment Alice Heath stepped back into the shadow of the cottage, then thought better of it and strode out. A girl in strange clothing visibly jumped and her hand flew to her mouth. Alice Heath peered at her more carefully. The visitor was a young-looking wench, small of stature and bird-like, with long dark hair which was held back in a decorative clip. Yet she wore the trousers of a man and some sort of bright, shiny over garment.

'And who are you?' she asked.

4

The young woman stood there, holding a clipboard to her chest.

'I'm Charlotte and I'm from the Council, I – Oh! I didn't realise there was a cottage here!'

Alice Heath pulled a face. 'Been 'ere since the last century. Byrd Cottage, one of me kin who owned it,' she added, narrowing her eyes. 'What council you from?'

'I'm on a Manpower placement with the County Council.'

'The what?' She looked perplexed. 'You ain't from the Commissioners are you?'

'What Commissioners?'

'Like you don't know.' She shook her head and began walking back into the cottage......

*

...... I had been surprised by seeing anyone there and especially finding this house, so I called after her, 'Would you mind if I looked around?'

'Why?'

'This is just the sort of place I was hoping to find,' I said, wishing the woman would stop retreating.

'Why?' The woman's eyes narrowed.

'Because this is what we need to find, to save this place,' I explained. 'Did you say it was built in the last century?' I was aware of the growing urgency in my voice.

The woman shrugged. 'Some four score and ten years, they says.'

I pursed my lips. 'So that would make it about 90 years old. It looks a lot older than that.'

'If you say so, Miss.' She stood by the low front door (the only door as it turned out), her arms folded across her chest. She was dressed in long, rather dirty skirts and an over-tunic of some sort, all dark colours. At her neck was an off-white cotton scarf. She sniffed, then wiped her nose with a quick movement on the back of her hand.

She went to speak, then hesitated.

'Yes?' I said.

'You says you want to save this place?'

'Of course, from that big developer who wants to-'

'I know all about *him*!' she snorted. 'And you could help?' She looked me up and down. 'How do I know you ain't from the Commissioners?'

I felt my bottom lip jut out a fraction. 'You can trust me, Mrs-'

'Widow Heath'

'Willow Heath?'

'Widow' she annunciated carefully, revealing several missing side teeth.

'I'm sorry.'

She sighed. 'So what do you want to see?' she asked, with a flick of her head to the cottage.

'Just a short walk around. Take a few notes, if that's okay?'

'What?'

'If that's acceptable to you.'

'Ain't much to see, but you can come in.'

I stepped over the threshold and stopped. The interior was surprisingly warm and clean.

'Just done me chores,' said Widow Heath. There was a small inglenook in the far gable wall where a soot-blackened, three-legged pot was steaming away over a fire suspended by a pot-crane, which jutted out from the side wall.

'Wow! You don't see these that often!' I marvelled. Widow Heath came up and stared into the grate.

'What you talking about?' she asked.

'The old cooking equipment,' I said. 'I've never seen them in use before!'

She gave a short '*Huh*' and added as an aside. 'Your type probably ain't.'

The interior was like the replicas you see in living museums. A slate-flagged floor which Widow Heath was clearly proud of. The flags were rather roughly shaped and of differing sizes but were swept clean to a near shining finish. The walls were

6

coloured with a thin dun-yellow coating. Here and there were small areas of missing plaster which gave a hint of rather rough stone walling beneath. Bunches of dried herbs hung from the rafters, and, at the other end of the room, was a roughly hewn ladder disappearing into the plastered ceiling.

'Oh a mezzanine!' I exclaimed.

Widow Heath looked at me as if I was unhinged. 'A *what?*' she demanded.

As I drove back to the office later that day, I considered what Hugh had told me about the bookshop. My husband Chris and I had moved to a fairly new housing estate on the edge of Stourton several months ago, and I recalled a conversation I had had with an older lady who lived by us. I had said, in passing, that I loved bookshops, how, wherever we went - on days out, or on holiday - I had to find one. Chris joked I had invisible antennae on my head for such things.

'What a shame,' the lady had said. 'There used to be a new and second-hand bookshop in Stourton High Street run by two men. Craig Lyle and Hugh Winfield – you may know them?'

'No. We only moved into the area last July.'

'The shop shut down last April, so you've only just missed it. What a pity.'

'Oh no...'

'It was a jolly nice place too, had very good stock. I used it a great deal.'

'The recession, I expect,' I'd said.

She had shaken her head sadly at that. 'No. It was as a result of a vicious hate campaign run by a woman called Hermione Mere, the big property developer's wife. It was an absolutely shameful attack.'

I thought about what Hugh had said and wondered how this ball of anger and energy had been able to sit still for long enough to run a shop. And then I wondered what exactly had happened, and why?

Hermione Mere stared down at the dial on her tread mill. Why the hell was she running on this bloody thing for anyway? She peered around her gym – *her* gym – and a smirk played around her expertly-coloured lips. She had the best equipment. It certainly cost enough - she made sure of that. However, at odd moments like this, she wondered whether pounding on this thing in this lonely opulence was - honestly - what she meant when she described her gilded life to her friends, one or two of whom still had the decency to show a modicum of interest. She knew, as they did, in a few years' time there would be the inevitable face-lifts and breast augmentations with the purpose of keeping her husband's interest, while a new decade of young women would emerge, spring-like, nubile and perfect. She gave an involuntary shiver, popped another of her slimming pills and turned up the speed of the machine.

Rowland Mere was driving his Range Rover along the top of Blackman's Moor, thinking of how he could build a whole estate of executive houses on this dreary piece of scrub land. Stopping the car, he surveyed the heathery expanse before him, working out how many houses and yards he could get into the space, and the approximate net profit he could make. It would be a lot. Rolling his eyes, he smiled. He liked using the American word for gardens: 'yards'. It made him sound cool, as though he had travelled all over the world, when in fact he had stayed at a big theme park in Orlando with the children and Hermione, and all he could remember were the splitting hangover headaches, the sunburn, and the kids whining on about having the next bunch of over-priced plastic toys. Ditto some island near Greece. Mere also liked using the phrase 'parking lot' for car parks when he was talking to clients, to which he would then add 'Whoops, spending too much time in the States...! I meant car park, of course.' And he'd laugh a little, and most of his clients would stare at him blankly.

Mere had had an expensive education in a minor public school in the Midlands. 'If your old man has the money, they'll take you, that's democracy of a sort!' he was keen on saying, but stopped that when one of his puce-faced friends had called him a Bloody Commie.

Driving back home, he parked outside his brick, porticoed house. He had grubbed out a coppice and ploughed up an old pasture to build this place, and now there was an extensive gravel driveway sweeping round, with parking for a fleet of cars. Around the back an emerald-green lawn stretched out, surrounded by expensive board fencing. If he were truthful, he would have said the lawn looked artificial, but it was not Mere's way to entertain any self-doubt. He slammed the front door – a thick oak door, the real thing – and saw his wife flicking through a magazine in the lounge.

'And what have you been doing all day, Herm?' he asked, slumping down in one of the armchairs.

'I do wish you'd stop calling me that!' she snapped, glaring at him. "You make me sound like a hermaphrodite.'

'Have you had a good day?' he tried again, saying the words slowly.

'It's been all right.'

She frowned. What had she actually done? She'd given the cleaner the list of chores; the gardener his; gone into town and had her nails done; booked an appointment for her hair; picked up a few things from the supermarket; bought another statement necklace, and then come home. The kids were back at prep school and away until the Christmas holidays so she had spent most of the rest of day on the phone to her friends. Had she really spent that long talking...? No wonder she was so exhausted.

Mere looked at her. She was gorgeous to look at, but, hell, she was dumb. Only recently at the County Fair dinner when one of his acquaintances, Alex, had brought up the subject of unemployment and said how there was work if people were prepared to shovel the proverbial shit, as he put it, and that the jobless were merely idle losers who did not want to work, adding 'Let them eat cake, she said!' At this Hermione had nodded and said with wide-eyed levity, 'Oh yes, Mrs Thatcher always says such marvellous things, doesn't she?' Alex's eyes had bulged as he choked on his pint.

Hermione had asked Mere about this on their way back home and he explained it to her. Mere's mother had often asked what was the point of educating the working class when they were all going to end up working in factories or as cleaners, or, more likely, be on the dole, and Mere's father had looked at his wife the way Rowland looked at Hermione now. She had had a private education at an obscure girls' school but to little avail it seemed.

'Guess what I heard today from Paul Smith?' Mere said.

'Row, how on earth am I supposed to guess anything about your day?' She put the magazine down.

'I found out that that Hugh Winfield character of the Stourton bookshop is on a Manpower Scheme,' Mere continued. 'Looking into the history of Blackman's Moor with some student-type with the idea of writing a book, or something.'

'*And?*'

'Doesn't it strike you that Winfield may just have an axe to grind with you, through me? That it's rather a coincidence that he's found a job working on Blackman's Moor?'

'Why the hell is a history guide – Women's Institute style - of any concern to you?'

'Winfield's also pretty hot on the natural history side, so Paul Smith tells me. What happens if he finds something rare – a worm or something – and it buggers up my plans?'

Hermione looked at her magazine. 'I don't think there's much chance of that. Blackman's Moor's a dump and the quicker it's built on, the better.' She settled back, and Mere knew he would have to make his own cup of coffee.

The axe-to-grind had begun a year or so ago, when an article in one of her red-topped daily newspapers had made

Hermione stop, read it intensely, and then dig out one her popular gossip magazines from the rack by the side of her armchair. There it was: 'AIDS the Next Biggest Killer' and underneath reports of how men were dying in London, and how this was a Gay Plague, but it could be transmitted to heterosexuals. Hermione was unused to the sensation of fear, but she sat bolt upright at that. The papers said scientists were not exactly sure if the virus could be transmitted and caught by even the most casual social interactions. Hermione had stared ahead, target-eyed. So did that mean you could be walking around the supermarket, and, if a homosexual had just touched an item and left the virus on it, and then you picked up that item and put in your trolley, you could catch it...? How the hell could she have been so unconcerned about it before? She read the newspaper article again. There it was: gay men dropping like flies on the west coast of the States and in London. And what about all the other towns and cities in Britain? There were two homosexual men running that bookshop in Stourton... Dots of sweat prickled on her forehead.

Hadn't she been in the supermarket behind the blonde, long-haired man recently? Hadn't she picked up a carton of milk after he'd been there? Could she have picked up one he had just touched? Had she not pushed the same door open into the shop, walked up the same aisles, breathed the same air? The newspapers said it was thought contamination came about through exchange of bodily fluids (the phrase made her want to swill her mouth out with mouthwash) but that was not what this article was implying. It was much worse. She got up and, walking into her pristine kitchen, scrubbed her hands, dried them, scrubbed them again. She looked at her cutlery, gleaming in the drawers, and opened the kitchen unit doors and examined her shining bone-china cups and saucers and mugs, and thought: what happens if the virus can stay alive on these things and then the children pick them up? She would have a word with her cleaner – a solid middle-aged woman who lived in one of the rented bungalows on the other side of Stourton – and ask her advice. She would also ask her to wash her hands thoroughly as soon as she came into the house and use rubber gloves everywhere from now on. Why had the danger of this virus never really occurred to her before? She had bought her kids books from that bookshop in Stourton High Street and seen those two men together. There had been talk they were a couple of homosexuals but she had not taken much notice until she'd heard them laughing loudly together. Then she had muttered something under her breath and stalked out of the shop. But that had been that. Why hadn't the danger occurred to her then?

Later that day she rang up one of her friends. Ally was a bit of a socialite and Hermione liked to be seen with her; only in quieter moments did she think Ally actually never contacted her, an uncomfortable thought which she dismissed quickly. They discussed this Gay Plague thing and Ally gave a little delighted laugh when Hermione discussed a poster campaign, after she blurted out all her fears of infection and risk. Then she rang another friend, Tammy, who agreed something should be done, especially when kids could be exposed to this virus. Thus, the campaign started. It was called 'Mothers Against the Gay Plague' and phones rang, lighting up in homes like little emergency beacons. Hermione and Tammy suggested the enormity of the threat and implied to the listeners that no one really knew how the virus spread.

They called a meeting at the local Community Centre and Hermione gave a sobbing performance of what it felt like walking around the supermarket behind that homosexual man from the bookshop 'You know the one with the untidy blonde hair and the biker's jacket, and, ladies, that's the problem, he looks so normal, so male-' 'In a rough-trade sort of way,' one of the audience called out. 'Which just goes to show,' said Hermione 'You can never tell who's carrying what!' She had then asked the question 'If any of them touched something that had been in contact with an AIDs sufferer, how likely was it that they would be infected too, and then what about our children?' The audience had recoiled into themselves, looked wide-eyed at their neighbours, and then the talking quickened. What if we produced a leaflet, posted it to the houses near the bookshop and perhaps put a few up on telegraph poles and in windows? It was only being responsible. Being community-minded.

Who had a computer with a printer? Several hands shot up. Who knew how to design a poster on a computer? No hands. They agreed to a meeting in the next week in the same Community Centre with suggestions, and, in the interim, would get their families to show them how to use the computers so they could produce *Media*.

Hermione was almost loathe to admit it, but she enjoyed the next days, meeting up with concerned mothers like herself, sitting in kitchens on new housing estates and going through the same spiel, with increasing embellishment. The women would thank her and the next meeting at the Community Centre was full and buzzing. Posters went up in the neighbourhood asking the residents to think about who might be carrying the virus and whether it was sensible, safe even, to go into shops where known homosexuals operated.

Then the bookshop was mentioned on the posters. 'Who would have thought that in such a nice, clean shop, which has such a bright children's section, the virus could be lurking in the air, on the books, on the door handle, just waiting to swoop?' That poster lasted 24 hours before being removed (by the police, it was said) and an officer turned up on Hermione's doorstep and told her why the posters had been destroyed and why she should not repeat her action. But Hermione was burning with the flame of community righteousness and stared down the officer. She remembered a film she had seen about Joan of Arc and her bodily stance of defiance and she tried to emulate it. Then she recalled: hadn't Joan of Arc been burnt at the stake? So she sagged a little, but still shook her head when the officer asked for her compliance.

The next day a Cease and Desist letter from the local solicitor representing Hugh Winfield and Craig Lyle was served to Hermione at her house, and Rowland had snatched it from her, opened it and called her a 'Stupid f---ing bitch!'

'You'd better pack that in now!' he warned. But Hermione tossed her head and went and phoned Tammy and Ally. They too had been served, and Ally had ended the phone call by asking Hermione not to ring again.

But if the posters were no longer visible, the whispering campaign went on beyond the group who had fermented it. The once buoyant trade fell away from the bookshop, like a lead balloon thrown from the sky. A few people carried on using the place, but the seeds of fear had germinated, and the nicest chose caution and argued with themselves that they would go back when it was all over. The trickle that came through the doors could not pay for the overheads on the place – the rent, the rates, the insurance - and thus, on a freezing, raining April day, the bookshop sign went to 'Closed', the blinds were drawn down and a 'To Let' sign went up a few days later. Someone filled in an 'i' on the sign.

'Happy now, are we?' Rowland had said in a strangely cold voice when he came back from the office that day and found Hermione putting the phone down. Good thing they went quietly. They could have sued the socks off you. Which would, in effect, means me.'

'They're homosexuals Rowland!' Hermione announced. 'They're all promiscuous'.

'From all accounts they're not, and these two are actually well-known in Stourton for their monogamy. Ever heard of that word 'monogamy', Hermione? It means being happy with who you're with, not shagging everything you fancy.'

She stared at him wide-eyed. 'Are you accusing *me*?' she demanded, stabbing her chest.

Mere gave her an odd look. 'Half of those scrubbers you hang out with are probably at it.'

Hermione snorted. 'Now who's being libellous!' she shouted back, and slammed the lounge door with a big, rewarding crash.

I returned to the council building from the Record Office as I needed to sign a form to show what I had been doing with my work time. It had been a disappointing day. On starting the research, I had imagined heaps of easy-to-read documents, all on the subject of Blackman's Moor and nowhere else. Instead, I chased tiny scraps of information in tightly-folded parchment documents, sporting nearly indecipherable, tight handwriting.

It had rained most of the day and I sat on the train back from the city (the council would only reimburse public transport, not petrol money) in the twilight light of that late afternoon, which was quickly turning into a cold, wet night. On reaching the council building, I pushed through the swing doors and went down to our windowless room, 'The Water Closet', Hugh had named it, which held our desks and an old computer (computer singular, you note). 'And you were lucky to get *that*!' Paul Smith had said with obvious resentment when Hugh had asked about getting another.

From the door I could see a long pair of legs in faded blue denims ending in large Rigger boots. As I walked in, I saw the owner was a man sitting with his arms crossed, revealing powerful forearms under the rolled-up sleeves of a heavy, hooded jumper, South American style. However, the most startling thing about him was the mane of blonde hair which fell heavily down his back in ripples, making him look as though he had just dropped in from any one of the heavy metal bands that were so popular. I stared and hoped, against all odds, my reactions were not showing up like illuminated score-boards.

'Hello,' he said in the flat, local accent, and held out a hand. 'I'm Craig Lyle. I'm picking Hugh up... Hugh Winfield.' He smiled up at me, revealing dimples which were rather at odds with his image.

Oh Hugh, you lucky bastard! I thought. I fumbled with my coat.

'I'm Charlotte,' I said, shaking the warm hand. 'I would offer you tea or coffee,' I added quickly. 'But I'm afraid the Council haven't run to that with us.'

Lyle looked up. He had kind, very light blue eyes. On hearing footsteps echoing down the corridor, he looked towards the door and revealed a profile with a straight nose and a strong jawline.

'Sounds like Hugh,' he said. 'Not one for a quiet entrance, is our Hugh'.

I smiled over at him.

'Sorry you had to wait,' Hugh addressed him as he swung in and snatched up his waterproof jacket, one of those good ones with a hood and integral chin protector. 'How's it gone today, Charlotte?' he added as we followed him out. Lyle held back to let me walk in front of him. We walked out into the dark. It was a wild night and the wind and rain whipped Lyle's hair over his face.

'Talk to me in the car,' Hugh said. 'I need to get some forms for you to sign for tomorrow, but I've left them at our house. Then I'll drop you off.'

Lyle opened the passenger door for me but I shook my head. There was no way he was going to get his six foot or so frame into the back seat. Lyle was not large in the sense of fat or even slightly overweight; he was big in a strongly-built way, if the forearms were anything to go by. A shire horse amongst neat polo ponies. He stood several inches taller than Hugh, but something about Hugh made you forget that as soon as you saw it.

He had been on site at Blackman's Moor doing a survey of fungi and it looked as though his day had been as frustrating as mine.

'So what did you find?' I asked, peering through the gap between the front two seats. Lyle's legs were flexed and he had his feet planted uncomfortably under the glove-compartment. I realised he had moved his seat forward, so I would have more leg room.

'Mr Lyle, do move the seat back,' I said. 'I don't need this much leg room,' I addressed the back of his head.

'Mr Lyle?' he said turning round and smiling with pleasure. 'Do call me Craig. The Mr bit makes me sound old and boring.'

'Craig it is then.'

'It means 'rock',' said Hugh for no apparent reason.

'Oh.'

'My name means 'spirit' or 'mind',' Hugh continued. 'What does yours' mean?'

'Feminine form of Charles, something to do with being free, I believe.'

'Hugh's got this 'thing' about words,' said Craig.

I frowned.

'It's called taxonomy, classification,' said Hugh. 'Very useful in the fields of flora and fauna study.'

'Oh...Is it?' I said.

'You did ecology, didn't you?' Hugh asked, looking at me through the rear-view mirror.

'Yes.'

'Well then.'

'I thought the study of words is called etymology.' I said. 'And the meaning of words is semantics. Surely classification/taxonomy is another sub-category, but not to do with meanings.' There was something about Hugh that brought out this school-girl competition in me.

'I suppose you're right...It's a bit late in the year for most fungi,' said Hugh, veering off to yet another topic. 'So I'll join you in the Record Office tomorrow. Do you want to come along?' he asked Craig, and even I could detect the eagerness in his voice.

Craig gave a reluctant shake of his head. 'I'm over at the auction tomorrow.'

'Oh yes. No, you can't miss that.'

We pulled up outside a red-brick Edwardian end-of-terrace. In the twilight it looked welcoming and safe. There was a lamp on in the front living room casting warm amber light. A row of heads were visible above the back of the sofa – three dogs with ears of different forms and at various angles.

'May I present Lyle's Mangy Mongrels,' Hugh said, unlocking the front door to an immediate uproar of yips, barks, and a whirlwind of swishing tails and paws. Three broken-coated lurchers of questionable ancestry bounced in and out of the living room.

'We'll have less of the mangy, thank you,' came Craig's voice.

Along the one side of the hall, cardboard boxes were stacked, in some places nearly touching the ceiling.

'Stock,' Hugh said, and disappeared into a kitchen at the back. Craig held his hand towards the living room. 'After you,' he shouted above the canine cacophony.

I sat in a large armchair by the bay window. A blonde, saluki-type dog with beautifully feathered ears and tail climbed up and curled herself in my lap. I laughed.

'Are you all right with that?' Craig asked, peering with concern over the dog's fluffy ears at me.

'I'm fine.' It occurred me how similar their hair and fur looked. Human and dog look-alikes.

A grey rough-coated lurcher, sprouting fur at all angles and with huge bat-ears, climbed onto his lap as he sat in the armchair close to the sofa.

'This is Bruce,' Craig explained while the dog washed his ear. 'And this one's Angus,' he said, stroking another untidy lurcher with a spectacularly wiry coat and sporting frothy eyebrows and a big canine smile.

I nodded, then noticed a sturdy Victorian desk by the lamp at the back of the room on which stood an Amstrad computer, linked to a dot matrix printer. On the floor were several piles of books.

'And what's this one's name?' I asked, pointing at the dog on my lap.

'Angharad,' he said, and rolled his eyes. 'Hugh gave her a Welsh name – apparently it means 'dearly loved'. But we call her Harry for short.' It came out as 'Arry. Craig widened his eyes, then said, as though noticing I had looked at the desk, 'One day I'll bring it to the window, but it feels a bit better back there for now.'

I looked around the room – it felt secure, with a warm burnt-umber colour to the walls and deep red Persian patterned rugs to the floors. Bookcases filled with irresistible-looking volumes lined all the walls, except by the desk where a large radiator poured out invisible heat. Big plastic dog beds filled with blankets were near this work area and, although the room felt womb-like, its sense of deep loneliness struck me.

Hugh came into the room, mugs of tea in hand. Craig visibly relaxed and let his arm fall over the armchair's side. Hugh sat on the end of the sofa by him, briefly touching the outstretched arm.

'I see you've met The Flossoraptor,' Hugh addressed me.

'Flossoraptor?'

Hugh raised his eyebrows. 'Harry can be a bit of a beast on the lead if she sees dogs she doesn't know. Those ears floss out like a dilophosaurus and she barks like hell.'

'Hugh's just discovered another new word,' Craig added. 'Di-lo-phos-aurus and he's *showing off*!'

Hugh grabbed Craig's large, socked foot and there ensued a bout of good-natured horseplay with said foot, and, for a moment, I sensed they had forgotten I was there.

I decided to visit Blackman's Moor first thing on an early November morning. I had been busy in the archives and wanted to check a couple of places. I had been studying the mid-19th century Tithe Award Map for the area – a huge tablecloth of a thing which took up the entire desk I was working on, and which showed the present extent of Blackman's Moor as 'Waste', while the original top half had the large symmetrical fields of Parliamentary Enclosure. I had been looking for the plot on which Byrd Cottage stood, but there was only a gap and the word 'waste' in smaller writing. Although my husband, Chris, delighted in my rather eccentric spatial understanding and the fact I often held maps the 'wrong' way up (what is wrong with turning the map the way you are going?), I was fairly sure I was searching in the right place on the Tithe Award Map. So before going into The Water Closet that morning, I took a detour and walked towards the boggy flush where the heads of cotton grass nodded over the bog which was now mainly greying and beige-brown as the vegetation died back. Hugh had made some interesting discoveries about the flora concerning this area and was busy in the office writing up a report on the ageing computer.

As I walked along the narrow causeway, which demarcated the bog from a strip of land that formed the western boundary of the moor, the sun came out unexpectedly, flooding everything with apricot-coloured light. For a moment it also seemed very quiet, the sort of quiet that comes after a deep fall of snow. But instead of snow, the sun was shining and I heard the singing and chirping of many birds and I swear I could see motes of gnats, the sort you get dancing in small spirals on summers' evenings. I passed an old sandstone rock which had been roughly hewn into a post and was covered in light bluish-green and grey lichen; where a small piece of the top layer had sloughed off, a dark orange-pink was revealed. It made an excellent marker post. I then passed the rounded hazel coppice and stepped into the Byrd Cottage plot and saw Widow Heath banging a rug out on a line tied between trees. She wheeled around as she saw me, shading her eyes against the low sun shafts.

'You found anything for me then?' she asked, without preamble.

I shrugged, holding my hands out.

'If you ain't got nothing for me, why have you come here?' The last word came out as 'ear'.

I stepped forward, noticing the rug. It was thick and made from twists of cloth in a variety of muted colours. Widow Heath leaned towards it, as though trying to work out what I was actually looking at. She was noticeably taller than me.

'That's a wonderful piece of work', I said, examining it. 'I've only ever seen them in pictures.'

Widow Heath gave something like a '*Ergh?*' sound.

'So beautifully done,' I said, touching it.

'It's only rags,' she said. 'Summat to do of a night'.

I looked around for power lines, but the little plastered cottage was nestled into its cocoon of hazel coppice with not a line or cable in sight.

'How do you work at night with no lights?' I asked.

'By the fire,' she said and the unspoken corollary was 'Stupid'. 'Give us a hand and we'll turn this,' she added, and we flipped the rug, which was surprising heavy and unwieldy.

'If I don't hit it every so often it gets full of muck,' she said, whacking the rug with a strange wide-headed baton thing. With every thud, a small billow of dust puffed out floating like the spirals of gnats. So that's where the motes had come from, I reasoned.

'I'm here, Widow Heath, because I was looking at the Tithe Award and Map entry for this place and I can't find it.'

She turned round, wiping away sweated strands of rough black hair from her forehead. '

'You can call me Alice,' she said. 'And I ain't got no idea of what you're talking about.'

'The Tithe Award Map, you know - '

'I don't know.' She clouted the rug with more wide, swinging blows.

'Oh, well it was a map drawn up in' – and I explained what it was, and why it was, to Alice, and I could tell she had stopped listening about halfway through.

'Well, the thing is, I can't find this cottage on it,' I said, hoping she would turn around.

'Ask the lord of the manor'.

'You mean Rowland Mere?' I giggled at her sarcasm.

'Ferris, ain't it?'

We looked at each other perplexed. Of course, the developer and the actual owner were different people. There was a lot I needed to find out.

'Ferris has been trying to get me out for a long time but I told 'is agent, you find the law documents, and then we'll see.' Alice stared at me and I saw how tired she looked. She was hollowed in the cheeks and the arms that stuck out from the voluminous layers of clothing were stick-thin. 'My kin bought this place, and I'm staying.'

'Do you know why it's not on the Tithe Map?' I asked. I could see we would soon be going around in circles.

'Well, you're the one with the learning, Missy,' Alice said. With that, she turned back to the rag rug and gave in a huge whack, muttering some about wishing this was Ferris' arse (pronounced as 'ass').

I walked back to the car park, passed the hazel coppice stand which obscured the cottage from the bog, back down the gritty sand path, and then onto the dark heather expanse of otherwise sandy ground, which splayed out below the scarp. This was an old river terrace, the river channel of which had, over millennia, moved snake-like across the ground of the lower moor, which latter was cut off from the rest by a main road, formerly the turnpike. The river had subsequently wandered further west and was now hidden behind an untidy gaggle of houses and small industrial units of various ages and tasteless modern designs. Hugh had said something about the sandy scarp being an important place for a type of nesting bird, but my mind was on my travails in the record office and I did not take much in, much less actually remember any detail.

The sun had gone in by the time I reached the car. I had to admit that in this light the area looked bleak and I felt a trickle of fear for the survival of this place. Rain began falling from thick grey skies and dripped onto the washed-out yellows and dun-browns of the dead summer's vegetation which was recoiling back into the ground. Worse still was the worn and stained mattress which had appeared overnight on the side of the main road. An old stainless steel sink had also been dumped and was lying upside down on the thin, fine grass of the lower moor. The mattress looked like a beached whale, half on and half off the road and the sink still had its pipes and hoses attached, like ghoulish metallic entrails. The moor had long been a dumping ground for unwanted household goods and appliances, which was odd as the nearest council tip was only a couple of miles away. Burnt-out cars were a regular feature of the upper moor area and were usually surrounded by a wide area of black singeing, as though their oily entrails had exploded. It was part of my duties to phone in any 'dumping episodes' to the council, and one of their trucks would eventually turn up and haul away the spoils.

The Manpower Scheme placements had - in part - been created in the hope that the moor's profile would be lifted and its wildlife and historical interest might deter at least some from using it as a tip. There were records from 19th century learned society journals which recorded some of the moor's more unusual plant and animal species and it was hoped that we would be able to track these records down and find out if the species still survived. This was to go in tandem with the council's bid to buy Blackman's Moor, the only other interested party being Rowland Mere, the successful property developer.

Chapter Two

'Lord Richard,' said a man, standing up from his desk and giving a small bow.

Richard Ferris took a seat opposite, crossing one elegantly-booted leg over the other.

'You received my communication,' Ferris stated.

Tobias Cookson, a man in his late sixties, took his seat. 'I did.'

'Well?' Ferris opened his eyes in question. Richard Ferris was a young man of exquisitely well-formed stature which was amplified by an expensively tailored cut-away coat which touched stockings of dove grey silk and cloaked a beautifully embroidered waistcoat.

Ferris tapped the top of his cane with his free hand.

'You have to abide by the rule, the Standing Order,' Cookson said.

Ferris gave a dismissive gesture with his hand.

'My dear Lord Richard, one has to be seen to abide by the law.' Cookson's eyes were drawn to the intricate embroidery around the buttonholes of Ferris' waistcoat – it must have taken weeks to produce such fine stitching. 'Indeed to live by it.'

'So I have to display *notices*.' Ferris' words brought his attention back. The spit of displeasure screwed Ferris' handsome features.

'I'm afraid you do,' Cookson said. 'The rule of law must be obeyed.'

Ferris snapped his tricorn on over shining brown hair and stalked out, the little black ribbon flipping up and down comically as he walked.

Who did Cookson think he was? A man of learning, yes; a man holding respect, yes. But in comparison to him, in terms of wealth, Cookson was but small fry. Yet Ferris knew he needed his advice. Since his parents had died, Ferris had gravitated towards him, used him to talk through ideas, as he used to do with his father, to get his opinion, to discuss plans. Indeed, Cookson had been a close friend of his parents and was a well-respected denizen of Stourton, living as he did in an elegant mid-18th century town house in the central square. Ferris had accorded him this standing several years ago, and it seemed the role of substitute father and son had been implicitly accepted by both. Cookson was widely known for his listening ear and sagacious observations. As a man of private means, he was comfortable in his own life, but aware of the plight of those less fortunate than he and it was in his nature to help and to advise.

A manservant stopped and made a little bow as Ferris strode out into the street. Ignoring him, he climbed aboard his carriage and sat back as the vehicle moved on with a sudden start; he kicked the opposite seat violently. An apology floated down. Ferris frowned.

When he had come up with this scheme for enclosing Stourton Waste (he disliked the name Blackman's Moor as this suggested gibbets and danger) he had not envisaged such resistance, especially from the people who were apparently in favour of the process. At every turn men were trying to extract money from him. It had started with his petition for enclosure.

Jamison, an old school friend, and he had had a fine old time, drinking wine and falling around with laughter as they composed the petition:

'I, Richard Ferris, do believe that the Inclosure of this waste will benefit all, from the poorest to the richest. Once inclosed and improved, crops will be grown on land which before was desert and desolate moor. It will

fill the bellies of babes and give their fathers more work and, by degrees, more comfort. By so doing it will reduce the burthen upon the Poor Rates. This can only be for the good and will transform what is wasteland and the haunt of footpads and highwaymen -'

Neither had ever heard of the waste harbouring the latter, but a little drama would not go amiss-

'- into a place of industry and agricultural plenitude.'

Jamison and he had snorted with laughter at this bit. The truth was that Ferris' wife was costing a lot more to keep than he had anticipated, and his gaming at the tables was stretching his purse, therefore an increase in acreage would fix that royally. And he was lord of the manor, lord of that dreary bit of wasteland which seemed to be used exclusively by the lowest classes and their mangy-looking livestock, so he could do as he wanted, could he not? Of course access by the poor would all change when it was enclosed, although he was not sure what he was going to do with the lower half of Stourton Waste. His land agent told him it was a loose, sandy place with a large boggy flush (yes, he did actually use that expression!) to its western side. Perhaps he could leave it for hunting, or something.

The carriage glided to a stop outside the marbled pillars of Stourton Hall, which lay to the west of the town. It was Ferris' main residence and was an ornate, early 18th-century building with a wide, white stuccoed front which contained many windows. The main doors were opened as Ferris stepped down from the carriage. Walking into the hallway, he handed his tricorn and cane mechanically to a servant and entered the drawing room. Georgiana, his wife, was sitting on a couch, looking like a beribboned whale in her silk maternity gown. Another child would be born soon, another son he hoped to keep his line going.

'My dear, what is troubling you?' she asked with genuine concern.

Ferris looked at her. She was certainly beautiful he thought, even in this state. Expensively coiffured blonde hair, a little frame of curls around her pretty, symmetrical face. Her arms, sleeved in the lightest silk, were slim and quite lovely to look at.

'Cookson tells me I have to put up notices of enclosure on the church door every Sunday for the next three weeks in August or September.'

Georgiana gave a smile. 'Rather like banns.'

Ferris thought. 'Yes.'

'Why is that worrying you?'

Ferris scratched his neck. How could he tell his wife that he wanted to push the Enclosure Bill through without notice. Jamison had explained that the fathers of a few of his friends at Cambridge had had the whole enclosure procedure petitioned, bill drawn, read, re-read, then passed in the House of Commons within a couple of months, and the first thing those affected by the enclosures knew was when said paters' men began physically enclosing their plots. The Standing Order had only been brought in a few years ago and now one had to be open and honest, it seemed.

'It give the commoners time to complain - '

'And put forward their concerns,' Georgiana interrupted him.

Ferris stared at her. Was she contradicting him?

'It gives people like that woman at Byrd Cottage the chance to cause trouble, what's her name?'

'Widow Heath.'

'Yes...She's a nuisance. The land agent still cannot get her out.'

'You do know that she lost her husband last year?'

'And how do you know that?' In fact he did know.

She shifted herself awkwardly on her opulent couch. 'My women folk tell me of what happens in the parish.'

'She's a nuisance.'

'And so would you be if you were in financial distress and being threatened by your henchman.'

'Are you arguing with me, Madam?' Ferris stepped back a little, a gesture he realised too late might be taken as weakness, of uncertainty even.

Georgiana continued her appraising look. 'No Richard, I am merely asking you to consider the plight of others.'

Ferris left the room, his hands fisted. Oh the wretched irony! It was Georgiana's kindness that had been one of the qualities he had fallen for, although he would have been loathe to admit it, even to his mother. But kindness over kittens or young children was one thing; consideration about a rough peasant woman was quite another.

Walking across his grounds to the field boundary he looked out towards the edge of the waste. It was definitely going to have to be enclosed. Today it looked bleak and dark, like some crouching, silent thing, deadly and ready to pounce. It needed taming. It was his duty to do that, to bring it into cultivation and make it become productive and fertile. Thinking of Georgiana, he pulled a face. Sometimes he visualised himself as a small boy, standing straight in front of his mother, hands smartly by his sides, being spoken to about the need for gentlemanly behaviour to those less fortunate. Perhaps he should treat her more harshly? To call her 'Madam' a few more times. He could see by the minute twitch in her expression that the word had vexed her. Perhaps...But perhaps not. Shaking his head, he realised he needed her continued approval, however he might want to rebel and posture. 'It's not fair!' Ferris heard the words of his four-year old son. Most of the parishioners could not read their own name, let alone read or understand a legal document. So what was the point of the Standing Order? People would get their dues in the apportionment. If he capitulated to his wife in this, the foundations for strife would be laid. No, the waste must be enclosed; he needed to make a stand.

Chris and I shared an old Ford Escort Mark II which I used when I had to be out in the field but which Chris needed most days for his work at an estate agents office in Stourton. On the non-car days, Hugh picked me up and dropped me off at home, and we mostly used the time to keep each other updated on our findings concerning Blackman's Moor. I noticed that during these journeys he often treated me as one might a slightly annoying younger sister, but during the last day or so he had been oddly quiet as we travelled. This surprised me, as we were working well with each other, and I had asked after Craig a few times. It was as though he was debating something within himself, whether to disclose a secret, so I was not entirely surprised when we were driving back from surveying the moor, and he blurted, seemingly from nowhere

'There were days when Craig could hardly get out of bed he was so down after the shop had to shut.'

'Was this after the hate campaign?' I decided to grasp the nettle.

'So you know about that?'

I nodded.

'All that vicious gossip nearly broke him and he just went into himself....Do you know what really pisses me off,' he said, slamming the gear into third. 'That Craig lost so much confidence. All because of that f--ing Hermione Mere and her revolting little mind.' Hesitating for a moment, he seemed to decide to go further. 'I think the final straw, on top of the mounting debt with that shop, was when two young women came in, pretended to look at cookery books, then clacked up to the counter where Craig was doing the accounts, and one of them stood, bang in front of him, and said straight into his face 'Pity you're a queer. You'd be quite shaggable if you were normal.' Then they screeched with laughter and, as they bolted out of the door, I heard one of them say 'You'd probably catch something from them.' Hugh had not drawn a breath in this delivery.

I swallowed, swilling my mind uselessly for something helpful to say, but all I could manage was 'That's bloody awful. Should never have said those things.'

'Damn right they shouldn't! Craig's one of the kindest, most gentle people I've ever met and he's got more compassion in his little finger than a whole town of those scrubbers. It had only been a few days previously that a woman had come in to pick up a book order wearing disposable gloves. So after that with Craig, I bolted the front door, pulled down the blinds and we just walked away.'

I shook my head.

'We were in arrears with the rent at the shop, so we had to take out a loan to cover it, which is why I'm working on minimum wage doing this.'

'Bloody hell, no wonder you're so angry!' I tried to look at him but he was still staring forward and I could see his knuckles were going white on the steering wheel. There was an uncomfortable silence and the rain started to beat against the windscreen. Hugh flicked on the wipers and their rhythmic motion seemed to calm him.

'Anyway, I heard about these three lurchers that had been tied up and abandoned on Blackman's Moor,' he continued in a quieter voice. 'So I went to the dog pound, paid the fees and took them home. And that's when Craig started to come back. The next morning he was out walking them, even before I'd got out of bed. So you see, I owe those dogs a lot.'

It was a few days later I returned from another sortie at the Record Office. Shaking rain off the sleeves of my outdoor jacket I walked down The Resounding Corridor (my name) to The Water Closet. The door was open wide and I saw Craig leaning with his back against Hugh's desk, arms folded, a surly, low-browed stare directed at a person who was out of sight, but whose voice, higher-pitched with anger, was familiar.

'This isn't a waiting room, you know! You can't just saunter in here and hang around and-'

Paul Smith stopped abruptly as I stepped in.

'Is he yours?' he demanded.

'I'm not sure of your meaning,' I said. I had been reading 18th-century documents all day and I nearly added 'Sir.'

Smith faced Craig who seemed to fill the room. Smith, I noticed, was pressed into the opposing wall.

'Are you this woman's husband?' he continued.

'No,' Craig said, and the unspoken word was 'And?'

'Then why are you here?' Smith pulled himself up; I swear he puffed-out his chest. A thin sheen of sweat was visible on his forehead.

'I'm picking Hugh up and dropping Charlotte off,' Craig replied, giving me a barely perceptible wink.

'Don't these people have cars?'

Craig shrugged. 'There's only one car between us.'

Smith frowned, trying to compute who the 'us' was, and why. Smith's eyes darted to Craig, to me, then back again, before he turned to me and said. 'I will be speaking to your superior about this, young lady.'

'For what exactly?' I asked. 'For being too poor to run two cars?'

'Insolent too! No wonder we have such a high unemployment rate among the young.'

I heard Craig make some guttural noise and decided not to catch his eye.

We heard loud footsteps coming down the corridor. Smith visibly jumped as Hugh swung in.

'Sorry for the delay,' he addressed Craig, and then looked at Smith with evident disdain. For a horrible moment I thought he was going to demand 'And what are *you* doing here?'

'Would you like to explain why we seem to have a taxi driver taking up the room?' Smith demanded.

'Craig's taking me home and dropping Charlotte off.' Hugh's voice was expressionless.

There was silence. Smith went to go but leaned in again before leaving. 'In future, you get your lifts to wait in the car

31

park. This is council property and we do not allow any old Tom, Dick or Harry to wander in as and when they think fit. Do you understand?' Smith's eyes were bulging slightly with exasperation, and I noticed he had large, yellow teeth.

'Understood,' said Hugh. 'Actually his name is Craig!' he called after him.

We waited for the footsteps to recede before relaxing.

'Bloody hell!' I said and realised I had been standing so stiffly my shoulders ached.

'Idiot,' Hugh said, signing the time sheet and handing it to me. 'I've heard all about him. Smith likes to get planning applications for housing estates and developments forced through at unusually high speed. It's the usual stuff: "Building homes for the masses", but most of the developments are for four-and-five-bedroom properties – the sort with double garages and built-in security alarms. Fuck knows how that is supposed to help the masses.'

'Hugh, watch your language,' Craig warned, nodding to me.

'Oh, don't worry about that!' I said. 'With Smith, I get the impression, the greater the potential profit, the greater his help, which would explain why he's so hostile to us.'

Hugh looked at me and grinned. 'Spot on, Kiddo!' he said, and, for a moment, I honestly expected him to pat me on the head.

'Smith's the snake's head, the most visible because he's such an aggressive bastard,' Hugh continued, 'but there are plenty more tucked in the crevices - '

'You want to be careful,' Craig interrupted as we walked out into the rain. 'Keep those back-hander comments between yourselves. If you want to protect the moor, do what you're doing, but stop courting trouble.'

Later that week we had the expected visit in The Water Closet. Jon Blake our supervisor from the Countryside department was in his late thirties, had a friendly face but projected a rather put-upon demeanour. Sitting on the edge of my desk, he gave an awkward smile.

'We had a formal complaint from Paul Smith, from Planning,' he said. 'And I have to follow it up.'

Hugh nodded, and I stared at Blake, waiting for more.

'Strictly off the record,' Blake said. 'Smith is quite hostile to this scheme-'

'We had noticed,' Hugh interrupted.

'-and he's looking for any excuse to get these placements cancelled.'

I felt my face colouring as I realised what we had done.

'In fairness to us,' Hugh said before I could even form my words. 'Smith really has the most belligerent attitude, rude and condescending. And I don't know why he's always lurking around where we are.'

But we all knew. Smith wanted us gone before we found anything to stop development. Therefore, we knew we had to dig deeper, to work harder, to find those things and we had less than a year, probably eight months before the sale of the moor went through.

Blake stood up. 'I do understand what you're saying, believe me, but, as a favour, please don't antagonise him any more.' I saw the strain in Blake's face, and nodded.

When he had gone, Hugh sighed 'I can't stand that Smith character – I'd love to punch his lights out.' I went to interrupt. 'I know, I know,' he said. 'That etiolated prat's not worth a prison sentence. I wish I was like Craig, he handles situations like this, manages them so well.'

But at a cost to himself, I thought. It came unbidden and unwanted into my mind.

The following day found Hugh and I in the Record Office. Hugh was at a loose end as it was raining hard, thus stymying any outside survey work, and he had finished his written reports to date. I looked at him sitting awkwardly in the chair, half-turned, looking as though he was about to bolt – he clearly wanted to be searching the moor for plants, tracks, its mysteries. By contrast I was quite happy to sit in the warm, while the rain spat over the wintering moor miles away.

The Record Office staff had directed us to a stack of boxes which they said might well contain information about Stourton Waste and Blackman's Moor, but it had yet to be looked through and catalogued. Therefore, if we were interested, we could be the first to search the boxes, but would we make a one-line note of the title of each parchment? Bound notebooks were proffered. The senior archivist had told us about this hoard. It had been found in the vestry of Stourton church in the late 19th century by a young scholar who was down from university for the summer. This scholar had been given permission to search through the church for any records or items of historical interest. Being the vicar's nephew, one imagines he had been tasked with that to keep him quiet for several weeks. I could only imagine the young man's delight at uncovering the boxes, which were found in an old cupboard where fold-up tables and brooms were stored. Notes stuck on several boxes in tight copperplate handwriting stated that, after some research, it was established that the boxes had come from a solicitor's office which had shut in Stourton High Street. The building had previously been a notary's office and dwelling in the18th century, if not earlier. Why the papers had ended up in the church vestry could not be ascertained, although I suppose if I had to leave something for safe-keeping, a church might have been my first choice.

I opened the first lid of the cardboard archive box and blinked. It was a researcher's delight. Dozens of folded parchment and paper documents, some with thick, blood-red seals, others tied up with fabric ribbon. I could feel my fingers twitching.

'I wonder when these were last opened?' Hugh said, standing over me and peering into the box. I noticed he was squinting.

'It could be a couple of hundred years.'

Hugh picked one up, put it close to his face and tried to read the writing on the front of a tightly-folded packet.

'Do you need reading glasses?' My voice sounded like an infant school ma'am. 'Is that why you can't sit down and start work?'

Hugh gave me an odd look, then. 'Yes.'

'Where are your glasses?'

'In the car, Miss.'

I joined in the charade. 'Well, go and get them, and no raiding the sweets machine on the way out.'

Hugh grinned stupidly. I tried to recall if he had been wearing reading glasses when typing up reports, but could not remember.

I unfolded a document. It was dated 1750 and dealt with a property of a family called Cookson in Stourton High Street. The text was amazingly fresh, as if it had been written very recently. Thankfully the script was legible in terms of handwriting and I soon realised that it was not relevant to the moor, so reluctantly I folded it back up and made a note of its title in the notebook provided.

I tried to picture where the old house in Stourton had been, but could only visualise the characterless concrete block which housed a recently-opened wine bar and a supermarket which had obliterated the site, above and probably below ground. If the old buildings had been preserved, Stourton would have been a very attractive town, but utility was the standard in this place which had suffered a good deal of architectural mauling by the Brutal School in the 1950s and 1960s – that brave new world, which in Stourton, now lay mildewing and forlorn.

Another packet of documents were bound together. I checked them individually. Some went back to the late 17th century with eccentric handwriting and phonetic spelling, thus in an inventory of household goods were 'cuborts', 'chayers' and 'cofers'. I was engrossed in one, which again had nothing to do with the moor but was still fascinating, when I sensed

Hugh slip into the chair next to me. Picking up a handful of documents, he opened one and stared at it.

'Interesting', he said. 'Mentions Stourton Waste.'

'*What?*' I took the document from his hands and studied it. Hugh was right. In the looped handwriting of a 17th-century parchment the words 'Stourton Waste' emerged. I turned to Hugh. 'I've been searching for weeks and you just walk in and find something within seconds!'

'It's these glasses,' he said. 'They're special fact-finding ones.'

I glanced at him. They were round gold-rimmed spectacles which made him look scholarly and revolutionary. 'They suit you,' I said.

'I look like a nerd.'

'You look fine in them. Stop being so vain.'

Hugh pulled a gurning face, then carried on reading.

'*The Waste is of vast expanse,*' he quoted '*and from it sand, and turves and wood are taken for use by the people. It stretcheth out beyond Stourton, towards Oakhampton near to the south and Mytton to the east, beyond into more fertile lands to the north. But that to the south is but a desert and it is said people of ill repute consort therein.*'

I stared at Hugh and then over at the document. It would have taken an hour or so for me to decipher it. 'Have you done this before?' I asked, my eyes narrowing.

Hugh raised his shoulders, held up his hands. I took the document from him and examined it. There were lines of minuscule handwriting wavering across the parchment. I made out a few words but the rest was like some ancient unknown code.

'Are you pulling my leg?' I continued.

'No... Look.' He stood by my chair pointing out the words, and it was like a fog lifting, as the letters seemed to reshape into coherent words. I sat back.

'I think you're a natural at this, Hugh,' I said. 'A natural.'

There had been an unspoken agreement that we should work separately: Hugh on the fauna and flora side; me on the historic records' side. There was nothing in our contracts to say who did what, merely a general outline.

Hugh was fidgeting in his chair again, gazing over to the windows, clearly wanting to be outside.

'How about if we work down here on days when you can't go out in the field; and on good days I'll help out on the moor with the ID. Did you say Craig was good at photography?

'Yes.'

'How about if he came along and photographed for the presentation and book the council want at the end.'

Hugh brightened immediately. 'I like that idea.' Then he frowned and added in a puzzled tone, almost to himself, 'Why didn't I think of that?'

We spent several hours going through the documents, Hugh reading and then jotting away in his notebook. For a moment I felt just a small curl of – what? Resentment that he did so effortlessly that which I found so hard? Why couldn't I be that good when I so desperately wanted to be? And yet, why should it matter at all?

I stole a look at Hugh's profile, static in concentration as he was now engrossed in another paper. There was no denying it that, although he was conventionally good-looking, there was a strange distance about him, a carapace which kept him apart. It was there in his dealings with everyone we had come into contact with. Only with Craig did his expression soften, his eyes open up from the guarded look they held, as if by default. With everyone else, even in close proximity, he seemed a step or two apart. But it was not surprising, I suppose, considering what had happened with the bookshop. I had not let on that I had heard all the details of Hermione Mere's campaign, although I sensed this distance in him had an older history. Belligerence, maybe, but if I had been in a similar situation as he was in now, could I have carried on with everyday life? I doubted it. Maybe this is one meaning of the word 'courage'? Carrying on in an environment when the average person would have escaped or run away. Carrying on with the existence of everyday life, amidst self-doubt, fear and injustice.

Hugh was in a buoyant mood when we travelled back, in fact he was unusually animated when he summarised what the documents had said about Blackman's Moor. It was originally much larger – at least twice the size, it had people with common rights to take wood, turves, and a few had grazing for a cow or sheep, whilst fewer still had the right to take sand, and also clay from *'the boggy flush that lieth to the west and bounds the waste from enclosed lands.'*

The Record Office was conveniently in the city centre so we caught the train to and fro, and handed the tickets in for reimbursement with the council finance office. Smith had insisted these were presented within 24 hours.

'Why not add, "and only reimbursed if dropped by a private helicopter in the presence of both great aunts and their parents,"' Hugh had sniped. 'But that would be a bit difficult for a moron like Smith to think up.'

Smith had also insisted we came back at the end of each working day if we had been out of the building. There we had to fill out a time-sheet which then had to be stamped by administration, whose offices shut at exactly 5.30pm. Smith must have known that the trains from the city were famously late most of the time, which meant we had to leave an hour earlier than necessary from the Record Office to get the sheets signed in time for that day. I was fairly sure both restrictions were nothing to do with the council or Manpower Service regulations, but were imposed by Smith out of spite; as he was senior in the umbrella department under which we were run, he had taken it upon himself to watch us.

Driving away from the office, we stopped by at Hugh's house for me pick up some flora identification books – Hugh had ones he had used at university.

Craig waved me to sit down as we trailed into the living room, looking up from the desk in the back of the room where he was using the Amstrad. The blond flossy dog, Harry, climbed on to me as soon as I sat down and curled into my lap. Hugh came in with several books and three mugs of tea.

'That'll keep you going, Kiddo,' he said, flopping down in the armchair by Craig.

'So you must have studied biology or something like that at university?' I asked.

'Biological Sciences, and a minor in earth sciences.' Hugh said. 'Craig was doing archaeology. It's where we met. We were both mature students which, in your mid-twenties, is pushing the 'mature' thing a bit, but frankly with all the 18-year-olds, I felt like someone's granddad, until I spotted Craig in the Students' Union bar. And from then on, life got so much better.' Again I was surprised at his openness, wondering where his accustomed distance had gone.

'Had to work on it a bit though,' Hugh continued. 'I even got myself signed up to do a hedge survey near one of the plots they were excavating – a piece of land that was up for development and we were there trying to show it was worth saving – bit like now really – and I would appear, tins of beer in hand at breaks. It took a while, then finally Craig got the message.'

Craig smirked, then coloured slightly.

'We've been together ever since,' Hugh said. 'When we graduated – we got 2:1s, by the way – what did you get?'

'A 2:1'

'We should start The 2:1 Club,' Craig said.

'Yes, regular meetings in The Water Closet,' Hugh replied, and their laughter was loud, and went on for a bit too long. Hugh turned back to me. 'We knew the chances of getting employment together in our fields was remote, to say the least. Then this shop idea came up, and we thought, why not?'

'Do you think you'll get another shop in time?' I asked as Hugh drove me home.

'Not a chance!' he snorted. 'Running a shop has to be one of the most boring things imaginable. No, when we get over all this, we'll find something away from here, out in the open. If you saw the plot our house is on, you'd know what I mean. You've not seen the garden yet, but it's fairly narrow and overlooked by two terraced roads further up the bank. Even in hot weather when we may want to lope around outside, I'm aware there are people a few inches away on the other side of the hedge, as well as all those houses looking down. We're also joined to next door by a wall all along one side of our house. It feels as though we're constantly at a vicar's tea party with all the social niceties. I know we're lucky in that we have good neighbours who have been very supportive, but sometimes it feels as though we're always tip-toeing around, remembering never to be too loud. Craig feels the same way. The only space we've got at the moment is the sky.'

We had been given permission to look through Stourton town museum archives. The museum was housed in a suite of rooms of the ground floor of a concrete civic building and was manned by an array of volunteers. On duty today was a man in his late seventies with grey straight hair (no balding) and wearing the mildly red complexion of a chronic tippler. His eyes lit up when we came in. I had the feeling we were the only visitors so far that day.

'And what can I do for you today?' he asked, getting to his feet. His old blue eyes looked at me with interest.

'We're doing a project on the history of Blackman's Moor and wonder if you have any pictures or records we could see,' I said.

Hugh stepped forward.

'Oh I know you, you're the chappie from the bookshop!' the man announced.

Hugh gave a tight smile.

'We're really looking for the oldest pictures you have to start with.' I interrupted. 'Paintings, sketches...'

The man led us to a set of card index drawers. 'Should be in there. It's a good place to start.' He looked back at Hugh

'I wondered what had happened to you and your friend, the tall guy with the girly hair.'

Hugh winced. There was a pointed silence.

'Very good bookshop though,' the man said. 'Pity it's gone'.

Hugh carried on flicking through the cards with a set expression, his revolutionary glasses perched on his nose. I pretended to busy myself with the index cards a few steps away, my mind not on the search. The old man hovered, then moved back to the reception desk.

Within half an hour we had made good progress and had ordered up three pictures by filling out request forms (Hugh beat me to it) and they were delivered by a silent young man who gave Hugh a hard stare but nodded to me in greeting. I did not return it.

The first two paintings were of some interest, being mid-19th-century pen and ink sketches of the area of the whole moor and heath, but which exaggerated the scale, thus small rises looked like mountainous enclaves, and the river terrace scarp looked as though it should be part of an Arabian wadi. They were interesting in that they were trying to portray the area as dramatic and extraordinary, even though it was just that, but in a more nuanced way.

The third picture quite literally took my breath away. It was an intricate line drawing of the western part of the boggy flush area and, when I looked to the site of Byrd Cottage, my heart gave a skip. There it was, tucked away with hazel coppice stools hiding the front, but with the chimney and the undulating tiled roof clearly visible. The artist had depicted the small pottery roof tiles in painstaking detail. And there to one side was a tall figure holding a stick which went into a barrel, arms raised as she – I knew it was a she – prepared to push down. The artist had got Alice's likeness, even though the figure was depicted in the distance – there the unmistakable tall, lean stance and the layers of clothes with the thin arms protruding.

'Hugh, look!'

Hugh stood next to me and peered at the drawing, stood back, then examined it more closely.

'It's Alice,' I said, and knew it was absolutely so. The pictures was dated 1774. A shiver of fear, delight - whatever it was - flickered through me.

'Alice who?'

'Alice Heath from Byrd Cottage.'

'I don't know who that is.'

I stared at him. Hadn't I told him about meeting the woman? About the cottage? Although how could this be Alice when I had recently spoken to her? My mind reached for a practical solution, an everyday explanation, but none fitted, and, slowly, a realisation began to seep through me like a cold sweat.

'The next time we can get out onto Blackman's,' I said. 'I'll show you the cottage. Oddly it's not on the Tithe Award Map but it is most definitely there, this picture proves it.'

Hugh studied the picture, his brow furrowing in concentration. 'I think we need to show caution,' he said. 'These pictures are artists' interpretations, so I don't think we can say this is definitely this or that. We need to walk around Blackman's with copies of the pictures.'

'It's Alice,' I said, and heard the edge of anger in my voice.

Hugh stepped back. 'All right, Kiddo...you've done a lot more research on this. Maybe we could get permission for Craig to photograph these pictures, if the museum or whichever department it is, is okay about it.'

I accepted the change of direction. 'We'll need Craig to photograph out in the field too on the next sunny day, if he has the time.'

Hugh rang me at home the evening before a sunny November day was forecast to announce that he and Craig would be picking me up at 8.30 the next morning. It was one of Chris' rare days off and, out of politeness, I asked if he could come along too.

'Sure,' came Hugh's voice down the line, but there was the hesitation I had sensed several times before. 'Chris knows about the shop and all that, does he?'

'Yes. he does. And I can assure you he feels as angry as I do about what happened.'

'Just checking, Kiddo,' came a friendlier voice.

It struck me then how much the hate campaign was still wearing away at them. I tried to imagine what it must have been like to have your life discussed like a salacious, red-topped newspaper story, to have people inching away from you because of the lies of someone who does not know you. Bring any danger to children into the question and the poison is bound to take maximum effect. I shook my head at the ripple of irritation at Hugh for showing he still cared about what people thought, that it still mattered to him. But how could it not? There would still be the nudges in supermarkets, the turned heads along footpaths, the blatant pointing. Why the hell didn't they just move away, change their names if they had to, get out of this festering environment?

Hugh answered that as we drove up to the car park on top of Blackman's Moor. Chris had just asked them if they had plans to open a shop anywhere else, even though I had told him that they would not. Yet Chris knew how to open a conversation and suggest we had not been talking about them – it was a polish that I wish I possessed.

'Not a shop,' Hugh said. 'But one day we'll go. At the moment we have so much debt that we need to work it off.'

Again, I was surprised at Hugh's openness.

'You need a good two to three thousand to sell and buy,' Chris agreed. 'When you take solicitors and all the legal stuff into consideration.'

'It's also the stress,' Craig said, turning to speak to us from the passenger seat. 'I don't think either of us can face much more of that at the moment.'

We murmured consent. 'You're right,' Chris replied. 'The amount of times we see people up on the ceiling because of house moves and their amazement at feeling like that. But then we get the serial movers and they seem to thrive on it.'

'Mad,' said Hugh. 'Of course you work in estate agency, don't you.' It was a statement.

'The least boring of a very few options,' Chris said.

'Would you keep your ear to the ground for us.'

'What sort of property?'

'As far away from other human beings as possible,' Hugh said. 'Preferably down a track in the middle of nowhere. Water and electricity optional.'

Chris laughed but I knew Hugh was not joking. 'I'll ask our partners in Wales to keep a look out. You can still find some interesting properties at good prices, especially in mid-Wales, and away from the coasts – if you are prepared to put the work in.'

'Chris, you sound like a television advert,' I said. A quick movement from Craig made me look over towards him and I saw him switch at something in his eye.

We reached the car park and Craig got out, holding his head down so his hair obscured his face and walked around to the boot where he started searching, and for too long. I looked at Chris; he pretended not to notice.

We walked around the moor for what seemed like hours, Hugh pointing things out, Craig photographing at will and becoming more animated with the walk, and then laughing at some truly awful male joke Hugh regaled us with as we walked towards the boggy area.

It was one of the brilliant late November days – a photographer's dream, when the ferns are fiery brown, and the leaves that still hang on the trees are a bright yellow, apricot-orange and all sorts of shades, from russet to beige. The sky was a high-summer's mauve-blue, and the sun was strong, but lying just above the horizon and casting fantastic shadows behind us. In one shadow Craig looked like a man on stilts. Hugh had visibly relaxed as the morning wore on, and he and

Chris were deep in conversation as I turned the corner towards the bog.

The dying vegetation was skeined with a multitude of delicate webs and I called to Craig to photograph them. Joining me, he knelt on one knee and started composing the pictures, and altering the exposure. It was a top of the range camera with exchangeable lenses, and he worked it like a magician. And the place did seem to have a magic about it just then, eerily quiet, with that same silence as after a heavy snowfall.

The longer vegetation in the bog was being drawn back into the ground and the rest of the plants looked dark, dank and frankly a little sinister. I saw Hugh pointing something out to Chris over the heathy area, and more animated conversation. I could always depend on Chris to ease any new social meeting and do it with sincerity. I was fairly sure he had seen what I had with Craig, and he had handled it perfectly.

I felt the sand granules crunch on the narrow path along the odd little causeway as we walked. I passed the old post of sandstone with its greenish verdigris of time, and was just preparing to do a wild flourish to introduce Byrd Cottage when I stopped dead. There was no cottage. The garden was barely distinguishable from the rushes and ferns that grew in this area of the moor. Surely I had not come the wrong way? Frowning, I retraced my steps in my mind. I even went back round the corner to the sandy footpath snaking along its causeway, then turned and walked back past the old sandstone post, over to the fat coppice of hazels and stared. The cottage had gone.

A trickle of sweat ran down my back and prickled over my forehead.

'It's just disappeared,' I said to Craig as he came over to me. 'I don't understand.'

'You all right?' he asked, peering at me. My heart was now thudding in my ears. I nodded, then stared about me.

Without a word Craig strode over to where the cottage had been and began photographing. I looked around. The garden plot was still discernible from the remains of an old dry stone wall which sagged in places and had collapsed in others. The small patches of grass that were visible were of a finer, cropped texture. Possible explanations kept going through my mind – had I become so hopelessly disorientated on other occasions, and there were in fact two places? But no, I knew I was not incompetent with directions, and the sandstone post proved I was in the right place. I shook my head. This meant that the only explanation left was that I had actually seen a ghost and walked into a time warp. But surely that was impossible?

'There's definitely a house plot.' Craig's voice cut into my thoughts. 'Look, you can see there's an outline of an oblong,' he called over, pointing to a sunlit area of fine, dark green turf where the submerged shape of stones stood out like the skeleton hidden below.

Chris and Hugh joined us. I tried to explain what had happened, as I sat on a tree stump, but Chris only laughed. 'Charlotte's not too hot on the old spatial awareness thing, are you, Charlie?' he said almost triumphantly, and I could have thumped him. 'It's the girlies' right and left problem.' My expression stopped the laughter in a second.

'Don't worry, Kiddo,' Hugh said, with unexpected kindness. 'You've obviously taken a wrong turning somewhere.'

'I didn't,' I whispered

Craig emerged from around the back of the house plot. 'There was a house here,' he said. 'A small cottage by the look of it. You can see it in the grass over there where the sun's on it. So Charlotte's technically right.' The others squinted and I could see they were struggling to make it out.

'Craig's an ace with archaeology,' Hugh said. 'If it's there, he spots it.'

'Not all the time,' Craig said. 'But that house plot's pretty clear.'

Chris helped me up.

I walked over to the plot. I looked around, trying to work out how I knew this place but clearly did not know it.

The outgrown remnants of the hazel coppice sprawled about. '*I gives the leaves to me cow as fodder,*' Alice had explained when I said how good the hazel nuts were. I turned to where the house should have been and walked over to where the chimney had been added, and there, under this strangely smooth grass, was the outline of the footprint of the chimney stack. I heard a snap of a twig behind me.

'I can't work out what's happened,' I said, expecting to see one of the others, but no-one was there. I looked back around; they were all talking by the track into the boggy flush. They could not have got there in the split second it had taken me to turn round. My heart thudded thickly in my chest, in my ears and another trickle of sweat meandered down my back. I stepped forward a little way into the hazel and elderberry copse that had grown thickly at the back of the plot. Two more twigs snapped. I jumped violently but then strained to see in the gloom of the tree cover. I could not see anything human, or otherwise. I wanted this to be someone playing a prank on me. Something everyday, humdrum. But there was that odd silence again, insisting on being noted. As I turned to go, I am sure I felt a faint squeeze on my shoulder. I fled.

'Thought we'd go over to the pub for a break,' Chris said, looking at me carefully. 'I think you could do with a sit down.'

I knew I stood there target-eyed, wanting to talk, but mute.

As we walked away, the sun went in so quickly it was as though someone had switched off an enormous cosmic light. We crossed over the main road, Chris held my arm and led me into the deep orange of the bar of the roadside inn called 'The Warrener'.

I drew in my breath and closed my eyes, opened them. I concentrated on the building's interior, tried to focus my mind on what I knew about its history. I had recently found out that the inn, or its forerunner, had been a warrener's cottage at least as far back as the mid-17th century. I looked around, kept forcing myself to focus on the detail. Although various revamps had been carried out (some quite hideous, others more in keeping) I could see old oaken timbers in the ceiling, former roof heights ghosted the gable walls. Inexplicable notches and the outline of plastered beams revealed themselves to confirm there was a shell of an old house hidden beneath.

Craig was at the bar getting the drinks. Hugh and Chris were talking about something but I hardly noticed because my attention had been drawn to the back wall of the room facing our table. I stared into the wall and saw the tell-tale small bulges in the plaster of an old window.

Then I shot back in my chair. A face was forming in the panel. It was Alice's face looking down in an attitude of immense sorrow, her hair half covering her face in blurred and uncertain outline.

Standing, I grabbed Craig's arm as he reached the table.

'*Hey*!' he yelped, and tried to steady the drinks he had been in the process of putting down. 'What's the matter?' He held me by the arm to steady me. It was a powerful grip.

I stared, pointing but the image was disappearing before my eyes. I could hardly get my breath.

'Charlie?' Chris' face peered into mine.

I pointed at the wall, trying to talk.

'Here get this down you, it'll help.' said Hugh passing me a glass.

'There was a face,' I said at last. 'In that wall. There!' I pointed.

'Charlie, you've got to calm down, Love,' Chris said. 'You're shaking.'

'There's definitely an old window in there,' Craig said, smoothing over the plaster with his hand and looking at me, and giving an odd shiver. And somehow I knew he understood who I had just seen.

Chapter Three

Hermione Meer had been at a bit of a loose end since the debacle concerning the two men running that bookshop. The friends she had made during the short campaign had gone, almost as soon as they heard about the Cease and Desist letters. Some women even had the nerve to cross over the road when they saw her in Stourton High Street, which surely was all the wrong way round? She had cast round in her mind for a way to re-establish herself over these types of people to whom, if she were truthful, she would not have even given the time of day, let alone visited them in their boxy housing estate homes, with their vulgar paved parking areas and no gardens...She pulled a face. Rowland had built most of them.

Talking of whom...he was now in greater competition with the County Council to get hold of that area of wasteland, Blackman's Moor, with its regular spoil of discarded fridges, cookers and washing machines. It was a particular problem on the scrappy land of the lower third of that moor where the road sliced that part off from the main area and gave easy access to the lazy sods who dumped the stuff. In recent years the council had started clearing up such eyesores, probably because they were in the process of putting forward a bid to buy the land and wanted to convince the local tax payers, like Rowland, that it would be a good investment. And now Rowland was a main player in buying it. It belonged to some institution she had not heard of, but she realised she could perhaps help with this bid.

Thus, she had recently met Paul Smith at the council offices to talk about how the area would be excellent for housing, implying there would be some financial reward for him. That Rowland would probably build facilities for the community (which she knew he would not). However, Smith had spent most of the interview looking at her legs and glancing furtively at her breasts. It crossed her mind that perhaps she could use her feminine charms on him, but then looked again at the late forties/early fifties Smith, with his receding black (probably dyed) hair, his sallow skin and large ears and thought *Gross! No way!* Rowland would have to do without her help here. There's only so much a wife can be expected to do to help her husband's career, and their bank balance of course, which she had only a vague idea about.

She had recently joined the local Stourton Ladies' Group, which she'd heard was embarking on a campaign to boost the traditional family: the two children, hard-working father, home-maker mother; the clean solid back-bone of what made this country what it was. As she had said at the last meeting it was going too far when a couple of gay men were actually so visible and had been running a business so successfully in a backwater like Stourton. This was not London, for goodness sake. Unfair, when there were decent, family men who had lost their jobs and were having to make do with second and third best. She would mention it again at the next Stourton Ladies' Group meeting, see if they could not make the campaign more attractive to younger women.

However, Hermione was rather deflated when she went to her next meeting. The average age appeared to be about eighty and she had to raise her voice constantly to be heard as half the old dears had forgotten their hearing aids. In truth she found the elderly irritating. They moved around too slowly, talked about boring stuff like the weather and arthritis, and hardly seemed to notice her.

Perhaps she could set up Stourton's Young Mums' Club instead which would focus on Traditional Values. The more she thought about it, the better it sounded. Encourage young mums like herself (she did not have to tell anyone she was the wrong side of thirty-five) to meet up and perhaps .... what? She thought for a moment but could not quite decide what this dynamic group was going to do. Helping out the church was too boring; helping out with animal charities sounded dirty and certainly not headliney enough, and you would probably end up with fleas or nits, or something. So what else was left? The aged (no, for reasons already given); the disabled perhaps (no, that was just going *too* far). She would have to continue to mull it over.

Out of boredom she popped another of her slimming tablets. She liked them. They gave her a buzz as well as keeping her desirably slim, or so she believed.

Rowland Mere sat in his Jag on the Upper Moor car park, parking as close as he could to the scarp edge so he could view the sandy plain below. One day all this will be yours, my old son, he said to himself, lighting a cigar and remembering to open the window and hold the cigar in his hand out of the car. Hermione would go on and on about the smell of smoke otherwise. Looking over this dreary expanse he wondered what all the fuss was about – it was a scruffy piece of wasteland and just ripe for a large executive housing estate.

In his mind he saw the place with mock-Tudor detached and semi-detached properties with their matching single and double garages. He thought having mock-Tudor garages was a nice touch; it might just keep all the historians quiet if he did get this place. In front of these houses would be block paving in herringbone patterns and there did not need to be pavements because the sort of people who would buy these houses would probably drive everywhere, so he could save money on kerbing and all that, just have a different colour in the road demarcating a pedestrian way for anyone to walk along whose car had broken down.

Stretching behind his lovely mock-Tudors would be immaculate lawns surrounded by expensive board fencing, just like he had, and Cotswold stone patios with double-door access to the dining room. Any fill-in areas could be gravelled with Cotswold stone chippings. For the more expensive five- and six-bed houses he could have half-height brick walls built at the front, topped with black mock-Victorian railings tipped with gold-coloured spray to the spikes and finials. Round the back there could be half-brick walls topped with decorative wooden fencing.

The most expensive plots would be up here on the scarp, which had dramatic views over towards the river (as long as you did not look too hard at the industrial units which had infested the edges of the lower bits of wasteland). Rowland Mere liked order, cleanliness and tidiness – nice new plots, nicely matching gardens. What a lovely place this could be...

Puffing on his cigar he looked over towards the boggy sludgy area and wondered how he was going to successfully drain it. Or would they have to build on concrete rafts? Sounded expensive. It would add to the costs, and, although Mere liked to build bright, new houses, he did not like spending too much on the infrastructure. Nobody saw all the underground and hidden stuff, so why bother too much with the detail, why not cut the odd corner or two?

Turning on the Radio (247 Radio One!) he leaned back in his seat. The next minute he sat up as he recognised an imposing figure walking up the scarp with three scruffy-looking lurcher-things in tow. It was that Lyle guy. Looking closer he envied what he saw – long hair being blown back by the wind, and a face which looked as though he was far away in thought. But what sort of bloke goes round with blonde hair down his back like that? Actually, the sort of tall, athletic man who fronts a rock band and pulls chicks and smashes up hotel rooms, and who Mere knew he would never be like. From his late-teens he knew he was going to be of average height, with what is euphemistically called a 'stocky' or 'well built' frame. Knew that he had a round, uninteresting face and boring brown hair. Maybe if he took some exercise he could drop some of the impending middle-age sag (he was only forty years old!) but walking dogs always seemed like a waste of time when you could be doing something in business, and joining a gym just was not his thing, too time-consuming.

Turning the radio up louder, he dismissed the thought and flicked his ash out of the window. Lyle looked around sharply and Mere slumped down and pretended to re-adjust the car radio.

He remembered the first time he had convinced Hermione to visit the bookshop. Their kids were six and seven at the time and their clear lack of reading at home had been remarked on by several prep-school teachers. It had coincided with a memorable occasion when he'd dined with the Chamber of Commerce. After a few drinks, the subject of the book store had come up. A lady said how good it was that Stourton still had a mixed High Street, including such an interesting bookshop and Mere boasted, 'I don't read books. Haven't read one since I left school!' The rather refined wife of the chairman, had turned to him and said in the sweetest voice, 'Yes, dear, it shows.' After that he dropped his favourite boast. It had annoyed him at school when the clever kids had nicknamed him 'Numbskull' and his boast had in some way been a fingers-up to them. Now he saw it had the reverse effect.

Thus on an early September afternoon, he and Hermione had gone into the bookshop and she, focussing like an Exocet missile onto the desk where the two men were working, glided over on her expensive high heels and stopped in front of them. Mere watched as Winfield looked up, bespectacled in professor glasses, and given a customer-greeting smile. She gesticulated, patting the top of her chest a few times, and Winfield had wordlessly pointed to an alcove which turned out to be full of new and second-hand children's books. Hermione sashayed over and said too loudly that her kids weren't having any second-hand rubbish, and Mere had shushed her with a wide-eyed stare. Together they picked out books with the age bands printed on the front and went to the counter where Lyle had taken them and smiled a genuinely warm smile at them both, which reached his eyes and dimpled his cheeks. Hermione had then flourished her credit card and smiled gorgeously at him, her hand subconsciously going back to massage her neck. Winfield handed her the carrier bag and Mere saw how she had given Winfield a little sideways, under-the-eyes, smiley-pout, and he stared back at her without expression. Hermione had then taken Mere's arm and called back as they approached the door. 'See you soon, fellas!'

'Wow!' Hermione had thought. The conventional one, whom Rowland called Winfield, was quite the works! If he got rid of the reading glasses, got contacts, then he would be even better-looking. It must be his shop, he had an 'in control, man-at-the-helm' air about him. Probably owned a chain of stores. That dopey-looking, long-haired man was probably just a low-wage assistant. For a moment she wondered if she could get a few hours there, help with sales. Then she thought, would she be able to get there at a set time week in, week out? Perhaps not then...

Later that afternoon they walked past the shop on their way back to the car park. It was raining and Hermione raised her pavement-filling designer umbrella. As she walked past the windows, she slowed down to tilt her umbrella so she could give a winsome, sexy smile. Then she stopped when she saw that the two men were sitting, facing each other, Winfield having moved his chair round to face the long-haired bloke, who was talking animatedly. Then Winfield threw his head back and laughed. They did not even glance in her direction, being intent on sharing this joke. Then, like some poison, the thought that they were actually laughing about her shot into her mind, and she straightened the umbrella and quickened her pace to catch up with Rowland, giving him her shopping to carry without a word.

That evening and still smarting from this imagined put-down, she sat close to Rowland on the large white leather sofa. Rowland shifted, trying to change channel on the new television with its remote control.

'Row,'

'What?' Rowland did not stop staring at the television, which he was finding impossible to work.

'What do you know about those men in the bookshop?

He shrugged, picking up the instruction manual and flicking through the pages. 'That they run a bookshop,' he said at last.

'Who are they?

'I don't know.'

'Doesn't that Winfield man come to your Chamber of Commerce meetings?'

He put down the remote. 'No, why should he?'

'How many shops does he have?'

Mere shrugged again. 'That's it, as far as I know. They both run it.'

Hermione frowned. 'What do you mean, 'they both run it'?'

'They're partners, or something.'

'You mean business partners?'

Mere gave a guttural laugh. 'Bit more than that, love. They live together.'

Hermione's eyes grew wide with disbelief. 'You mean they're a couple of...*poofs*?'

'Everyone knows that,' said Mere. 'It's no big deal. There's quite a few of them in the business world,' he continued, and was about to add that there had been several at his school, but was cut short when Hermione jumped up, and, going over to the drinks trolley, poured herself a stiff whisky, forgetting of course, that her husband would probably want one too.

I went to bed early on the night I saw Alice's face at The Warrener pub. I had tried to explain to Chris what had happened, what I thought was happening, but this brought only a worried expression, an exhortation to get to bed as I 'looked fit to drop' and the promise to bring me up a hot drink shortly. I went to sleep almost as soon as I had climbed into bed and dreamed of Alice. I was sitting on the oak stump in the neatly-tended garden plot with the cottage in front of me.

'I made you jump, didn't I?' Alice said as she emerged from the cottage and leaned against the wall.

I looked up sharply. I was wondering why this was happening to me, why me, why now?

'I thought it was in bad taste, doing that,' I said. I was surprised at my reaction. Shouldn't I be running around, screaming or shouting? I could see a ghost house and its occupant and that was supernatural, and, by anyone's book, that was frightening. But it felt as though Alice had just got one over on me.

'It weren't.'

'You think appearing in walls is not at all freaky?'

Alice frowned at me. 'What?'

'You appearing in a wall, you don't think that's just plain odd?'

Alice shook her head. 'I was trying to get your attention, Missy.'

'Well, you certainly did that!'

Alice smirked. 'Didn't quite go how I wanted.'

'Why didn't you appear in front of the others, like you did with me?'

She shrugged and scratched the back of her head as though in deep thought. 'Don't know.'

'Are you here all the time?' I had to know.

'Yes....I'm here.'

'Did you see the three men who were with me?'

Alice gave a gappy-toothed smile. 'The long-haired man is nice; he knows I'm here.'

I stared at her. 'Pardon?'

'Might not actually realise it, but I can see he's knowing I'm here.'

I sighed. 'So we're playing games, are we?'

Alice pulled a face. 'What you talking about?'

'Why did you materialise in the pub wall?'

'Pub?'

'*Inn*. The Warrener pub.'

Alice sniffed and wiped her nose with the back of her hand.

'Why there?' I insisted.

'Is that what they calls the place?' she asked.

'Stop changing tack.'

'What?'

'Stop trying to change the subject.'

'Used to be The Royal Oak Coaching Inn,' she said. 'They held the manor courts there.'

'Why is that important to you?'

Alice gave me a measured stare. 'You'll find out...As I said I was trying to get your attention, but you wouldn't see me.'

'It's not a case of wouldn't...couldn't. I heard the twigs cracking and-'

Alice guffawed. 'That were a bit obvious, I warrant you... but you were pushing against me.'

Was I? Did I? 'It would have been much less scary if you had just walked out,' I said.

'I was trying,' said Alice. 'But I couldn't get through.'

'Through what?'

'Don't know. I could see you, but you weren't seeing me. They was blocking me.'

'How?'

'Don't know. The long-haired man is sad.'

I looked over to Alice, cocking my head. 'Do you know why?'

'I seen it.'

'What happened in Stourton with the bookshop?'

Alice nodded. 'I hears the stories when I sees the person. I hates injustice.'

She went into the cottage and came out with a carved wooden bowl which was full with hazel nuts.

'I also eats the nuts,' she said, cracking one with her back teeth. 'Have some.'

I leaned over and took a few, and she pressed a handful at me. 'You needs fattening up,' she said and, going into the cottage, brought out two three-legged stools and we sat against the wall, which had the full sun. It was pleasant to feel its rays, even in their late autumnal guise. We cracked nuts with our teeth and Alice told me about her three daughters, whom she clearly adored, about her husband, who had died of consumption over a year ago. How she had nursed him through weeks of sweated pain and increasing difficulty in getting his breath. How she had left her eldest daughter, Harriet, in charge while she roamed the coppices, heath and moor for herbs to concoct salves and poultices to aid his breathing. How he always held her hand when she sat by him, even on the last night when in the early hours he had silently passed over, and his thin hand had fallen from hers.

She had sat in the flickering rushlight of the room for ages, in the warmth she always made sure he had, stoking the fire as soon as the first damp bite of evening air had come, and which would have set him off coughing painfully. Now she stared into the fire and wondered how on earth she was going to carry on without him. They had met as children and grown into adults together, and now he was gone and she could not imagine her life without him. Alice had said all this in a quiet, almost emotionless voice and only once did I see her eyes get teared, but she retreated from that quickly.

'But I had to get back for the childer. And so, after I'd laid him out, I went up into the sleeping loft, woke up the girls and told them. My eldest went for Cookson and he came over at first light and we got him ready. Cookson's a good man and said not to worry about burying costs - he'd see to it.'

The sun was sliding down towards the horizon, casting long shadows over the plot, making the cottage glow with a gloriously wheaten colour.

'This was our only home,' Alice said, looking round. 'And I love it very much.'

'I know,' I said, and knew fully what I had to do, and why.

As I got up to leave, she tapped me on the arm. 'Tell the long-haired man not to be sad; he's deeply loved, that's clear to see.'

I had woken from the dream with that sense of falling off a cliff which made me sit bolt upright, my heart racing. I stared into the thick black of the room, so dense it felt oppressive and matt – it was before the dawn. I felt Chris was asleep on his side, only the red numerals of the clock alarm were visible. I drifted back down but my heart began banging in my chest, in my ears, and, as the grey light of morning seeped into the room, I got up, dressed and, ten minutes later, leaving a note for Chris telling him that I would be back before he needed the car for work, I left the house and drove to Blackman's Moor.

Rounding the corner, past the old sandstone post, past the fat hazel coppice, I expected to see the overgrown patch, but the cottage was there, bathed in early morning sun, complete with the finely grazed turf and a little vegetable plot to one side. I felt a ripple of panic. Alice was working at the washing barrel, thudding the laundry with a great stick. She looked up.

'Why did you do it? I asked.

'Do what?' There was an edge of irritation in her voice, as though she did not want to be interrupted.

'Frighten the wits out of me.'

'I've already told you,' she said and went on with the laundry.

'I dreamt about you - '

'I came to you last night, told you what you need to know.'

I stared at her. 'Pardon?'

Alice carried on with her work. I glanced down to see my hands were trembling. I looked up, and Alice, the cottage and garden had gone.

It was on a January afternoon, not long after Alice's husband had died, when the puddles were frozen and a low sun barely made it over the treetops, that Alice met Richard Ferris on a track that ran from the top scarp of Blackman's

Moor and went through a tunnel of grown-out hazel stools. The ice in the puddles splintered as she plodded towards him with a large stack of dried twigs and small branches tied to her back. She looked like a strange hedgehog with boots. Estovers it was called. She thought of the word as she saw Ferris, sitting high up on a gleaming horse, and felt the vibration of the horse's hooves in the ground, even though they were only trotting, ambling even. When Ferris was in front of her, he pulled the horse up and leaned down.

'Do you have a date when you will be vacating your cottage, Mistress Heath?' he asked, his breath smoking in the freezing air.

'Byrd Cottage is mine, as well you know,' Alice said, staring up from the thatch of twigs. 'My great, great grandsire bought it off them that was there before you.'

'And you can prove that, can you?' Ferris smiled at her, then his expression recoiled. 'I do hope you're not taking more than your fair share of firing wood, Mistress. This seems rather a large load.' Ferris brandished his horse whip at the burden.

'I takes what I'm entitled to,' Alice said and wished she could move on as the load was dragging down on her back painfully; when she walked it felt a little easier. And her feet felt as thought they were burning with cold inside her boots and freezing solid to the ground.

'You have the documents do you, proving this sale?' he persisted. 'Deeds?' Ferris took a closer look at her. When he had first spotted her she had looked like a mountain of firewood moving along, with a pair of shabby black boots sticking out from the hem of dirty, long skirts. She walked with her head down and her bony arms akimbo, presumably to ease the load, looking more like a walking rag doll than a human.

Alice shrugged. 'Don't know about no deeds, but I do know that cottage is mine. It was given me by me father.'

'Mistress Heath, let us stop this nonsense, shall we? If your father was indulged by living rent-free by my own father, then that is all very well. But I am the lord of the manor now, and I cannot allow my tenants to live rent-free. I am good enough not to back-date your rent but, Madam, I will need paying from now on, or you must leave the place.'

'It's me home and I ain't got nowhere else to go.'

'The Poor Rate will assist you, I am sure.'

Alice put her hands to her waist. 'And I tell you that is my house and you've no right to it.'

Ferris' horse was growing restive. Ferris tutted as he tried to manage it. The animal threw its head up and down, even though he was holding the reins tight. It occurred to him that horses were unsettled by witches. Perhaps this woman was one. Checking this thought quickly, he said

'If you think you have a claim, then go to law and prove it. The law is there for everyone.'

'No it ain't,' Alice snapped. 'It's there for the likes of you, and run by those with the money. And you knows it.'

Ferris smirked. What a ridiculous woman she was. 'Go to law, Mistress Heath!' he called, kicking the horse into a canter and pounded off down the track.

Alice plodded on. The load was biting viciously into her lower back and the straps holding the load were cutting her shoulders. She could almost feel them incising her skin. Her feet felt numb in her boots, making it harder still to keep walking. The horse had turned up the ground beneath the ice in areas of the track and she slithered along and then sank into the torn, soft mud. Foetid, freezing water trickled into her boots. It would take all night, possibly all the next day to dry them out.

As she walked on, she remembered her father telling her that the cottage had been sold to his great, grandfather, some sixty or seventy years before by the previous family who had lived in Stourton Hall and had been lords of the manor. The cottage was on a small piece of land and in disrepair, and the owner had asked her great, great grandfather if he wanted it for a pittance otherwise he intended to pull it down, as it was not worth his while repairing it. The plot was next to the bog and on damp, difficult land of little agricultural use. Thus the transaction had taken place.

This previous lord of the manor, whose name she could not now recall, had said the sale should be recorded properly and engaged the notary from Stourton to draw up the deed of sale. Alice's great, great grandfather had signed it with a mark, paid the small amount, and all was done. Alice's father had said he'd left the deed with the notary as it would be safer with him. When she walked into Stourton to find the offices after Ferris's land agent had first approached her, she found that the notary had long since died and no-one knew where the deed to her house would be. Another notary had opened up further along the street but she was told that he had not taken over from the previous man and would not have inherited any of his documents. It was many years since the previous notary died and no-one seemed to know much about him. As she walked back along the dusty turnpike road, with carriages and horses billowing up incessant clouds of fine, choking dust, she realised viscerally that the last bit of security she had clung to was now under deep threat. Indeed, she was being threatened by a man who had so much, and could not possibly need more. And she felt like the fox driven into a coppice with no escape, surrounded by dogs that she knew would rip her limb from limb and drink the life's blood out of her, just because they could.

Richard Ferris stood to one side of the grand windows which overlooked the sweeping lawns. An early fog was creeping up over the sward, like nebulous ghosts crawling along the grass, seeking the light, the comfort.

'I have heard about you trying to get Mistress Heath and her daughters out of Byrd cottage, Richard,' Georgiana addressed him.

Ferris carried on looking out, wordlessly preparing his answer, staring at the rolling mist.

'It is necessary,' he said at last.

'Why is it necessary?'

Ferris sighed, then looked at his wife. 'If I allow this woman and her family to live without paying the rent, then what do you think will happen with all my other tenants? I am not a charity, Madam.'

'That is abundantly clear.'

Ferris folded his arms and his expression soured. 'The enclosure procedure is already costing money, my dear, and where do you think that money comes from?'

'Don't patronise me, Richard. The decision to enclose is yours, and, from what I gather, it is most unwelcome.'

Ferris raised his eyes. 'And how would you know *that*?'

'I go into town and I talk to my friends.'

'Who told you that there were objections?' There was an edge to his voice; he too had heard about the dissent and had hoped he'd quelled it with a few small gifts of money, here and there. It hurt doing that, but he wanted the extra land from the top half of the moor, because, properly resown, it would make fairly reasonable grazing. The bottom half looked useless.

Georgiana met his cold gaze. 'I will most certainly not break my confidences.'

'You are my wife. You have to tell me.'

She shook her head. 'You need to be very careful, Richard. By evicting Mistress Heath you will make the situation a good deal worse. What possible use can that plot be to you?'

'It's the principle,' Ferris said, and knew it sounded lame. In truth this peasant woman's truculence offended him, and he would not countenance it.

'Principle?'

'Where do you think all this finery comes from!' Ferris snapped. 'Does it suddenly appear, and for free? How much do you think that gown you are wearing cost, Madam?'

'And what is the rent you would be asking for the cottage?'

Ferris told her.

Georgiana smiled. 'I don't even think it would buy one of the ribbons in my hair,' she said, and arched her eyebrows at him. 'I think you are treating this woman atrociously. I am ashamed of you.'

'Oh, be ashamed then!'

'I also hear that there is talk that Mistress Heath's great, great grandfather bought the cottage from our predecessors-'

'Oh do you indeed! And may I ask where you heard that?'

'Several people have said so.'

'Who do you think you are to meddle in my business affairs? 'Ferris shouted at her. 'Your place is the home and raising our children, and mine is making this estate work.'

'And my role is also to challenge your behaviour when I see you acting in a vindictive and reprehensible manner, *Sir*!'

The 'sir' made Ferris momentarily draw back. Blinking, he made for the door, remembering to slam it as he strode off.

On the next fine day we drove over to the moor. Hugh had picked me up at 8.30; Craig was joining us to take some more photographs of the place. The previous ones had been processed into prints and slides, and, from the former, I could see that Craig had an unusually creative skill with the camera. The pictures of the bog were magical, some even looked as though they were stills from a fantasy dream, with a soft haze illuminated by the slanting rays of the sun. Then there were razor-sharp close-ups of plants – the downy, wispy heads of the last cotton grasses being gently drawn in the breeze; and there was the incredible detail of the forests of minute moss filaments, like some strange miniature country we never notice. I congratulated him on them, and he smiled diffidently and did not seem to know what to say.

Today we were in riotous mood. Craig was driving the old Ford estate which grated through its gears as it did when Hugh drove. We were discussing the coming day's work and Hugh was talking and stuffing handfuls of savoury snacks into his mouth out of what was euphemistically called a party pack. I waved away the offer of these acid-orange UFOs and monster-shaped aliens.

'Hugh!' Craig protested, shaking his left arm. 'You've just covered me in crumbs.'

Hugh had the habit of talking while eating, which, when shovelling in cereal-based UFOs, really was not a good idea.

'They're nice,' Hugh said in muffled tones. 'Want some?'

Craig shook his head. 'You know those things are full of garbage?' he said, carefully negotiating the car around a tightly-packed side road. 'Full of those E numbers.'

Hugh looked up. 'What?' Another spray of crumbs. We yelped, I too brushing off the arm of my jacket.

'Artificial colourants,' I said. 'Will make you go hyper.'

'Not that he needs any help with that,' said Craig as he pulled into a parking space on the Upper Moor car park. 'It's like living with a coiled spring as it is.'

There was crumb-spraying protest from Hugh.

'Not that I would have it any other way,' Craig said, turning to grin at Hugh.

We walked down the scarp to the heather-clad sandiest part, which I suppose should technically have been called a heath. We stayed with the colloquial name, Blackman's Moor, often shortening it to 'the moor' or 'Blackman's'. As we slithered down the slope, Hugh came to a sudden stop.

'Interesting,' he said, putting a pair of binoculars that he habitually wore around his neck, to his eyes. '*Very* interesting.'

'What is?' I asked.

'We have Rowland Mere, Paul Smith and some guy with a theodolite working around the bog. And that will be the area that'll defeat them.'

We both knew what he meant. The history of this place was clear from the records, but it was its fauna and flora that were exciting and might well now protect the site from development. However, there were a number of leases dating from the mid-17th century which gave the inhabitants of properties close to this area leave to dig drainage channels and conduits to drain some of the excess water away, which suggested it was then a troublesome area for those who lived on it. We also felt that the made-up land of the 18th-century turnpike road would have frustrated such water drainage schemes and thus in the 20th century, builders and engineers were now having the same problems as their predecessors.

'I wouldn't have thought Smith should be seen consorting with a developer so openly,' I said.

'Why not?' Hugh said. 'They think the deal's in the bag. They think they can just throw money around and we'll back off. But those bastards have a big surprise coming.'

'Do you think we should get out of sight?' Craig said, and I could see the muscle in his jaw tightening.

Something in his voice drew a serious look from Hugh and he nodded. 'You're right.'

As we walked over the lower area of the main common we made sure we kept out of Smith's view, knowing he would report us for being out together, given a chance. We could almost hear him 'And *why* do you both need to be in the same place? And why is that other man with you? Why aren't you maximising your time – you in one place, you in the other? It's tax-payers' money being frittered away here, subsidising your escapades!' Smith had actually said as much one day when we'd all checked back in to admin after a long day of drawing up plans and photographing the scarp rising to the upper moor.

I noticed that Craig's hands had unballed and the tension had eased from his jaw as we reached the lower moor. This area was mainly one of moorish, rough grasses and isolated patches of heather. I looked over to where Mere and Smith still gesticulated in the distance, gloriously unaware of our presence. While I delighted in keeping out of view, I could see that for Craig it was necessary.

The ground was behind The Warrener public house and had been heavily used in the past. There were the grown-over remains of sand pits which pock-marked the surface close to the road and salt cutting pits on the very southerly border towards the river. Stretching from the back of the pub there had been a rope walk (where hemp was twisted on a wheel with a man walking backwards to make the rope lengths) in the 18th century. The long, thin triangular plot was marked out on the Tithe Award Map and helpfully named 'The Rope Walk'. Towards the river, and in a field bordering the lowest possible boundary, was a plot called Tanyard Field. Hugh suggested we look for remains of the associated tan house and works in the immediate area on the moor. I had read about it in documents from the 17th century at the Record Office while Hugh had found the tan house and works mentioned in deeds from the 16th century, which he read with effortless ease. Tan-houses were often on the edges of settlements as they were notoriously stinking places using urine and excrement to produce supple hides. These concoctions were left in tanks for weeks to fester. One can only guess how this stunk. I was fairly sure that hemp was retted (left to rot in water to release the usable fibres) in or around the same area, suggested by the presence of the rope walk, which may have come after the tannery.

Hugh had almost instantly homed in on a small but strong-flowing stream to the main river.

'There's your water supply!' he announced, for I had just been saying a regular water supply was necessary in the tanning process. From reading the deeds for the tannery, I pictured those who processed these hides as probably being men of few words and working long hours at their difficult, heavy work, while the rest of society kept their distance. I do not know quite what we were expecting to find, as any sign of a building or works had long gone. Indeed the tannery disappeared from the records after 1750.

The stream flowed in a deep channel with the patchy remains of old stone walling shoring up the sides, but it was densely overgrown, and tangled among the vegetation were the remains of carrier bags, crisp packets, plastic sweet wrappers and beer bottles – the everyday detritus of mankind.

Hugh jumped into this watercourse and crouched, trying to work out if there were any other tell-tale signs of the tannery from that level. Craig was working in the wider area, examining the well-grazed turf. The sun was strong and casting long shadows from the smallest bump or ridge in the ground. Suddenly he started taking photographs.

'What is it?' I asked.

Craig waved me over and pointed out the nuance of lines in the fine turf, of rectangular outlines further down, and it was as if the past was slowly revealing itself.

'Hugh!' Craig called. 'Come here and look.'

Hugh's head popped up from the stream further up and, hopping out with the grace of a deer, he hurried over. There followed a discussion on where the tanning tanks might have been and the location of the tanner's house and sheds. Hugh was writing things down in a notepad he kept in the bib of his waterproof jacket, and he started to pace along possible building lines while telling me to hold the tape measure, and getting Craig to take it further along and out, while he moved another tape here and there over the turf. At one stage I wanted to shout out 'Oi, the history's my field! You stay with your plants and birds!' and it was as though he heard this thought, because, after talking to Craig, he said 'You don't mind me taking over this bit, do you, Kiddo?'

I stared, eyes wide open and was about to say. 'No, it's fine!' until Hugh added with a grin 'It's important to get our bearings right, like north and south. We can't have it facing upside down or moonside up,' and feined a yelp as I pretended to kick him.

'You've been talking to Chris!'

'Yes, Chris did warn me about your rather unusual spatial awareness,' he added, jumping back down into the safety of the stream bed.

It was deemed that the tan house stood on, or near, The Warrener pub. Perhaps it was the original core of the building Craig and I had sensed. But then I thought of what Alice had said about the manor courts being held in the building and that would be most unlikely - impossible - if the tannery was still in operation, although, with 1750 as the cut-off date for the tannery, it was just feasible. I went to tell Hugh and then stopped. I had not told him or Craig about Alice. Hugh's scientific and practical demeanour cautioned against any form of supernatural explanation, and Craig's sensitivity made me hesitate for reasons I was not sure of. So I merely added that I had heard that manor court hearings were held in The Warrener pub in the late 18th century and I could not find any further evidence of the tannery being in use after 1750.

It was lunchtime and getting very cold on the exposed ground, it was early December after all. With claw-like hands and faces so cold we could hardly talk, we decided to go to The Warrener to warm up. Before going in, Craig took me to one side.

'Are you all right about going in?' he asked, and his voice was kind. 'We can go somewhere else if you feel uncomfortable.'

I smiled at him. 'I'm all right,' I said, and knew I would be. 'But thanks for asking.'

'After you,' he said, holding the lounge door open.

We sat at a table by the fire and looked through into the dining area. Smith and Mere were just getting up after finishing a meal. Hugh raised his eyes at us in enquiry. As they walked through, Smith saw us and shot over like a hawk after prey.

'What are you doing here?' he demanded. 'Is this what we tax payers pay you for, to hang around in pubs?' Smith aimed this at Craig and Hugh, and somehow I knew that Mere had told him they were together, and what had happened with the shop, or whatever version of the story Mere had concocted.

'It's the dinner hour,' said Craig, looking Smith straight in the face. 'It's their time, not yours or the council's.'

Smith stared at him, bug-eyed. I could sense that, for once, he was actually lost for words.

'And as a rate payer,' Craig continued. 'I might ask why *you* are here?'

Smith's colour rose like a livid-purple stain from his neck up. I was expecting Smith to start ranting on about telling our line-manager about our rudeness and insubordination, but with a look of contempt, that can only be achieved after decades of practice, he turned and walked out of the pub, ostentatiously slamming the door of his new black Mercedes and screeching off down the road with Mere in the passenger seat.

'Thanks Craig,' Hugh said, his eyes alight with obvious pride.

'Yes, thanks,' I said. 'Smith needed that.'

'Probably pissed-off because we caught him consorting with the enemy,' said Hugh, drinking with pleasure from his pint. 'Remember, the council is the other contender for buying this land.'

'Which puts a very different complexion on their meeting, doesn't it?' I said.

Craig went up to the bar, which was now getting busier with lunchtime trade.

'It's really good to see Craig coming back,' Hugh said.

I nodded. 'It is.'

'For ages after we shut the shop, Craig was struggling, I mean really struggling.' We both looked at his tall, impressive figure. 'Hard to comprehend, I know, but he's actually quite shy.'

'Does he have any Viking ancestry?' I asked carelessly. Glancing at Hugh I saw a big smile breaking out on his face.

'Oh, he'll love that!' he laughed. 'Yes, he certainly looks as if he should have.'

I slithered down in my seat.

'Oh, wait till I tell him!' he continued with glee.

'Don't,' I said, my face getting hot. 'Hugh, please don't.'

The tone of panic in my voice made him frown.

'Really, don't say I said that,' I urged.

'I wish I could,' he said, and now there was unusual seriousness in his voice. 'That Mere woman's campaign knocked the stuffing out of him, he lost a lot of confidence in himself.'

'*What*? But he's so handsome!' I blurted out again. 'Look, if you think it will help, say something about the Viking bit.'

Hugh nodded. 'I probably shouldn't be talking to you like this-'

'I'm glad you are.'

'- but there was a lot more than the posters, you know. On several occasions we were spat at in the street, and the town's cavemen used to wolf-whistle and abuse us verbally if they spotted us in the shops or in the pub. It got to the stage that I would go to the next town for the essentials, and Craig just stayed in.'

'That's bloody awful....'

'And completely unfounded,' Hugh said. 'The rumours couldn't have been more off the mark if she'd tried. Even if we had been promiscuous and had AIDS as she implied, that sort of harassment would have been disgusting, but the irony is that we have always been the opposite of what Hermione Mere was suggesting. Apart from being gay, of course.'

I was about to say, 'You don't need to explain yourself to me,' but he turned and said, with unusual awkwardness which he covered by a sharp laugh, 'That's probably rather too much information, isn't it?' Luckily Craig returned holding two more pints, and a Marston's Low C for himself. I looked over to the bar and was glad that no-one was turning around to look at us, at them. Glad no-one was whispering behind hands and staring. It said something about the waning interest in Craig and Hugh, and what had happened because of Hermione Mere. At least I hoped so.

Chapter Four

Richard Ferris and his friend Jamison decided the lower half of Stourton Waste was not worth the effort of enclosure, with the exception perhaps of the western side. However, just to make sure, Jamison had suggested that his friend, Watts, should join them on a perambulation around the waste. Watts was a surveyor and ran his father's large farm and certainly knew a thing or two about land. Jamison and Watts had studied Classics at Oxford, Watts obtaining a double-first. However, Ferris was surprised when he saw him for Watts was a rabbit of a man, small, wiry and skittering this way and that, pointing out this undulation and that rise. He wore spectacles, the lenses of which looked as thick as the bottoms of old wine bottles. Ferris would never have befriended a man who looked and acted like him; but Jamison was a bit of a soft fellow. In truth Ferris was still put out that his own father had sent him on the Grand Tour with a dreary tutor, instead of sending him to university. It was this, if he had been perceptive enough to realise, that was the root of his dislike of Watts. But Ferris left soul-searching to the poets and philosophers, not to the man of business he believed he was.

Ferris was having difficulty keeping up with Watts who swerved like a hare over the lower moor. Ferris was used to riding his fine chestnut horse everywhere but when Watts had stated they needed to walk Stourton Waste in order to appreciate the land in detail, he had only half-heartedly agreed and within a mere half an hour of walking, he had felt his energy sagging. It was a grey, late summer's day, humid and hot; he could feel sweat trickling down the sides of his face, soaking his hair and dribbling down the middle of his back. This lowest area below the turnpike road was a dreary prospect. The turf that managed to cling to life was fragile-looking and thin, and probably no more nutritious for any grazing animal than ashes. Scattered bits of furze clung on in places but the peasants with common rights were like damned locusts and even on a sweaty day like this, they were bent over, cutting it for the fires back in their hovels.

'I hardly think it's worth the time or money to enclose this,' he heard Watts' reedy voice through the thick air.

Ferris caught up with him. 'My land agent tells me this is the best land of this lower half of the moor,' he said, dabbing his handkerchief around the sides of his face and over his forehead. None of the peasants looked up to greet them as they passed. Ferris thought of that peasant woman Alice Heath and how it would please him to see the look on her face when he finally gave the woman her marching orders. What a fool she was - if she had asked him nicely, he might have let her carry on living there at a peppercorn rent. Georgiana was right – there was virtually nothing to be gained from taking over that scrappy bit of ground. But that Heath woman had drawn the battle lines and, if she wanted a fight, he would certainly take her on. It would be her own fault if she became homeless.

'This land is -' began Watts.

'Valueless,' interrupted Ferris. 'I'll leave it for the peasants, and pretend I am doing them an enormous favour.' Watts had looked at him oddly and caught up with Jamison, who was staring at the roughly circular pond on the other side of the turnpike, where scrawny-looking cattle were drinking.

'Just as well my new enclosures will be fenced,' Ferris addressed him, simultaneously turning his back on Watts. 'I don't want my livestock mixing with this mangy, moribund lot.'

They walked over the middle moor, which gradually inclined up to an old river terrace scarp which was now purple with heath. Or was it pinkish-purple? What did it matter? The place was of no use to him whatsoever. Stopping, he looked it over and wondered if he could perhaps squeeze in a racetrack, but then seeing the old river terrace rising in front of him, he gave up that idea. Too much work to flatten the area; the costs of enclosure had already started to dent his fortune. And it would not matter how much marling, manuring and resowing was done, it would be like trying to farm a sandy beach. This observation was only underlined when he struggled up the sand of the scarp as it was like walking up an enormous sand dune, so loose in places it dragged him back as he tried to push on upwards.

'Want some help, old man?' Jamison said, coming back down the slope and holding out his hand. Ferris allowed himself to be hauled up. It had rained overnight. The flat upper moor area surprisingly held water in scattered, shallow puddles and the sandy paths through these had the consistency of fudge. It occurred to Ferris he had never walked over this part of the heath before, only ever seen it from his carriage on the turnpikes, or up high on a horse from a distance. It was even worse than he imagined. A blasted, dismal plain where the wind whipped around viciously in winter gales, if the tortured, forward-leaning forms of the few hawthorns and oaks were anything to go by. Watts was digging a stick into the path.

'Very hungry soil, Lord Ferris,' he said. 'Not worth the effort. Let's see if the area up towards the mill pools is any better.'

They tramped on, Ferris ignoring any peasant who chanced to look up; he had already been slighted today and he was damned if he was going to start acknowledging any of them. Jamison looked through them. Only Watts gave a little bow of acknowledgement to anyone who wished him good-day.

Ferris studied Watts: he seemed more imp than man, much shorter than he was, and a hand shorter than Jamison. And Watts was rather untidy in a way that only scholars are allowed to be. As he walked, off came his jacket which was thrown over his shoulder and his cravat was unceremoniously unwound and used to mop his face. How Ferris wanted to copy him, but knew he could not. Would not as he must not give his tenants anything to laugh about behind their evening mugs of ale in their various drinking dens. Watts looked like a character in a pantomime with his boldly chequered breeches clashing terribly with his stockings and his voluminous cotton shirt billowing in the breeze which at last sighed over the moor, giving a moment's relief from the oppressive, sweating humidity. Ferris waited for the few people on the heathery plain to make some sort of comment, to laugh at this ridiculous man, but they did not. In fact they wished him good-day and turned their backs on Ferris, whether by design or by accident, he was not sure, but guessed at the former. How *dare* they.

They reached the eastern side of this higher area of ground which gave into more continuous and even dense mats of bristly-looking grasses.

'Sheep's fescue and bristle bent.' Watts said immediately when Ferris stooped to examine them. 'Grows on dry, rather poor soils.'

Ferris felt his mood, which had momentarily lifted when he saw areas of grassland, plummet. The idea of enclosing this and cultivating improved pasture trickled away when they joined a wide sandy track. It was almost pure sand. Watts kicked it with his booted foot and shook his head. Jumping sideways into the purpling heather, he plunged a corer into the ground and, with surprising strength, drove it in, and then, with one enormous heave, pulled it out in one go. Taking out a knife, he smoothed down one side and stared at it in dismay.

'It's almost all sand! Afraid you've got yourself a bit of a problem, agriculturally speaking,' Watts said, addressing Ferris. 'But from a geological, natural history side -'

'Oh I'm not interested in *that*!' Ferris blurted, feeling his face go red and become even hotter. 'If it doesn't earn me money, I'm not interested. Move on.'

Watts was being paid by the hour and he was damned if he was going to hear this fool's opinion on the place's natural attributes. To him it was a miserable, worn-out piece of ground that he could throw to the peasants to shut them up and to appease his oh-so-good wife. They walked on in silence into a shaded area under oaks and thorns, down a long slope to a reedmace-fringed pool. Reedmace always looked as though they were man-made to him, dark brown cylinder heads, like fat cigars, bobbing around on tall, thin green uprights. As a boy he had delighted in pointing them out to his governess, or, on the rare occasions when his mother joined them, showing them to her. She had always had the grace, he realised now, to look as if she had never seen them before. The pool was one of three that ran Oakhampton Mill, a few hundred yards away. Even to Ferris' world-weary eye, he had to admit the pool was rather attractive, despite this flat, sultry light. Perhaps he should suggest that Georgiana and the children should walk here from the carriage on the turnpike. Looking up, he saw the thin bodies of dragonflies skittering over the water, and one, iridescent and greenish-blue, hung motionless in the air; he would describe it to Georgiana later. A heron stood, as still as a statue, on the further side of the water. The mill, he knew, had once processed oak bark for the tannery which had preceded the coaching inn. Now it had switched to corn grinding.

'And this is one of the pools to the mill, is it?' came Watts' voice. Ferris was aware he was addressing him.

'Yes, I suppose so,' Ferris murmured. He was not going to assist him in any way, why should he? He grimaced. Even he knew how ridiculous that was, as Watts was being paid by the hour.

Watts made a funny noise between a sigh and a snort, and looked at a rough map and then at his pocket compass.

'This is Oakhampton Mill,' he declared and led the way, not stopping to see if Ferris had deigned to follow. Jamison fell in with Ferris.

'You seem rather out of sorts, old friend,' Jamison began.

'I didn't realise how useless this place was,' Ferris confessed. 'I've had Georgiana reminding me constantly about how I should consider the poor and their common rights. Well, at least I can now say to her that they can have half of the moor. This part is no use to man nor beast.'

Jamison looked around and then mopped the back of his neck.

'Yes it's a sparse old stretch, to be sure,' he said. The sky was curdling in front of them, a dark bruise-purple. 'And I think we're about to be royally pissed upon.'

They jogged over to Watts, who was raising his tricorn to a young woman picking herbs. She gave him a glorious smile and then turned to carry on in her search. Ferris felt like switching the woman on the shoulder with his cane, to make her acknowledge him, but knew that Jamison would not be impressed, and he did not want Watts looking at him with even more half-concealed dislike.

They followed a thin, sandy path that snaked over the eastern edge of the moor and was mercifully cool under the thick curtain of hazel and oak leaves. A greenish light was moving through the leaves, and he realised a wind was picking up. They walked up to the turnpike where their carriage was waiting by one of the roadside inns. The horses were eating from nose-bags.

The driver doffed his hat as Ferris approach.

'We're going over the top half of the moor,' Ferris announced. 'Water the horses and wait here.'

The servant wordlessly assented.

The area on the other side of this turnpike, which seemed to cut the useless land off from that of promise, joined the lower turnpike by a short stretch of road which bounded the waste on its western side. The view over this top half of Blackman's Moor was far more promising and Ferris quickened his pace to catch up with Watts, who was even more animated than he had been.

'Now this is more like it!' he said and Ferris detected genuine pleasure in Watts' voice. Looking at him more closely, he thought maybe Watts was not such a fool.

The top half of Blackman's Moor comprised rough, moorish grasses which grew continuously to a lowering horizon. Watts drove the corer into the ground and pulled it out with a flourish.

'Oh good!' he chortled, scraping the side of the implement and showing the brown, gritty soil to Ferris, who gave the ghost of a smile. 'Not the best soil in the world, but free-draining and good for crops that don't like getting their feet wet. But you will have to spend time and money on getting this land marled and manured if you go in for arable,' Watts added more seriously. 'You understand that, I hope?'

'Yes,' said Ferris, bristling at the impertinence of the man.

They walked over the moor, correctly named now Ferris thought. A maze of little paths incised the grass, going thither and hither and Ferris wondered at their number. There were also conspicuous bare patches where commoners had gathered turves, evidence for the right of turbary, but not for much longer, he thought. It occurred to him that these people were also making off with the soil attached to these turves, which he needed for future crops. Just as well the Standing Order notices would soon be attached to the church door in Stourton and to the little Chapel of Ease towards the confluence of the turnpike roads, to inform them of the enclosure of this part of the common and the extinguishing of their common rights. Their right to roam over this land would also be stopped. The quicker he got the notices and the Enclosure Bill written, read in the House of Commons, and passed, the better. And if the peasants did not like him now, wait until they read *that*!

The day had been a difficult one in the Record Office. It was a chilly, rainy day in the latter half of December. Hugh had been sluggish all morning and we had opened archive box after archive box to find, after careful reading, that the documents related to properties on the other side of Blackman's Moor and were not associated with it in any way. Enormous mortgage documents the size of table cloths covered our desks with pages covered in small, neat writing espousing some incomprehensible legal monotony. There was a feeling of winding down for the break which, for council staff – and by implication us too - would last for about ten days. Even the expected visit from Jon Blake with renewed warnings not to upset Paul Smith had not materialised. Blake had indeed popped into our office a few times to see how things were progressing and seemed genuinely pleased with what we were finding. However, the time was ticking for this project – the current owners of Blackman's Moor were willing to hold off from a sale until next autumn, by which time our research and reports should be ready. We had heard obliquely that Rowland Mere was agitating for a quicker sale, and was being enabled by Smith. It was cheering that the sellers seemed to be on our side.

'Do you want to break for coffee?' I whispered to Hugh, who was looking even more pale and lethargic. There was a light film of sweat on his forehead. He nodded and we made our way into the common room area, where there was a coffee and tea-making machine.

'You're looking washed-out,' I said, peering into his face. 'Do you want me to drop you home, and I can go into the office and explain?'

Hugh shrugged. There was an unusual helplessness about him. 'I think I'm getting Craig's cold, and I can't.'

I frowned.

'If I get it, then we're stuffed,' he said. 'The dogs need walking -'

'I'm driving you home now,' I said, getting up and packing my backpack. 'Wait there and I'll get the documents put back in.'

Hugh sat with his head down, and I felt a shiver of concern. A vile 'flu bug was doing the rounds. I had had 'flu in the past and knew the look and how prostrate it could make you.

The staff in the Record Office were helpful and did everything to ease our quick departure.

Luckily Blake had intervened about the travelling expenses and it was agreed that, if we claimed the bare minimum per mile, we could get to the Record Office by car. 'One in the eye for you, Smith!' I'd wanted to shout out as I danced outside his very plush office. Of course I didn't. The rule of signing in and out with administration stayed however.

As Hugh and I walked out to the car, he stopped and I thought he was going to be sick. I told him to sit on the bench and I would get the car.

'D'you mind if I lie down?' he mumbled, as I opened the door for him. I helped him into the back seat and, pulling a blanket out of the boot, put it over him. Within minutes he was asleep.

I drove as carefully as I could back to Stourton, slowing before known potholes and drain covers standing proud. It was getting dark when I pulled up outside their house, even though it was only four o'clock in the afternoon. I fumbled with the keys to the front door after waking Hugh up and helping him out of the car. Craig appeared, coming downstairs in a large towelling dressing gown, looking pale and unusually drawn, and black around the eyes. Why had they not asked for help? the question flashed irritably through my mind. I guided Hugh into an armchair; he was shivering. Craig sat by him, helping to take his shoes off and easing him out of his jacket.

'You should have said what was going on,' I said, as Craig sank back into the opposite armchair.

'I thought it was just a heavy cold,' he said, and I could see he too was sweating.

'I think you two have 'flu,' I said, looking around for more blankets. I found some folded on a chair behind the door, and handed one to each. Luckily the room was warm and comfortable. The dogs were milling around, with concerned expressions. I went into the kitchen, which was in disarray, with washing up in the sink and open dog-food tins on the counter tops. I washed up while the kettle boiled and put more food out for the dogs. Having made Lemsips and heated up tinned soup, I carried it all in, to hear Hugh saying something about the dogs in a fretful, worried voice.

'Chris and I will walk the dogs after work,' I said. 'I've just fed them and they've come in from the garden, and they're now settled in the kitchen. We'll take over until you're up and around.' It was not a suggestion, and brooked no argument. 'So where do you walk them?'

They told me.

'I'll ring in to work now,' said Hugh. 'Tell them I've had to come home.'

'I've got to go back,' I said. 'So I'll tell them that I've had to drop you off. Do you want me to call a doctor?' Hugh shook his head. I looked at Craig.

'I don't think there's anything they can do for colds or 'flu,' he said. 'But I could do with some painkillers, my head's splitting.'

I went to the drawer in the kitchen where he said they kept the tablets. There were only two left.

'I'm coming back after work to drop some more off,' I said, handing them to him. 'If you need anything after that, leave a message on my home phone, will you?'

'Okay Mum,' said Hugh, and gave a weak smile.

I quietly left the house.

I reached the council offices before the administration office closed for the day and explained about Hugh.

The main receptionist, Mrs Little, looked at me with a knowing expression. Despite her name, she was a thick-set woman nearing retirement who wore large glasses and had her fairly short hair permed into unbecoming corkscrews.

'You want to be careful,' she said, and raised her eyes to a much younger woman, her clerk.

'Yes, this 'flu is a vile bug,' I said.

'I wasn't referring to the 'flu,' she said. 'If you get my meaning.'

I stared into her jowly face, at the thin-lipped, mean mouth.

'I don't get your meaning,' I said, but knew very well what she was referring to.

The woman gave a nasty little laugh. 'The man you work with probably has AIDS,' she said. I was momentarily stunned by her directness. 'Lives with a man,' she continued. 'I've realised who he is. One of those that ran the bookshop that that property developer's wife was warning us all about.'

The clerk gave a slight jump.

'Do you know what you have just said is slander?' I warned. My voice was dangerously low and expressionless. So Smith had been busy spreading hate, had he?

'Only if it's untrue,' she said, and a triumphant smugness settled on her face. 'Funny how he's gone down all of a sudden, isn't it?'

'Mr Winfield has 'flu,' I said. 'I would strongly advise you to stop spreading any more of these rumours.'

We stared at each other, like two dog bitches ready to attack.

'Huh!' she snorted. 'As though I'm going to be told what to do by a Little Miss like you, a Manpower Service recruit.'

I glared at her steadily and, in the end, she looked down. Wordlessly I walked away.

Each day after work Chris and I dropped in. While Chris took the three dogs out, all muffled up for a bewildered walk around the quiet residential streets, I did the bit of washing up, made hot drinks and warmed soup for the patients and cleared up after the dogs outside. One late afternoon I called in as the local doctor was just leaving. Hugh had developed a painful, hacking cough and Craig had called for a home visit. The doctor remarked that they were exceptionally busy at the surgery as the 'flu bug had taken hold and spread fast. Hugh and Craig were sitting nearly supine in the armchairs. I was glad that the room was warm and they looked comfortable. As I drew the curtains, Hugh sat up a little.

'Charlotte, you don't have to do this,' he said. 'It's quite likely you'll catch this. It's 'flu - you were right.'

'I knew it was. I had it when I was coming up to Finals,' I said, and recalled lying, sweating in bed for five long days, unable to move as my limbs ached and my head throbbed unbearably with a blinding viral headache.

'The doctor's written out a sick note for ten days,' Hugh said, picking up a piece of paper. 'Would you hand it in?'

'Of course,' I said, taking the certificate. I must have looked concerned as he added. 'I have a small heart problem which adds a few problems with this sort of thing,' he explained. 'Don't look so worried, it's a minor thing I was born with.'

I could see Craig looked unusually serious.

'Hugh's problem is that he never cuts himself any slack,' he said, unsmiling.

Hugh waved him away. 'It's a small problem -'

'Which is why the doctor's coming back to check on you tomorrow,' Craig interrupted. 'Which is why you might have to go into hospital.'

'*What?*'

'Craig!' Hugh snapped and turned to him. Then he looked at me. 'I have a chest infection, on top of the 'flu - '

'Which, if you had taken time off sooner, wouldn't have happened,' Craig retorted. 'I told him not to go into work,' he said, addressing me.

Hugh was about to answer back, and I held my hand up. 'Now children!' I said with assumed joviality. 'What would you like to have: tea, coffee or chocolate?'

For the first time in days Hugh's eyes lit up. 'Chocolate. Oh, and some of those UFO things.'

'And me.' Craig chipped in, and thankfully the atmosphere changed.

I was aware of muttering and sideways looks as I went alone into the canteen during my dinner hour the next day. The admin woman, Mrs Little, and her clerk were sitting opposite and staring unashamedly at me, even pointing me out to a couple of other women who had just joined them. They swivelled around and studied me hard. I felt like waving. But then thought how important the Blackman's Moor project was, and decided to ignore them. However, as I walked past on the way out, I heard the words 'Dirty Bitch'. I swung round, but the gaggle were feigning intense conversation.

I got out of the car that evening at Craig and Hugh's to find a piece of paper wedged under the door and almost hidden under the door mat. I pulled it out and unfolded it, half concentrating, but then gawped as the words 'DIRTY AIDS RIDDEN BASTARDS' jumped out. Scrunching the paper up, I stopped myself from tearing it into shreds.

The doctor pulled up as I stood there, frozen on the doorstep. Moments later he joined me, frowning. I realised I was shaking. I tried to tell him where I had found it. He read the note and shook his head. I could see his jaw tensing.

'I wouldn't say anything to them, if I were you,' he said. 'But I think you should take it to the police. Some of the people in this town,' he added, as though to himself, 'need a scapegoat for everything.'

I followed him in and spoke in what I am fairly sure was a too loud voice as I saw to the dogs, while the doctor walked upstairs. He was down a few minutes later.

'Better news, they're looking a lot brighter,' he said and gave me a warm smile as he left.

'Our little friends get any notes, did they?' Mrs Little said, smirking at me the next morning.

I appraised her. 'Notes?'

She gave me an evil smile.

'Oh, you mean the hate mail shoved under the front door?'
I said. 'I took that to the police station before work this
morning. They're dusting it for fingerprints as we speak.'

Mrs Little's face seemed to wobble beneath the thick layer
of powder and foundation.

'They're going to do handwriting analysis on it too,' I lied.
'They asked me if I knew anyone sick enough to send such
a thing.'

She blanched.

'They said they would check workplaces for handwriting
examples if there are any more such notes. Or rumours for
that matter,' I continued. 'They're keeping the fingerprints on
file so they'll be able to match them up with the perpetrator in
the future. Amazing what they can do with technology these
days.' I stared at her, then walked out of the building.

Richard Ferris knew there was going to be trouble with
his enclosure plans when he spotted a Standing Order
notice he had affixed to an old oak tree by the upper moor.
Someone had daubed THE POX ON YOU FERRIS in
ungainly black pitch. At first he had stared blankly at the
piece of paper, which was flapping in the wind, then a sweat
of anger and even a twitch of fear welled up through him.
His mind raced over the likely culprits, of which he realised
there were many, but they were all illiterate, unable even
to sign their own names. He thought of the people in the
lower orders who could write, the various scribes and clerks,
but all of them seemed unlikely daubers. They were, as a
rule, mousy, unassuming people who seemed permanently
hunched over desks in badly-lit buildings. The words on the
notice were formed crudely, as though the dauber was unused
to wielding a brush, let alone a pen. Ferris moved his
horse over to the notice and tore it down in one violent tug.
Ripping it up, he threw the fragments in the air for effect and
cantered off.

Tobias Cookson, Ferris' unofficial mentor, was holding a meeting that evening at The Royal Oak coaching inn. He persuaded Ferris that he should attend, mainly to assuage the fears and answer some of the questions that the people had been asking about what was going to happen to them if the top half of Blackman's Moor was enclosed. What an utterly stupid thing to do, thought Ferris, to deface the notice that very day. If there had been any goodwill left in him – which in truth there was not – that insult had done for the lot of them. He turned up twenty minutes late out of spite, a gesture which went against him as he had to walk the length of the long back room to the table set on a small platform. The floorboards resounded painfully and he was surrounded by droves of parishioners. As he walked he felt, rather than saw, their silent, sullen stares. Taking his place at the head table, he ignored Cookson, who stood at right angles with his head slightly cocked, as though waiting for an apology for his lateness. Ferris merely stared ahead at nothing. On one side of him sat Watts the surveyor, and on the other side, his friend Jamison, who would be elected enclosure commissioner when the Bill was passed in the House of Commons. There was an awkward silence, then Cookson coughed and the meeting got under way.

It was as Ferris had thought it would be: case after case of inarticulate peasants trying to get him to see their point of view. He had to stifle a yawn several times as they complained about their soon to be lost common rights, their livelihoods, independence, their whole way of life in fact. Ferris was secretly rather surprised, when he deigned to listen, at how dependent these people were on a bit of grazing here, a bit of wood gathering there. How a bit of 'herbage in the pot' can stave off this or that, and how the milk from a cow grazed on the common could make this or bring them that in barter and exchange. If it was not standing in the way of what he wanted, he would have found it all rather quaint, even charming. But if they thought he was going to give up his plans for enclosing the upper half of the moor and putting it to the plough, they were deluding themselves. Occasionally he smiled blandly during the proceedings, thinking of the drinking he would do afterwards, then he remembered the morning's daubing on his poster and his expression soured again.

Watt was explaining the proposed allocation of plots for the cottages which had common rights – he looked to Ferris when somebody asked about leaseholders' common rights. Ferris had mumbled that he would see that they were 'all right'. When pressed further, he snapped that these were the details that would be drawn up in due course. Did they not realise that the lower half of the waste was being left as it was, and common rights would be in operation there, as they had always been? There were a few laughs at that, and several comments about the lack of good grazing on this lower, heathy half of the moor. How could one carry on, with the same stints (allowed numbers) on half the land and a much poorer type of grazing? Ferris had wanted to get to to his feet and bawl to them to go and seek their fortunes elsewhere, go to the cities where labour was needed, but he recoiled. He remembered what Cookson had said about listening to people, about not appearing to be aggressive or patronising to those who voiced quite legitimate fears. And yet Cookson was clearly drawing battlelines, always introducing the next whining peasant with consideration and tact. Cookson the turncoat. Go and find your own land, thought Ferris, picking at his thumbnail. Stop taking something for nothing from me.

It was Alice Heath's gruff voice that made him look up from this slouching ennui.

'This man is forcing me out of me home,' she announced from the floor. 'Byrd Cottage is mine by rights and this man is trying to claim it as his.'

It felt as though a hundred eyes were trained on him.

Cookson looked at her and then at Ferris, who stared him out.

'Does this relate to the proposed enclosure, Mistress Heath?' asked Cookson, trying to keep the situation equable.

'Course it does. Ferris wants the best bits of the moor and the boggy flush, and my plot which is hard by.'

Cookson looked to Ferris, who shrugged.

'My great, great grandsire bought that cottage,' Alice continued. 'And the plot from those that were at the Hall before -'

Ferris got wearily to his feet. He would stare the hag down. 'And as I have said to you, Mistress Heath, show me the deeds, show me the paperwork - '

'Ain't got no deeds.'

An old man raised his hand. 'I remember summat of that,' he said, as Cookson nodded. 'I remember old man Jones, Mistress Heath's father, and I remember he said his own great grandsire had bought it for a pittance.'

Ferris seemed to wake up. 'Can you prove that?'

The old man thought carefully. 'Not with papers as such.'

Ferris waved him away. Cookson turned to him.

'I think, with respect, Lord Ferris, that you should at least consider this as a possibility.'

Ferris scratched his forehead. 'It is my understanding that my father was more than generous in letting this family stay rent-free, but times have changed and I am afraid I can make no exception. Rents must be paid.'

'If you evict me,' said Alice, staring at him, her dark eyes like black diamonds. 'You will be making me and me daughters homeless -'

'Then pay rent, and you can stay.'

'Pay rent to stay in me own cottage!'

'Mistress Heath,' said Cookson. 'We can talk about assistance from the Poor Rate if you need help with payment of rent.'

Alice stepped back. 'It's my house. If he takes it from me, it's theft!'

Cookson held his hands up. 'Let's calm down...I am sure something can be sorted out, but perhaps now is not the best time.' His voice was calming, gentle almost.

Alice snorted. Ferris fixed her with a look of contempt and he saw the answering curl of her top lip.

'I tried so hard to save that cottage.' I heard Alice's voice as I woke with a sudden lurch from a deep sleep. I could feel a crackle of energy, like some strange electricity and I stared, again, into the thick blackness of a freezing winter's night. I knew I had to go back to where the cottage had been, and I did when it grew light, a midwinter's sun just appearing in the sky.

It was one of those glorious winter's mornings, with the sun shining on the frost which iced the puddles in the bog, and skeined the cobwebs and dried-out seed heads like a rime of delicate sugar icing. The ground was iron hard. The whole area seemed to twinkle with thousands of diamonds under an ice-blue sky. The frosted vegetation crunched underfoot as I rounded the corner to Alice's plot, and there she was, hanging up a sheet over the bare branches of the hazel coppice.

'Anything yet?' she asked, as though she was expecting me.

I shook my head.

'You keep looking?'

'Of course. We're finding a lot, but there's still a lot to go. Do you know anything about the tanner and the tan house?'

'Me father knew of some that worked there, but that were years ago.'

'How about the rabbit warren?

Alice wrinkled her face up, then shook her head. 'I heard some of the old people talk about a warrener but that were before me grandsire's time. There's still plenty of coneys – you can't miss them. They eats me vegetables if I ain't careful.'

I was relieved Alice was being friendly – I had not been here for a while. I was ploughing through reams of documents but nothing came to light that I could fit in with this place. I felt as though I was letting her down. I'd made a note of her father's surname Jones, but in this westerly district that was not a great help. Every other surname seemed to be Jones.

'How's the long-haired man?' she asked. There was that gappy-toothed smile again.

'They've just got over the 'flu.'

'The what?'

'Bad cold—cough, um... runny nose, head aching, aches in - '

'Oh that!' she exclaimed, still looking at me quizzically.

'Craig seems much happier,' I said.

She grinned.

'Thanks again for everything you and Chris did,' Hugh said, as I climbed into the car. It was the week after new year and we were back at work in the dull grey light of a Monday morning. 'I know we couldn't have managed the dogs without you both, or the clearing up.'

I waved him away. It had been a quiet Christmas break, with Chris and I travelling to see both sets of parents, who lived over 60 miles away, stopping over with one, then visiting the next. It was a bit of a blur watching too much television, going for walks in the local countryside known since childhood, and a lot of thanking parents for the food, putting us up and entertainments, as well as assuring them we were (a) eating properly, (b) sleeping enough and (c) not arriving late at work.

We travelled back in that strangely expectant time between Christmas and New Year when most people seem still to be in holiday mode and are cheerful and ready to chat and meet up at the pub. I was pleased when, among the post on the doormat, I saw a card written in Hugh's copperplate handwriting – he never disclosed where he had learnt to write so well. It was an invitation to his birthday celebration, which was on Sunday 5th January. They invited us round the previous evening so potential hangovers could be slept off the following morning. We had not seen them since before Christmas when they had recovered from the 'flu in time to enjoy the festivities. I was relieved to see that both of them looked well, and appeared to have put on a little weight. I was expecting to see 'flu-hollowed cheeks but their faces were fuller and had a good colour. We had a lovely evening, sharing stories about childhood and backgrounds. It transpired that Hugh was an academic high flyer, had gone to a rather well-respected grammar school, and then on to clerical jobs in offices, while he worked out what to do with his life. Then, in his mid-twenties, he applied and got into university easily.

Craig by contrast had been a quiet and rather shy boy, despite his natural good looks and easy-going personality. A much less confident student, he had gone to a large, brash secondary modern school, where he was good-naturedly teased by the other boys for being quiet. Most of the girls from the school over the road tried to befriend him when he lost his boyish cuteness ('a real bugbear looking like that') and grew tall and heavier-framed than the other boys, who, not surprisingly, stopped their teasing. Leaving school at fifteen (the school leaving age at the time) he took various low-paid jobs, but saved up money and decided, aged twenty, that he wanted more in life. For several years he strove away at night school and worked long and hard to gain enough A levels to get into university to follow his boyhood passion of archaeology. At the age of twelve he had announced, in his rather squeaky pre-voice-breaking tone, that he wanted to be an archaeologist when a supply teacher had asked them all what they wanted to do when they grew up, and he was promptly beaten up in the playground in the next break. After that he had kept his mouth well and truly shut, on a lot of things.

I described our rather conventional backgrounds: good comprehensive schools, met at university, studied together, got married, and here we were now.

We had a superb evening, ate well (whichever of them did the meal was a dab hand) and drank good wine and beer.

I was inwardly very pleased when Chris said it was one of the best evenings he had had in a long time.

So to the freezing mist of the Monday morning when the light had only started to filter through.

'Difficult time of year to be born,' Hugh said as we drove along the dual carriageway. 'Craig's birthday is at a much better time, late August.'

I considered. 'Yes, but he would have been one of the youngest in class at school - it would make him nearly a year younger than the oldest.'

Hugh considered this. 'Yes, and he was the seventh of eight children. It wasn't until he started school that it was discovered that he didn't like talking very much.'

'Probably didn't need to in a big family.'

'And he was an undemanding child by all accounts,' Hugh said. 'People spoke for him, and he got used to that.'

'Doesn't seem to have held him back.'

'But he's still quite shy, and I put that down in part to being the youngest in a big group all the time.'

'Could also be part of his natural personality,' I suggested.

Hugh smiled. 'I've seen pictures of him as a child – he was adorable, no wonder he was everyone's pet – teacher's pet at infants and junior's, big sister's pet, parents' favourite child as he was good-natured, and so little trouble. Unfair perhaps, but also unfair on him in a way, as he was cast as the pleasant, no-trouble child and little was expected of him.'

'What?'

'Think of it – he's from a big family, went to a big, rough and tumble school where there were always noisier, more demanding and pushier kids getting the attention, and a quiet, well-behaved childlike Craig gets overlooked, and, being - okay *naturally* shy - never pushes himself forward. I think school smothered him, it certainly didn't do him any favours. But then he puts himself into gear when he's had time to consider, and off he goes. I really admire that.'

'So do I,' I said. 'How were you cast?'

'Oh, as an awkward little sod, I should think.' Hugh gave a short mirthless laugh. 'When I was younger, I never knew when to keep my mouth shut, even have trouble with that now.'

'Could be interpreted as sticking to your guns.'

'I think in my case it was seen as sheer bloody-mindedness. In fact, the words I remember most with reference to me were "awkward" and "answers back". What about you?'

I pulled a face. 'Pleasant, hard-working and friendly.'

'Damned by faint praise,' said Hugh.

We were greeted kindly when we walked into the Record Office and it struck me again how different the staff were here from those like Paul Smith and the harassed linked departments, where mistrust thrived and gossip infected the air.

We ordered up four boxes of documents and I glanced over to see Hugh settle into work, with a set expression, bouts of careful reading and sudden explosions of writing in the notebook the archivist had given him. A coiled spring, as Craig had described. We worked on until the dinner hour when we sat in the common room area and ate pre-packed sandwiches and drank machine coffee.

'Found anything?' he asked.

I scrunched my face up. 'Some things look promising, but then it fizzles out. You?'

Hugh shrugged. 'I'm still making notes for the Record Office catalogue, but zip in terms of Blackman's Moor.'

I scratched my forehead. 'I suppose such dry times are to be expected but with a time limit it feels we're treading water at the moment, and we really can't.'

Who said there's no thing like coincidence? We had barely taken up our seats when I opened the top of the next box and a late-17th-century parchment revealed itself with *Hemp Retting Stourton Waste* written in large, loopy writing on the outside.

'Hugh!' I squeaked, waving him over. Leaning towards the document he read it carefully and I heard '*Wow*!' whispered under his breath. He dragged the chair to him with his foot without even glancing round. For the next few minutes he was uncannily still, and then he looked up, his professor glasses on the end of his nose and his green-brown eyes wide open, popping almost. Moving to one side so I could sit, he read out:

'There is to the south of the rope-walk the retting pools in the boggy flush and hard by the Kings Waye to Stourton, and it is here that the hemp grown to the south of the rope works is laid in these pools to forment, thus dividing the fibres for ropes from the hempen waste. The rope maker Thomas Jones doth use these ponds, placing the bundles of hemp into to decay for upwards of fowerteen days to the distresse of the people who live hard by.'

'Jones,' I said. 'Alice's paternal relatives were Jones.'

'Which is one of the most common surnames,' cautioned Hugh.

'I didn't ask Alice about rope-working,' I said to myself. 'Only about tanning and the warren.'

Hugh put his glasses on the desk. 'Pardon?'

I glanced at him; he was looking at me with barely concealed disbelief. I fidgeted.

'Is this the Alice who lives in the house which isn't there?'

'Scoff if you want.'

Hugh shook his head. 'You know you sound half-baked when you go on like that?'

I felt my lower lip pushing out a fraction.

'And let's have none of the little-girl behaviour, it doesn't work with me.'

I felt my face redden. I was genuinely taken aback by that remark.

Hugh seemed to sense that and sighed. 'If it's any consolation, Craig felt some presence when he was over there too, which means I'm surrounded by nutters at home and in work.'

I pretended to give his foot a playful kick.

'Oh, now I'm being attacked by a girlie!' he said, and waved his arms around in mock alarm.

There was a sharp '*Sshh*!' from the next desk. We stared at each other with round eyes and I looked away as Hugh's shoulders started shaking with silent mirth.

Chapter Five

'Thomas Jones hath agreed that he shall forthwith not rett the hempen bundles within the pools hard by the road on the lower moor, or use the watercourses running to north by east of his house. Instead he shall have cause to be built a small pool of about twenty two feet across at the lower end of the boggy flush on the north side of the king's highwaye and one hundred and thirty feet east of his tenement. Thomas Jones shall also build a bank above the northern part and shall from this time rett his hemp in this, his aforementioned poole.'
Deed of 1685.

I was standing by Hugh's side, peering over his shoulder at the lines of looped handwriting which revealed the forgotten activities of this old world.

'Three hundred years to the year, bar one,' Hugh said.

'Apparently the retting pools stank like hell,' I said. 'All that decomposing vegetable material.'

'And the toxins released by that process,' Hugh butted in. 'No wonder they didn't want the stuff decaying in running water.'

Once again, I sensed we were trying to out-do the other in detail, and this time I backed down. After all, Hugh did have the Biological Sciences degree and was twelve years my senior. However, I had noticed that neither of us wanted the other to have the last word in general. Yet there was also a sense, shared by both of us I think, that this friction was propelling our work forward.

'They might not have understood the biochemistry, but the smell would have been enough to warn them,' Hugh continued.

'You know, there's a field just down from the bottom end of that area -'

'You mean south-east?'

Did I?

'Just below the old warrener's cottage,' I said. 'In the field between the bottom end and the river.'

'South then.'

'I suppose.'

'You need to be more precise, Charlotte. This vagueness is all very well, but in science precision is necessary.'

'This is history -'

It had been like this most of the day. Me trying to sound as though I knew everything; Hugh acting like an irritating know-it-all.

'And it's our job to present the facts as accurately as we can.'

'What's up with you today?' I asked, glancing at him sideways.

Hugh pushed his glasses further down on his nose and looked up. 'Nothing...Why?'

'You've been catting all morning.'

'*Catting*,' Hugh said the word as though he was tasting an unsavoury wine.

'Over-critical.'

'About your supposed ditzy sense of direction?' he retorted.

I stared at him, unblinking.

'I know you have a solid sense of direction, and so do you. But you just can't be bothered working it out.'

'Oh, thanks for that.' The sarcasm virtually ran from my words.

'It's irritating, because I know you can do it, and I don't know why you chose to act dumb.'

'I don't.'

We didn't talk for a few minutes. I looked through more documents but took nothing in; my mind was smarting. Hugh meanwhile carried on reading as though there was nothing wrong.

After a few more minutes, he asked, without taking his eyes off the page. 'So what about that field just south of the lower moor?'

'It's called The Oil Field.' I pointed it out on the copy of the Tithe Award Map we always carried with us. 'I wonder if the name had anything to do with the retting process, for instance if any oil-like secretions were released from decaying hemp. Also if that area was waterlogged, there would be decaying vegetation giving off oily substances in anaerobic conditions. And, looking at the map, if you carry on with the arc of the boggy flush, so-called, from the present bog, wouldn't the natural trajectory pass through this field? And, if this was a waterlogged area, it might explain why the main routeways ran further north and north-north-west.'

Hugh gave a satisfied smile. 'Knew you could do it--'

I pulled a face at him.

'And I think we'd better go back and have a more detailed look,' he said. 'This is the best time-'

'Because the vegetation is right down,' I interrupted.

In the car on the way back I broached the subject. 'You can be a bit over-critical, you know,' I said as I drove. 'Picking up on things all the time.'

'It's the way I am.'

'It can be hurtful at times. A bit patronising.'

Hugh sighed, and I noticed he coloured up a little. 'Sometimes in life you have to take it on the chin, Kiddo.'

I rolled my eyes. 'Would you like it if I picked you up on things?'

'If it was going to help, yes.'

'Well, I am pointing something out now.'

'Okay, point taken,' he said, and folded his arms. 'Craig says I'm a nit-picker.'

'Well?'

'I'll try not to pick too many nits then...But if I think you're letting yourself down, then I will pick the nits – okay?'

'I suppose.'

We went back to the lower heathy area of Blackman's Moor on the next sunny day with Craig to photograph. It was a still morning with a metallic light blue sky and a cold sun. It was late January, and even the sand seemed solid. Can sand freeze? I had never considered that before.

We walked on to the end of the present bog by the road and, there, among the winter-bleached grasses and rushes, was the outline of a small bank around a low depression – on its western and southern sides.

I pointed it out to Craig, who saw what I meant and leaned forward and took several photographs. I noticed Hugh clambering around in a ditch which ran alongside the western side of the bog to the main road. I went over to investigate and was met with the sight of a deep-sided ditch, liberally dosed with beer bottles, drink cans and sun-faded carrier bags and sweet wrappers. At the bottom of this litter ran a small stream. A high board fence closed off the adjoining garden from view.

'I think I've found it,' Hugh said, looking up. 'The watercourse Thomas Jones was told not to ret the hemp in.' Jumping out of it, he waved Craig over. He joined us immediately, and we showed him the pictures we needed.

'The pond Jones built is only a stone's-throw from this,' Hugh said, watching Craig appreciatively.

'Makes you wonder if any run-off from the retting would have seeped into it,' I said, trying to get Hugh's attention. 'Do you think this was used for drinking water?'

'Really don't know...'

Craig was leaning down to photograph the flow of water and Hugh stood back, hands behind his head, watching him and smiling approvingly. I was trying not to look at Craig's superb be-denimed behind. Suddenly Hugh blinked, as though remembering I was there, and pretended to examine the map.

'This ditch begins where the path comes out near Alice's cottage,' I said. 'I've checked the ditch's course, south by south-south-west.'

'Don't push it, Kiddo.'

'Could it go into the bog, into the middle, and join up with one of the pools there?'

Hugh held his hand in that direction. 'If you really want to jump in and look, be my guest.'

I did so, squelching through the foetid-smelling water which came almost up to my knees. The surface oozed with a hidden world of filaments and fronds and I tried not to think that anything alive might be wriggling through the depths. Several times my wellingtons were caught fast in the clay and I pulled them out with a loud flatulent noise, and hoped that Hugh and Craig had not heard. I staggered to an open stretch of water, metal-smooth under the bronze disc of the sun. It was here that I saw the remains of a ditch flowing into the open area of water, and, looking back, the faintest suggestion of it running through the low vegetation of the drier areas of the bog. I beckoned Craig over, suggesting he took the footpath on the edge, the narrow sandy causeway that led to Byrd Cottage. Jumping in, he walked with some difficulty towards me, he too nearly losing a wellington in the process. The disturbance created more unsavoury wafts.

'I can see a junction from here,' he called. 'Stay there and I can use you as a scale.'

Composing the photographs with care, he took several. Crouching low, he then started photographing the little bundles of sphagnum moss-heads. I stooped down to examine them: they were like watery, miniature forests. Craig then stooped by patches of cross-leaved heath on the drier areas and took several close-ups. I crouched with him to look at these plants which still held the dried-out remains of the flowers, which, when fresh, would have appeared as tiny fleshy, pink lanterns. Then I looked at the remains of the cotton grass flowers which nodded like stranded tiny ghosts over the bog. Usually I was too busy to notice any of these things, but now I stared at the delicate, amazing structures. In the water the top of a long fish snaked silently below and I jumped, not expecting to see any fish here. Quite why, I didn't know. A pool of water equals fish, doesn't it?

It was a few days later and we were in Stourton supermarket at my request to pick up milk and bread. It was a concrete monstrosity of a building, open every night until 8.30 - a big glowing tanker of a place that had destroyed an elegant block of early Georgian town houses, one of which Cookson had lived in. Hugh accompanied me into the shop and picked up two packets of cakes, which made me smile because he had been complaining about gaining weight over the Christmas break. I waited for him at the check-out. As we were going out through the automatic doors, a group of not-so-young men did a double take at us.

'Oh fuck me, if it ain't the poof!' one man announced at high volume.

'Keep walking,' I whispered to Hugh, who had tensed by my side.

'Oh look, he's got a pretend girlfriend, the wanker!' the man persisted.

'Oi *poof*! We're talking to you,' shouted another.

They stopped in front of us. Hugh stood stock still and I could feel him staring the others out. I felt my insides clench.

'*Bum-boy!*' shouted the ringleader, a going-to-fat, late twenties man with very short hair. Jabbing Hugh in the chest he hit a wall of hard muscle. Flinching, he turned away, trying to keep out of sight as he shook his fingers.

Fortunately, the manager emerged from the shop.

'Get out!' he shouted at the group. 'I don't want you lot in here. Get lost!'

The ringleader was about to speak.

The manager wheeled round on him. 'If you're not off these premises in one minute, I'm calling the police, do you understand?'

'*Go fuck yourself!*' bawled another. Then, amazingly, they sloped off, cat-calling and wolf-whistling, until they knew they were out of earshot. The manager disappeared into the shop without a word. We carried on walking to the car.

'I'm really sorry about that,' I said as we climbed in.

Hugh looked puzzled. 'It's not your responsibility.'

'If I hadn't stopped, this wouldn't have happened.'

In truth I had naively thought that the animosity towards Hugh and Craig was over. Mrs Little in the admin office now avoided my eyes, said the conventional courtesies, and no more, and nothing had happened since.

Hugh gave a short, mirthless laugh. 'Now the papers have got their claws into the AIDS epidemic, it looks like I'll have to get used to it. Which is why we go out of town, to where people don't know us, as a rule.'

'Bloody hell!'

'Hermione Mere couldn't have timed her vicious little campaign any better.'

I paused, wondered if, indeed, that was the case.

'Don't say anything about this to Craig,' Hugh said. 'What he doesn't have to know about all this crap, I keep from him.'

'Of course. But you shouldn't have to put up with abuse like that,' I said.

'You haven't noticed the red-topped gutter press howling about AIDS and gay people?' Hugh asked, cocking one eyebrow.

Of course I had. I had seen the relentless coverage on television, noticed the hysterical banners in tabloid newspapers, but it was surprising how little it had impacted on my own life. But what if it had shone a full beam on me? How would it feel if people considered they could comment loudly on my most intimate life, on my very being? Felt it was acceptable to criticise, because the media had given them the permission to comment, to pry, and a reason to hate? The media. The red-topped papers and those clever, privileged journalists who sat in the moral gutters with the red-necks, feeding them poison because it meant a wider readership, and more *money*. The very people who wrote articles about scroungers and whores, and who parasitised off distress and disaster, and grew fat on it.

'But it's so bloody unfair!' I said, and knew how feeble that sounded.

'It's all about money and fear,' Hugh said. 'And most people want a scapegoat.'

'Have you thought seriously about moving?'

'What, running away?'

'No, not running away, going somewhere where this doesn't happen.'

'Show me that place and Craig and I will go there.'

Hermione Mere had been very busy. Her idea of setting up the Stourton Young Mums' Club had gone down well with the older ladies from the Ladies Luncheon group, who were glad to be rid of the stupid, preening woman, to quote just one. Hermione had Rowland photocopy flyers on the office machine for the first meeting, which she decided would be at her house, and after that they would meet at the home of each of the attendees. It would give them all the chance to poke around in each others' houses. It did not cross her mind that no-one might turn up. But they did because her flyer asked:

YOUNG MUMS OF STOURTON
Are you fed up with all the doom and gloom?
Fed up with hearing about the AIDS
Plague and the Economic Downturn?

Well, why not come along to mine to
form the Stourton Young Mums Club?

Meet at each others homes every month
and swap stories over drinks and nibbles
My aim is to bring back traditional family
values, to share stories, and to help.
Interested? Phone Hermione on * * * * * * * * * * *

Our first meeting is at 1pm on January 30 1986
Rochester House, off Sheepwalk Way, Stourton

The phone had been going regularly since she had posted the flyers around town and left neat little bundles at the hairdressers, the beauty salon, the two children's clothes shop and the two bakeries in Stourton.

As she pointed out on the phone, she had suggested one o'clock to fit around school and nursery picking-up times. The ladies were keen to meet up and asked what they should bring.

'Oh just nibbles and things,' Hermione said casually. She would, of course, make sure everything was from Marks and Spencer, or at least Waitrose. In fact she would have it delivered and sod what Rowland said about the extra cost. She spent ages organising the dining room, making the spread look as though it was from the best hotel or wedding venue. She wondered if she should photograph it, with the idea of starting up some sort of catering venture, but soon dismissed that idea as it would get in the way of her already hectic life. As the time neared one o'clock she popped another of her slimming pills – her 'fuel', her very necessary boost.

The first gaggle of Girls, as she liked to call them to herself, came in just after one and spent the next quarter of an hour giggling and preening themselves by the many mirrors. It was patently clear that none of them were mothers. What Hermione did not know was that they were noted for partying at any available venue, and when that place was exhausted of booze and food, they would move off abruptly to the next potential location, landing like a wave of party-loving locusts.

Minutes later the next group arrived. These were a rather surly bunch – the Dowdies, Hermione decided to name them - who were dressed down and glared at the preening Gigglers on the other side of the vast, open-plan living room. Another contingent followed, fashionably late and tossing their hair about, expecting to be noticed and waited upon. The last group, the outdoorsy fraternity, arrived seriously late and stared at the ensemble as though they had just come across something mildly vulgar.

'Ladies,' Hermione said. The disparate groups looked around. 'Perhaps we should all introduce ourselves. I'm Hermione and I'm a stay-at-home Mum.' It struck her that she had not actually seen her children for nearly three weeks.

The others followed suit. The first giggling group introduced themselves through explosions of laughter and sniggering, then drew back together immediately, like a shoal of fish.

'I'm Amelia and I'm married to the County Councillor for this area.'

Oh Get You! thought Hermione.

Amelia was a thick-set woman from the Outdoorsies, sporting an expensive skirt and blouse and an Alice band. The Gigglers fell about laughing; Amelia stared at them stonily.

'I'm Henrietta,' drawled one of the Fashionably Lates. 'I like riding.'

I bet you do, Hermione felt like saying, smiling as she handed around glasses of wine.

'I think it would all be rather interesting if we said what professions or careers we follow,' said a woman who introduced herself as Rebecca. 'I write for *The Lady*.'

Lady who? Hermione wanted to ask.

'I run a catering outfit – mostly business lunches and dinners,' said another from the Fashionably Lates.

'We just concentrate on being *Gorgeous*!' shrilled the Gigglers. Hermione gave them a filthy look. This was not going to plan, she thought. A load of Airheads and closet-lesbians.

She waved them through, pointing to the seats and sofas in her extensive lounge.

'I don't know about you, Girls,' she started. 'But I just feel that we're going too far in the inclusive thing. My son told me the other day that his little friend at Prep school had been given a children's book about two men setting up home together and-'

'Oh yes,' one of the Outdoorsies boomed. 'It's that bloody Greater London Council, trying to make us all into homos!'

Hermione looked around at her, wide-eyed. 'Yes, exactly. Where is it all going to end?'

'I'd say live and let live,' said one of the Fashionably Lates.

Bet you come from London, Hermione thought.

'But now we have AIDS,' she said. 'I mean...' Hermione shook her head, suddenly muddled. 'What I mean is...that AIDS is in our community, so I think we need to talk about going back to traditional values. Mum, Dad, Children, Granny and Grandpa.'

'I think you'll find AIDS is not just a disease of homosexuals, darling,' drawled another of Fashionably Lates. 'Anyone who has sex can get it. Apparently.'

Hermione stared at her. Dirty cow, she wanted to say loudly. Fancy saying that in a first meeting! This really was nose-diving. Extraordinary. She thought they would all be eating out of her hand by now. She rounded them up again and moved them back to the dining table. Perhaps if she got them all eating, they would shut up and then she could have the floor.

One of the Dowdies helped her.

'I think Hermione is right,' she said - she was a be-spectacled lady in her thirties. 'Everyone has been so tolerant over the last twenty years, and look what's happened, a plague of sorts brought in by people with *very* unpleasant life-styles.' There were a few grunts of approval. The Gigglers were in the background by the drinks-trolley, necking down as much wine as they could possibly drink.

'Yes, and now we don't know if anything's safe,' said Hermione.

'Hang on a minute,' said Amelia munching a big slab of cake, half the bloody thing by the look of it. 'Aren't you the girl behind that campaign a year or so ago?'

Hermione smiled, twinkled even..

'Shut down the bookshop, didn't you. Bloody bad form, I'd say.'

Hermione flinched.

'Run by a couple of gays though, dear,' said one of her friends. 'Goodness knows what *they* were getting up to.'

'Nothing, from the sounds of it. Been together for years, apparently,' Amelia remarked.

'Ahh, but you never *know* what they do, and *who* with,' said the friend. 'Never know who else they might be seeing on the side.'

Amelia looked at the woman with contempt. 'Think you could level that at the mass of the whole bloody population, dear. Rutting like pigs, most of them!'

One of the Gigglers peered in. 'And it's none of your business, neither.'

The rest of the Gigglers exploded with laughter.

Hermione clapped her hands. 'Anyway,' she said. 'Lets get back to the agenda.'

'Didn't know there was one,' observed Amelia.

The Bill for Enclosure had been written up and Richard Ferris looked at it and thought of all the money it had cost so far, for the surveying, the scribes, the draughtsmen.... Of course he would get as much back from the people who were going to be given plots in lieu of common rights, or in lieu of the cottages on the upper half of the moor, which he intended to pull down. Cookson and the Poor Rates contingent had leaned on him and he had eventually agreed to build a range of cottages for the poor, the dispossessed ones Cookson had called them. The cottages would go up facing the turnpike on the lower part of the moor immediately west of the boggy area, so the inhabitants could literally fall out of their back doors and get their free firewood, rushes and turves, or whatever else they thought they were entitled to. With his contacts he could get builders to throw the range up cheaply. The finish did not matter. As a final slap he would insist they were called The Poor Houses.

Watts had been surveying for what seemed like weeks as late summer merged with a warm autumn and the leaves gradually yellowed and browned on trees and bushes. By the time the Bill went to the House of Commons for its first reading, October had come and gone, and it was now November. The nights were long, and Stourton Waste looked sombre and hateful to Ferris' eyes. Jamison was a member of the House of Commons and, keeping a house in Chelsea, was able to oblige his old school chum and round up his MP friends to attend the reading. The Enclosure Bill was to be read on 12th November. All that day, Ferris had walked up and down the morning room, then around the park, then hacked over the countryside on his favourite chestnut horse, and, when night had truly fallen, he walked into drawing room, and sat silently staring at the fire, ignoring his wife.

It went on like this for another two days and then, late one afternoon, a note was delivered stating, 'First reading of Bill – voted for. Prepare for second reading on 24th November. Yours, Jamison.'

It was only when Jamison returned to Stourton that Ferris was fully apprised of the situation.

'It'll be after the second reading that a committee will be set up to examine any petitions against,' Jamison said as he stood warming his slim behind by the fire. It had been a bone-chilling ride over from his estate. Ferris sat staring at him, the corners of his mouth turned down. Drumming his fingers on the arm of his chair, he suddenly got up and walked over to the window.

'I don't think you have anything to worry about,' Jamison said. 'Most of the House know you, or at least know of you through me, and they won't be about to upset your Bill. Think, it may be me sitting there, considering their petitions in a few months and they will want my support, Richard.'

Ferris turned around to him at the unusual mention of his first name. Jamison was a decent chap, always had been at school. Fair.

'My problem is Cookson,' Ferris said. 'Ever since I brought up the idea about enclosing he's been at me, subtly but always there. Like a portable conscience, which I can well do without.'

'Is there any way to get him to see your point of view?'

Ferris smiled. That meant bribes, or coercion (the polite word for bullying). But Cookson had no financial interest in the enclosure so intimidation would not work. As for bribes, he knew, without being told, that Cookson could not be bought. Georgiana was of the same hue, and for weeks now they had hardly talked, beyond the usual civilities. Had he not spent weeks trying to get her to see reason? Where did she think the money came from? he'd asked many times. It did not just turn up and keep renewing itself. She had looked at him with thinly-veiled dislike, and her look reminded him that she had come with a large dowry. And there was the unspoken question 'and where has all *that* gone?' He felt he was being goaded on all sides. The cost of enclosure had surprised him as he thought he had kept the expenditure down to the minimum. Employing Jamison as the sole commissioner had helped. There had been rather awkward conversations over rates of pay and they had eventually agreed that Jamison would be paid a guinea a day every day he worked on the enclosure process. Watts also agreed to those terms, and Ferris had smirked, thinking how quickly the man moved, and thought he would be getting a bargain there.

But now he had to face the prospect of the wretched committee and possible objections. Ferris knew if the commoners had put in a petition themselves that the committee and the House of Commons would have found it easy to throw it out; their objections would sound small and scattered. The committee could be easily talked round by the promises that enclosure would bring more work to the parish and create permanent jobs, as the upper half of the waste would be put to the plough. Then crops would have to be sown, tended and harvested. Everyone would win. Damn it, he was even going to provide 'The Dispossessed' with homes. Of course, the committee did not have to know that any land given in lieu of common right and plots would be on the worst land and in the most inconvenient locations, or that the poor houses would be thrown up using the cheapest materials and methods. Or that he intended to add the cost of building onto the beneficiaries' final payments as enclosure costs, disguised under another unavoidable charge. Who was going to find out, or do anything about it even if they did realise? Ferris would deny it, ask them to prove it, which no-one would be able to. If he just kept repeating the mantra that enclosure would make the land more productive, that it would feed the poor and provide more work, then the committee would agree. Everyone else did the same, and it worked. The only fly in the ointment was Cookson who was articulate and highly educated. In addition, his brother was a man-at-law, so advice and instruction could be gained, free of charge or with greatly reduced fees. Ferris had pondered the way to get Cookson on his side on innumerable evenings as he stared into the fire, but the man seemed to block him on every turn, on every plan that went around in his head.

Now, more than ever, he needed Jamison to help him through. Jamison had advised him to keep his head down over the next few weeks, keep away from the parishioners, not court more ill favour. There had been enough already. Unkempt men and women stared at him hard-faced as he trotted past them along the muddy, unturnpiked roads. Their faces were pinched. It did not occur to Ferris that this was through hunger. He assumed it was because of their insolent dislike of him, and he may have been partly right. One or two had started calling things after him but he could not make out what they said, although he knew they were criticisms. They should be grateful to him for providing more jobs and a new building, and not put out because their source of free fuel, and whatever else they pilfered, was coming to an end. Did they think his land was some boundless resource which they could plunder by right?

As November drew on, he increasingly spent most of his time in his own house, sending his men servants off to do the little errands he used to enjoy, as it had given him a chance to ride in the countryside, that countryside which he was about the change for ever.

'I've just found a deed that mentions the turnpike road over the lower half of the moor,' Hugh said, a week or so later in the Record Office. It was early February and belting with rain, which put a halt to any field work. Without ever saying anything, it was now implicitly understood that we worked together. On inclement days we would research in the Record Office; when the weather was fine we would be out in the field, trying to find the locations of the things we had discovered in the documents. It was also understood, tacitly, that Craig would join us on sunny days to photograph. I started to associate him with good weather and it occurred to me that 'sunny' was an apt description of his personality and bearing.

I knew that on the next field visit we would concentrate on the old roads, as we had found a few maps and records of the 18th-century turnpiking. These included the route that crossed the lower part of the heathery area, and the upper main road which was the northern boundary of the present moor, but had once cut the former extent in half.

We found that the boggy flush by the lower turnpike had been a problem as far back as the early 1700s, at least. A document had revealed that in 1710 the warrener had been given leave to improve the ditches and generally drain this land. We had been told by an elderly man who talked to us as we squelched around in the bog, taking measurements, that, as late as the 1960s, a stream had flowed over the land which was now a housing estate, and then flowed into the bog. The present main road was clearly made-up land, but when this was done we could not find out. Thus I visualised this part of the 17th-century moor as an expanse of heathy sand, interspersed with tough grassy areas, with a wide smear of boggy land coming from the north-west and meeting the river to the south. The road - or was it then just a big track? - probably meandered around the impassable bits, roaming past holes cut for clay and pits dug out for sand. It occurred to me that because of these uses – abuses? – this moor had a richer flora. The bare patches would have been colonised by rarer plants adapted to such conditions. On a 1770s map a sizeable track was shown in the line of the present road – would this have plugged the bog so that it became wetter and more waterlogged? If there was no barrier like a turnpike road before then, the water may have flowed freely from the boggy area and across the moor to the river.

We had discussed all this in the car before our visit. On arrival Craig pointed out the embanking at the southern end of the bog, below Thomas Jones' retting pool. There was also a culvert that ran from the end of the ditch that Hugh had previously examined which took water from the ditch away to the river. But when had that been put in? We could not find out.

It was a bitterly cold afternoon out on the lower section of the moor. Craig was photographing with fingerless gloves on. It was his blue-tinged cold face, and the fact that he was jumping on the spot to keep warm, as Hugh and I tried to take further measurements in the incipient evening light, that made me suggest removing ourselves to The Warrener to warm up. They agreed immediately and almost ran for the pub, and then sat close to the radiators while I got the drinks at the bar.

Hugh was shaking his hands to get the blood moving in them. As I turned, holding the drinks, Paul Smith appeared from the dining area.

'What the hell are you lot doing in here again!' he demanded. 'It's still part of your working day.'

I put the drinks down.

'We worked through our dinner hour out in the field,' said Hugh annunciating his words carefully as though talking to an idiot. 'Now it is getting dark so we can't do any more work outside-'

'And don't take that line with me, Winfield.' Smith interrupted. 'What's your *boyfriend* doing here?' The word 'boyfriend' came out as one might spit out a foul expletive.

'Mr. Lyle is here as the photographer – and Mr. Lyle is working voluntarily,' he replied in the same voice.

Craig leaned back in his chair, crossing his arms. Smith moved back.

'And does your line manager know about that?'

'Mr Blake thought it was very generous of Mr Lyle to give his time *gratis*.'

Smith snorted.

'Can I ask you, why you're in here, Mr Smith?' asked Craig. '*Again?* A public house during the day hardly seems the most fitting place for a senior county council official. Especially when he doesn't work in the vicinity.'

Smith's expression drew in. 'I am working in the area.'

Craig smiled. 'Oh yes, look there's Rowland Mere in the next room!' he said, pointing towards Mere, who was trying not to be seen around one side of the bar.

Smith leaned in towards him.

'I would be very careful if I were you,' he hissed.

'Really? Why?'

'What you are suggesting is slanderous.'

'I didn't suggest anything,' Craig said, opening those light blue eyes wide in mock surprise. 'If you made any connections, that lies with you, not me.'

Smith stepped back, his bottom jaw worked as though he was building up to answer back, but he turned and walked away, letting the outside door swing into the next customer.

I could see the tension in Craig's jaw. There was an awkward silence.

'I probably shouldn't have said that,' he said.

'What?' I squawked. 'You absolutely should have. Who the hell does that fucking man think he is!'

Hugh grinned. 'You say it, Kiddo!' Turning to Craig, he put his hand over this arm. 'Thank you.'

'Just hope he doesn't start mixing it with your managers, or whatever he calls them,' Craig said.

'Oh, I don't think he will – he'll want to keep this very quiet.'

Rowland Mere had insisted they met at The Warrener public house. It was convenient for him, and he was not known there. When they had arranged to meet, Smith suggested they went further out as he did not want to bump into those '*environmentalists*' again. Mere had decided it was time to dig his heels in; he was getting mightily fed up with Smith's condescending ways, making him feel as though he had to ingratiate himself to get his plans for Blackman's Moor through planning. After all, Smith was the traitor here, not him, he reasoned. A traitor to the organisation who employed him and paid his salary, who would eventually pay his generous pension. Mere was merely adding a few 'sweeteners' to help his cause. He was selling nobody down the river. As he did not trust Hermione to keep her bloody mouth shut, he could hardly invite Smith over to his home. In truth he never knew when Hermione would be in, or out shopping. Mere had never heard of anyone with the extraordinary capacity to shop as she did. Thus it was the The Warrener pub or nowt, he had said to Smith. This skinny, pasty-faced turncoat needed a kick up the arse. So when he heard Winfield, Lyle and the young woman come in, he had nearly gagged on his bitter. It was not helped by Smith rushing over to them like a rattlesnake and drawing attention to them both. Mere had seen that Lyle character with the long blonde hair clocking him. Glancing over to Winfield, he winced as he thought of the near miss he had had with the police through his wife's hate campaign. Stupid, stupid bitch. To be served like that was one step away from the courts and possible bankruptcy. Or something.

Mere had concluded his deal with Smith by handing over a bunch of papers, hidden in which was an envelope containing one thousand pounds in £20 notes. He winked at Smith as he fingered the paper clip which attached the envelope to the architect's plans for the executive housing estate. Another £1,000 if the plans were passed in outline, and an extra £250 if they were passed before two months were out, by April 1st at the latest. Smith had bleated about the latter. Who did Mere think he was, a magician? Mere had just looked at him, his round bland face inscrutable (he hoped) but, in truth, appearing like an insolent schoolboy who knows he has one over on the teacher. It was at that moment Smith knew he was in Mere's pay, and in too deep now to pretend he had misunderstood his motives. Mere had felt it too, felt the net close with a jerk. When the first payment was made, Smith was bound to him, and Mere knew he could continue applying nudges of pressure to get the sale and the planning permission through. Smith could not be all piss and wind. Not now, not when the key had just been turned so resolutely in the manacles.

Not surprisingly, the committee Jamison helped arrange was favourable to the Enclosure Bill going through. Well, it would be, wouldn't it, because it was made up chiefly of Jamison's friends and people who knew of Ferris. They were bright enough to understand that one day, probably soon, they would need a petition or bill passed in the House and they would need all the friends they had. This was a jolly good way of ensuring such future support. The committee went through the usual formulae for such proceedings:

Yes, the Standing Order had been observed and complied with. No-one there knew about the 'Pox on You Ferris' addendum to the one Standing Order notice, not even Jamison.

Yes, the Committee found the arguments to enclose were sound. But, again, of course they would, they would use the same mantras in the not-too-distant future. Those who knew Stourton Waste told the others, in private, that the lower half was like an Arabian desert, and not worth spitting upon. Yet all agreed in public what a darn good fellow Ferris was for letting the poor continue to use it.

Yes, they found that consent had been gained from those concerned with the enclosure. They knew of, course, these consents were done depending on how much land each person owned, therefore Ferris, who owned about 80% of the land, had 80% of the 'votes'. This made sense because they all wanted the easy passage of the Stourton Waste Enclosure Bill through the House.

'I must say,' Jamison remarked as he sat opposite Ferris in the morning room. 'Cookson gave a bloody good performance in putting forward a petition on behalf of the commoners and their rights. The House heard him out. I thought, at the very least, there would be amendments, but they voted it through with a strong majority.'

Ferris smiled broadly.

'Cookson also raised the point of the difference between the cottage owners who had rights of common and would be recompensed in the enclosure apportionment, and the leaseholders who also had common rights but would not get any recompense. And he pointed out that the Poor Rate would go up because these leaseholders would then seek extra assistance in lieu of these lost rights, and the man of middling income would, in effect, be paying more, *pro rata*, than the most wealthy.'

Ferris shrugged. Had Jamison only just realised that? Was he really *that* dull?

'*And?*' Ferris snapped. 'They'll always be winners and losers.'

Jamison blinked. 'Oh....Well at least you're providing the poor houses.'

Ferris looked at him in an open and direct manner, which he had learnt encouraged trust. 'Yes, of course.'

There were two further petitions against,' Jamison said. 'One was from a few cottagers, pleading that their livelihoods would be ruined, that they'd lose their independence -'

'Who the hell prepared that for them? That lot can't even read or write.'

Jamison shrugged. 'The second one was from a few of the proprietors who had originally signed the petition for enclosure. They argued that they had been led to believe that enclosure would benefit all, including the poor, but now, to quote,' - here Jamison referred to a little notebook - '"They find that enclosure would be a mistake, and would ruin the livelihoods of many."'

Ferris coloured up. 'And who signed *that?*'

Jamison held his hand up. 'Richard, calm yourself. The petitions were left on the table when the Bill was passed-'

'Meaning what?' Ferris stared up, under his eyelashes. Jamison knew that look from school – then it meant: 'Did *you* rat on me?'

'They were ignored.'

Ferris breathed out.

'The petitioners against were told that they could take the case to court for appeal if they wanted, but were warned that could be very expensive for them if they lost, as the costs would be awarded against them.'

'Probably a good idea to remind Cookson of that at regular intervals,' Ferris remarked.

'The subject of encroachments came up,' Jamison continued, as though he had not heard. 'It was determined that if any could be established as being between forty to sixty years' standing, the encroachment would stay with the possessors, but any right of common would not be conferred.'

'What about those over sixty years' old?' interrupted Ferris, thinking of Alice Heath.

'They'd be treated as old enclosures with rights of common.'

Ferris thought of the lack of deeds, the lack of hard evidence, and smiled to himself.

'Encroachments within forty years would be deemed to be a part of the waste to be divided, but then allotted to the current holders as part of their apportionment,' Jamison droned on. Ferris knew he should ask exactly what it all meant, but waved it away. This was getting dull....dull....dull.

'Several acres have been allotted for stone and sand for the making and repairing of highways,' Jamison reminded him.

That could come off the lower moor area, Ferris thought. There must be stone enough towards the river, and of sand there was far too much.

'The fencing,' Jamison was saying, 'will need good planning and execution.'

'Why?' Ferris asked wearily.

'It's one of the most expensive aspects-'

'So what? I'm getting most of the land.'

'Because,' said Jamison.'You would not want other people's livestock invading your crops, or mixing with your cattle and sheep. And it does occur to me that the people with the smallest plots will, in effect, pay relatively more for their fencing than you, for example, who will have whole swathes with only one perimeter fence.'

'Those with apportionments will have their own plots and they'll have to fence them,' Ferris retorted. 'You don't think they actually believe I'm going to *pay* for all that as well, do you!'

Jamison did think, well, why not? You're going to be the only true beneficiary in all this. Instead he said 'I think it is general practice that those with plots awarded to them pay for the fencing.'

'And what happens if they don't?' Ferris snapped.

'You can distrain the land-'

'Meaning?'

'Seize it and buy it for a pittance. You can even mortgage it back to the person, so they can then afford to fence it.'

Ferris smiled, it was a slow smile which crept like a sweet poison around his mouth. At the same time he could feel something tightening around his chest, something like a long, skeletal hand.

'What about lease-holders with common rights?' he asked.

'They don't get anything.'

'Good.'

'And the old roads and footpaths?'

'You can close any, and lay new ones to suit. Technically I, as commissioner, have that power.'

Ferris gave him knowing look. 'But we know who has the real power?'

'Yes,' said Jamison.

Ferris lost no time after the Bill was given Royal Assent. Within days of Jamison informing him that all was done, Ferris rode along the top area of the moor, leading a man who led a cart, pulled by two horses. In the cart were posts and ropes, picks and shovels. Behind was a line of labourers, mostly men on the Poor Rate in Stourton, aided by more who had been brought in from the next parish. They were to lay out the posts, ropes and rails at places which had been indicated by lines of pitch on the waste. Ferris had had two of his labourers do the rounds the day before, pouring the pitch along unflinching lines. Cottagers came out of their homes and grouped together wondering at what Ferris was doing. They knew why, but they could not understand how it had all come about so rapidly, and so completely.

Chapter Six

'I need a word,' said Jon Blake, leaning against Hugh's desk in The Water Closet. We stood, leaning against mine.

'There's been a complaint that you haven't been signing in or out for the last two weeks,' said Blake.

I had been expecting some complaint from Smith, but this threw me. I glanced at Hugh who was staring at Blake in surprise.

'We've been signing in and out as normal every day, without fail,' he said, his voice slightly higher than usual. 'Check with that woman from admin.'

'The complaint is from her, via Smith.'

'Eh? I don't understand."

Blake shifted uneasily. 'There have also been reports that you're using work time to meet friends and go to the pub.'

Hugh gave a tight smile. 'Thought so...Paul Smith saw us warming up at The Warrener pub after a very cold day surveying on the lower moor. We explained to him we had worked through our dinner hour.'

Blake nodded.

'We only went into the pub at quarter to five, so we had actually worked a quarter of an hour overtime, if you want to be picky. Which we're not.'

'Why was a friend along?'

'That's Craig Lyle, my partner, he's the person I told you about who's doing the photography for free. We need good pictures for any presentation and book, and Craig is a highly skilled photographer.'

Blake nodded. 'I thought that was the case-'

'Would you phone the Record Office?' Hugh interrupted. 'They'll be able to verify that we have been there on days when we couldn't get out into the field because of the weather.'

Blake went to wave it away.

'I'd rather you did, Mr Blake,' I said.

I could see him dither and then 'Okay, I'll ring from my office and get back to you in a moment,' he said, walking out.

We waited, I could see Hugh's expression contracting.

'Smith,' he hissed. *The little shit* - he's a bigger idiot than I thought. I'm tempted to tell Blake we've seen him consorting with Mere. Blake must know what happened to Craig and me, and the bookshop. Everyone else seems to.'

'Yes, tell him,' I said, and wondered whether I should also tell him about my run-in with Mrs Little. But what good would it do, even if we could prove to Blake we were where we said we had been? Hadn't Hugh been exposed to enough already? I decided to hold my counsel.

'Do you have any objection if I suggest we sign in and out with Blake from now?' I asked.

'No, not at all,' he said. I could see the muscles tightening around his jaw.

Blake came back in. 'Well,' he said in a much more upbeat tone. 'There's no doubt you've been there at the times you said, and I've seen you on the moor working when I've been driving over.'

'This may or may not be relevant,' Hugh said. 'But we've seen Paul Smith in The Warrener pub on two occasions with the property developer Rowland Mere, one during a lunch-hour, and the late afternoon he told you about.'

Blake's expression grew more alert.

'And you may be aware that Craig and I were put out of business by a homophobic campaign led by Mere's wife, Hermione Mere.'

Blake now looked very serious and nodded. 'Yes, I do know. If Mr Lyle would like to come and see us in Countryside,' he said. 'I'll see if we can come to some arrangement about reimbursement and expenses. And perhaps discuss something on a freelance basis, as and when we need him.'

Hugh smiled.

'Can we sign in and out with you each day?' I asked as Blake moved to the door.

Again he hesitated. 'Yes, okay, but do understand that it's just for the records. I have the highest regard for your work and your integrity.'

As he walked out, Hugh started rummaging through his desk drawer and took out several new floppy discs from a box and formatted them. Immediately he started backing up all the work we had done on the computer to date. It took longer than I thought. When he had finished he gave me two discs.

'Keep these safe. Bring one in with you every day and keep the other at home,' he said. There was a hardness in his voice, a barely disguised anger. 'I'll do the same. I'm also going to back up on Craig's Amstrad every evening. I think I get what's going on here.'

Ferris' men had worked hard and long putting the pitch lines over the upper moor. Now plough teams raked up and down, the ploughshare gashing brown, unswerving lines. Gangs of men dug holes for stakes between which other men slung thick rope, demarcating Ferris' massive gain. Soon he would get the thorn setts put in and a fertile land would be created from the waste.

On the side of the connecting road, west of the bog, builders worked from dawn until dusk throwing up terraced houses in a large, unwieldy block– two-up and two-downs which led straight onto the boggy area below Alice's cottage. Ferris was keen to get these houses built. The Poor Rate could take over any payments of rent to him, and he could throw down the hovels on the newly enclosed moor and get more arable. The work was coming along nicely, and he had intimated that if the houses were ready in double quick time there would be an extra payment for the builders. A vague promise of course, one that he would 'forget' when the time came. Drawing his horse up outside, he looked at the block. It was shoddy work to be sure, with only cursory attention to the mortar between the bricks, which he could see were of porous, inferior quality. Some of the roof timbers were up and they looked barely adequate. But it would be a cheap construction and get Cookson off his back. It might also appease some of the bad feeling that emanated from the parishioners – he was getting more irritated by the day with their belief that he owed them something.

Riding up to the upper moor, he could see an altercation and decided, as lord of the manor, he should be seen to intervene and settle it. As he rode closer, he saw that two of the Poor Rate men from the next parish were trying to smash down a picket fence surrounding a hovel and a young woman was trying to stop them.

Ferris came to a stop and, looking down at them, asked. 'What exactly is going on Mistress?'

The woman, dressed in worn-out clothes, looked up. 'These men have got no right to tear this fence. No right.'

Ferris shrugged. 'My workers have every right. You have been given notice of eviction and when the poor houses are ready you will move into them.'

'But they ain't ready, are they? And this is still me home.'

'It's mine Madam. You merely rent it.'

She glared up at him. 'I pays the rent, and while I does that, it's mine.'

'I think you'll find you're wrong there.'

'Then you give me back me rent then.'

These people were quite unbelievable, thought Ferris. Always wanting something for nothing. The way the woman was staring at him with that insolent dislike made him grimace. Who the hell did she think she was?

'You're paid up until when?'

'Until the beginning of next month.'

'The poor houses should be ready by then, and then the Poor Rate can have you.'

Ferris did not hear her reply as he cantered off over the turf which was as yet unploughed. Stopping by the top of the old moor he looked back over the ploughed, monotonous plain.

'This is all yours, Ferris', he thought, 'all yours. Each row sown with wheat will be money for next summer.'

Looking south he noticed two copses cluttering the eastern side of his newly ploughed land. Seeing a gaggle of workers erecting a fence along the northern boundary of the turnpike, he motioned them over. One looked up and put his hand over his eyes. Ferris held up his riding crop and motioned them to come over, impatiently. A few men peeled away from the group and ambled over.

'Come on, run!' Ferris shouted. 'I'm not waiting while you idle around.'

Putting them on a daily fixed rate had been a mistake, he thought. Jamison had suggested it, the fool. They should have been on piece work wages – that would get the idlers running.

The men jogged over.

'What?' said one, peering up moon-faced.

Ferris winced. 'See those copses over there,' he said, pointing with the riding crop.

'Yes.' It came out as 'yerr'

'I want them grubbed out within two days.'

'But we're working on the fencing up there!'

Ferris leaned down from his seat on his horse 'Then damn well work faster,' he hissed. 'I see enough of you standing around doing nothing.'

The men wandered back to their group. They were not from this parish. Ferris knew that if they had been, they would not have dared to speak to him like that, or look back in the way they did as they crossed the shrinking remnant of the moor.

The next day the men started hacking down the copses, which had for generations provided nuts from the hazel coppice, mast from the beech and acorns from the oaks. These oaks had provided timber for houses for centuries. Two of them were lofty pollards, and there was one in each copse. Yellow and beige leaves hung stiffly from twigs, surviving winter gales and rain, but not the axe. A myriad of small animals peeped out from tiny burrows and scampered back in panic as their world crashed down above them. A few birds of prey, who fed off the small animals, circled in the sky, watching the trees, their customary perches, being laid low by axe and saw. The copses were remnants of enormous woods that had once covered wide and ancient vistas.

The men who chopped the trees and hacked the bushes were aware of the flurry of activity from within and above, and many tried not to think about what they were doing. A few did not care. As the first oak crashed violently to ground, some were appalled at what they had done, and the few were pleased at their mastery over nature. Branches were sawn off and Ferris told them to cut the side twigs off and put the useful pieces in the low wagons he provided. The trees were split on site and hauled away for sale. One man looked with silent awe at the beautiful wood that was exposed by the splitting, staring at the strands which had separated on the edge of both parts, and wondered how the water and goodness from the soil was drawn up from the ground and into the tree. But another crash from the adjoining copse made him forget his awe and carry on with the destruction.

By the end of three days there were piles of brushwood covered with skeins of dead leaves. Piles of branches would be suitable for logs for the commoners and the poor. The felled oak carcases were dragged away by Ferris' men, followed by the wagons of usable timber. When Ferris rode over at the end of the work, he surveyed the destruction and thought of the acres he had added to his kingdom of arable, and the money it would make him.

'Can we leave the branches for the poor folk to take?' asked the foreman.

Ferris thought of the many small affronts he had suffered from these people and said. 'No. Burn it now.'

The foreman stepped back, clearly surprised.

'But it's drawing down night, Sir. Wouldn't it be easier to let the poor folk take it, if word goes about this evening?'

Ferris stared down at him. 'I want this mess burnt and cleared away now. If it takes all night, I don't care. It's to be burnt to ashes. You can spread the ashes on the land. Do you understand?'

The man nodded. Ferris looked at him with his eyebrows raised, waiting for a reply.

'Yes Sir,' the man mumbled.

But of course they did not burn the usable logs. The foreman waited for Ferris to disappear and called the others to him, directing them to go around the cottages and tell the folk to come over quietly and take what they could. A few older boys were posted as look-outs to alert the gatherers if any of Ferris' men appeared, but none did. All night people came and went, and only the useless bits were burned to ash. While Ferris lay in his bed smirking at his nastiness, the wood gatherers were smiling to themselves, knowing that at last they had one over on the bastard.

The next morning however, a good many mourned the loss of the copses as they surveyed the muddied, ash-smeared bleakness, knowing that the very land on which they stood was no longer part of their world, that they were now trespassers in a place which was quickly becoming unfamiliar and illegal to them.

A few weeks later I noticed Mrs Little had disappeared from her perch in the administration reception cubicle. I went over to look in after a few days and asked where she was. Her assistant clerk visibly jumped as she looked up at me.

'She's gone,' was all she would say.

I met Jon Blake walking down the corridor and asked him. Jiggling the change in his jacket pocket, he hesitated and then said it was all a bit awkward to go into at present.

Hugh was typing on the computer in The Water Closet. I asked him, but he shrugged and muttered something about 'Probably retired' and I could see he was engrossed with what he was doing. It occurred to me that Mrs Little's absence would mean nothing to him.

Rowland Mere had been behind all this. Since the bribe to Smith he had been able to apply more pressure and Smith had implicitly understood this, or had seemed to.

'I need those two gone,' Mere said to Smith when they met up in a car park out of the area. They agreed this was probably the best way to meet, change the venue each time, possibly 'bump into one another' in the supermarket or leisure centre car park in Stourton, then people would think they had met by accident, rather than by design.

'I can't just sack them,' Smith said. 'From what I gather from Blake, their supervisor, they're doing a thorough job. Finding far too many unusual species on the bloody moor and lots of history. Apparently.'

'Then we need to take more direct action against them. The only other party interested in buying the moor is your council, so we need get the Manpower employees off the case and I – we,' Mere said the last with a smirk, 'Are home and dry, and seriously in the money.'

'Well, I can't order a hit on them, can I?' Smith retorted, a little colour, like clown spots, appearing in his cheeks. 'What do you suggest?'

'Make out they're not turning up for work,' Mere stated. 'Say they seem to be gallivanting around a lot. Lose the time sheets, or something.'

Smith considered this, his expression wrinkling as though he had just smelled something unpleasant.

The next morning Smith called Mrs Little over, having heard her opinions about Winfield. She had been vocal in her intense dislike of him and the AIDS virus she suggested he was carrying. Oddly her opinions on that had gone silent, literally overnight, but Smith did not trouble himself with the reason why. Smith's impatient nature made him overlook things a seasoned criminal would have followed up. Attention to detail was something he lacked, and why he would always be caught if he chose a life of crime.

Smith put it to Mrs Little that she might like to help him. She had looked at him with dislike.

'What do you mean?' she asked, making sure they were out of anyone's hearing.

'I understand you don't like Hugh Winfield,' Smith said. 'Don't like his...um, *lifestyle*.'

She wrinkled her face. 'I think people like him should be locked up, sent away to a quarantine place somewhere. They're disgusting.'

'Do you know much about him?'

'I know he lives with a man! I read in the paper what those sorts get up to. Everywhere you go we keep hearing about this AIDS thing.'

Smith gave a thin smile. 'So you would be pleased if he went.'

'Of course I would. I went to those meetings run by that Hermione Mere before the authorities shut her up.' If Mrs Little had been at all perceptive she would have noticed the little jolt in Smith, but, like him, she did not notice unspoken cues. 'She talks absolute sense. We don't want those sort of people around here. Not round normal people.'

'One way to get rid of those Manpower people is to show they didn't show up for work perhaps?'

She thought about it for a moment. 'They have a time sheet each to sign in and out with the admin department each day. If those time sheets weren't there, or blank, they can't have come to work, can they?' she said. 'They haven't been working in the building for some time, as far I can see. Who else monitors them?'

Smith gave her a knowing look. 'As soon as you have something sorted out,' he said. 'Give me a nod and I'll do a spot inspection.'

'Right you are.'

'And remember,' said Smith, putting his finger to his lips. 'Not a word to anyone.'

She nodded, unsmiling, and walked back to the administration office.

Smith smiled to himself. Could it really be *that* easy?

About a week later when Mrs Little was called in by the sectional boss and his deputy to explain why she had not said something about the Manpower Service Commission employees apparently not turning up for work for the first two weeks of the month, she was genuinely thrown. At first she stuck by her statement that Hugh and Charlotte had not been in for that period. The man interviewing asked her whether she wanted to reconsider what she had just said. A panic rippled through her. She shook her head, too confused to know what to say.

'I have a signed statement from their supervisor Jonathan Blake,' said the man interviewing. 'Stating that during the weeks in question he saw them signing out on two occasions, one of which was his daughter's birthday, so he can be specific about the date as he made a joke with them and your assistant about clearing up after the birthday party. You were not in the office at that moment.' The interviewer looked down at the statement and then up again. 'Blake states on that last occasion he could also see the time sheets were fully signed-up for that month to date, and yet the ones you have given me are blank. Do you have anything to say about that?'

Mrs Little began to feel light-headed. 'Maybe I've got my dates wrong,' she said.

'Really?'

She again veered off with the explanation that she probably had the dates confused as she lost the time sheets and had had to do them from memory. They both knew how ridiculous that sounded.

'I have checked the computer logs for these two employees and they have also been wiped,' said the interviewer. 'We can get them looked at by specialists to see what was deleted and extract the original data.'

Mrs Little had never had to think two steps ahead like this in her life. She plodded along with her various prejudices, too ingrained in her own sense of what was right and wrong. She was of the 'no-nonsense, say it as it is' school and did not notice, or care to notice, that her opinions often wounded the people around her. As far as she wanted to believe, this was the first huge lie and deceitful action she had been involved in; she thought she had made it right with herself by believing she worked for the common good.

'Paul Smith from Planning made me do it,' she blurted. 'Asked me to disappear the records and falsify the time sheets.'

The interviewer studied her carefully. 'Can you prove this?'

'Smith spoke to me in private and asked me to give him a nod when it was done.'

'Which you did?'

She worked her mouth, then said flatly, 'Yes', and was escorted out of the building by two security guards.

Paul Smith was called in on the same afternoon, and questioned.

'I did a spot check on the time sheets,' he told the same interviewer.

'Was that your job?'

'I sometimes oversee the work of supervisors,' Smith answered, trying to be as vague as possible.

'The woman in administration, Mrs Little, said you asked her to falsify the time sheets to make it appear the Manpower employees did not turn up for work for at least two weeks.'

Smith gave a smug inward smile. 'I did no such thing.' Indeed technically he had not; he had let her suggest it.

'Why do you think she said that about you?'

'I have no idea,' Smith lied.

'So why do you think she did it?'

Smith sat back in his chair. 'She's made it perfectly clear she did not approve of Hugh Winfield's lifestyle.'

The interviewer looked at him with dislike. 'Mr Winfield's private life is just that, *private*.'

Smith looked at him open-eyed. 'But of course! However, this woman seemed to have it in for him from the beginning.'

'She told you this?'

'In so many words. She made her antipathy towards him very clear and fuelled it with the fear of the AIDS virus epidemic.'

The interviewer studied him and then wrote something in a card folder with 'Private and Confidential' stamped on it.

Smith later emerged from the office, job intact, and smirking at his success.

The first thing Mrs Little did the next day was to telephone Hermione Mere and arrange to meet her in a traditional tea-and-cakes cafe in Stourton, having picked up one of Hermione's 'Traditional Values Forum' flyers at the hairdresser the previous week. Rowland Mere was later to rename it the Trad. Vamps Club.

Hermione had again been very busy. The Stourton Young Mums' Club had disappeared after the first meeting but, being Hermione, she was not going to be dissuaded. What she needed was a group of people of age thirties upwards, who would meet socially and form a pressure group to act on councils at parish and county level, to make sure that the traditional values of Mum, Dad and Children in one family, helped out by the extended family in another, was back at the top of every agenda. This was being suggested on national television and in the daily newspapers, and now seemed the best time to strike with a local campaign. She was daily appalled at the lengths the Greater London Council were going to make out gay relationships were normal – it was all in her red-topped national newspapers. What was normal about two men (or women) living like man and wife? And even more ridiculous was the idea of them raising children. Crazy. What would two men know about raising a baby or a very small child? Corrupting madness, and now they had the AIDS plague to go with it. Thus she was pleased when she received a phone call from that woman from the council and heard about her plight. Mrs Little was pleased to have an audience and thought how she could play the victim who was forced out of her job for speaking her mind, a victim of liberal-minded madness. Thought how she was being made a terrible example of. She even started to believe it, and the fact that she had been sacked for a fraudulent offence hardly occurred to her any longer.

Hermione received a few phone calls in response to her most recent flyer, merely a rehash of the Stourton Young Mums' one. She arranged a meeting in a room of the local wine bar, and this time she made sure she only bought her own drinks, and anyone attending had to pay £2.50 each towards the room hire. The Stourton Young Mums locusts had drunk her dry and eaten bloody everything, the greedy cows she thought, and washed down two slimming tablets with a slug of wine. She had renamed them her 'power pills' and liked the feeling they gave her.

It was a few days later when I picked Hugh and Craig up and they sat in the back of the car, smirking like schoolboys. Hugh grabbed a photocopy of a page from a Victorian flora from his backpack.

'Craig, listen to this!' he squawked. 'The plant *cannabis sativa* was still being found on a track to the moor in the 1890s!' They started laughing hysterically, and I glanced from one to the other in the rear view mirror, not getting the joke.

'That's the hemp used for rope-making, isn't it?' I said.

'Amongst its other uses,' Hugh said. There was another explosion of laughter.

We had read about rabbit warrens on the moor from the 17th century in the Record Office and, as it was a sunny day, and I could see that Hugh wanted Craig with him whenever possible, we had decided to photograph any possible remains of pillow mounds (the artificial mounds made by warreners for the rabbits to burrow in). Hugh was in a strange giggly mood when I picked them up, and Craig was blissfully cheerful. I was driving, as their car had unexpectedly broken down, and big time. The garage had advised them to scrap it as they found sugar had been poured into the petrol tank. As Hugh said, it would have cost many times more than the car was worth to strip the engine down. I did not ask who they thought had done it, as I felt it would only underline what had happened. And it may have been a random act of vandalism – Stourton was known for such things. But now, being car-less, they were stuck. Hugh had phoned to ask if I would mind picking him up and dropping him off until they bought another car. Of course I agreed, and batted away any suggestion of petrol money with a 'I might need you to do the same thing in the not so distant future'. The state of the bangers we drove had become another good-natured competition between us. However, I sensed they did not have the money to buy a replacement and all thanks to Hermione Mere.

This morning, though, their secret humour, which did not allow anyone else in, was frankly irritating, and by the time we reached the car park by the bog I was all for leaving them to it and working on my own, but the cheerfulness glowing in Craig's face as he got out of the car banished those thoughts.

'You can lead,' said Hugh to me as they stood back to let me by. They followed, laughing about something. I glanced around at one point to find Craig holding Hugh in a loose horse-play head-lock. I wanted to shout at them to be careful, not to be so open, that the wrong people might see. Then

I thought what a coward I was, what a wet blanket. But this fear for them at first wheedled, then insisted, itself into my mind. I was all too aware at how the press were daily ramping up their campaign of fear about the AIDS epidemic, trying to pit people against others, trying to scapegoat, and I wanted to shout at them not do anything to draw attention to themselves. Then I realised the utter arrogance of my fears – they, more than anyone, knew all about this, and probably thought to hell with it. I certainly hoped so.

As soon as I pointed out the first thing to photograph, Craig became serious and focussed on the composition of the picture. There was a mention in 1298 of a rabbit warren 'on the waste' but which part we could not determine, although we agreed the sandy nature of the middle moor and scarp were the most obvious place. Rabbits were raised commercially in areas like this as they were thought to do well in meagre places.

An hour went by and we searched in vain for anything we could photograph or fit in with the history. In the proposed book I planned to quote the surveyor Norden whose work I had just read - in 1607 he stated that '*As for Warrens of Conies, they are not unnecessarie and they require no rich ground for feed in, but mean pasture and craggy grounds are fittest for them.*' I tried to quote this to Hugh as Craig photographed the scarp, but he was staring blankly ahead and did not seem to hear me. I wanted to ask what the hell was wrong with them this morning? But something held me back. When Craig rejoined us, a big smile broke on Hugh's face, and they followed me robotically along the terrace. The scarp seemed the most obvious area for a rabbit colony as this would have been a bank on a huge scale in which to burrow, but the sand was so loose that any mounds or enclosures would have been eroded away long ago. We searched the flat area of the upper moor, over its fine grass and heathy growth, but the sand was unlikely to have preserved the outline of any structures.

As we sat down for coffee from Thermoses on a backless wooden bench, Hugh turned to me, and I knew he was back. The alert look in those greenish-brown eyes had returned, the hawk-like expression of being just about to drop down on prey.

'We need to go through what the leases said,' he announced, pulling out a notebook and, reading from it, said 'So we don't know the location of the late 13th century coney warren, even it was actually on this remaining area of common. It may well have been in the later enclosed part.'

Craig, I noticed, was sitting back on the bench smiling inanely at the sky.

'The first lease for a warren is in1695 and refers to a man called John Jones who is given a lease for the "warrenable grounds". Was he of the same Jones family as our Thomas Jones the hemp retter?'

Craig was leaning even further back, his arms stretched backwards, holding his face up to the late winter's sun.

'Could be,' I said, glad to re-engage at last.

'Believe it or not there - '

A great thud behind us made us both jump and look round, to find Craig on his back, laughing.

'Whoops!' he said, and tried to sit up. 'Do carry on.'

'This John Jones was given the right to build a warren house or any structure he thought necessary over the warrenable grounds - '

'Bunny hutches!' Craig interrupted, and sat on the bench with uncharacteristic clumsiness.

'John Jones was also given the right to cut a watercourse or channel,' Hugh continued, 'through the waste, as long as it didn't impede any of the roadways.'

'Could that be the ditch we were looking at by the bog?' Craig said, as though suddenly arriving back with himself.

Hugh held his hand up. 'Ah, I'll come to that. This 1695 lease also mentions a cottage on the warren, a hemp plot -' more laughter – 'and a plot of ground called the nutland – spelled 'nutte-lond' – I thought of the hazel coppice by Alice's house.

'In 1725 there is another lease to Thomas Jones (the retter?) which states "the most southerly end of the heath betwixt the kings highway and the river" which has got to be the site south - '

'South by south-west -' I said.

'Yes - thank you, Kiddo – of the lower main road.'

'On the lower moor then,' said Craig.

We all stared out at the dry heathy expanse below.

'So why are we up here then?' I asked.

'Fuck knows,' said Hugh.

We trooped down to the middle section and Hugh came to a halt by the boggy area.

'Believe it or not, the 1725 lease talks about rabbits in the area of the bog where the lessee was given the right to let his rabbits graze on the "moorish or boggy grounds".'

'Probably needed a drink,' said Craig.

Hugh nodded and grinned at him as though still in collusion. 'This Thomas Jones was also given the right to take sand and to cut turf and clay from the bog with "tumbrells to take it away".'

'And the ditch Craig mentioned earlier may relate to a watercourse dug by Jones,' I said.

'Yes, and -' Hugh stopped, as though forgetting his words half-way through the thought.

Craig began photographing the boggy area.

'The cutting of clay and turves would account for the unevenness of the boggy area and would account in part for the bog flora,' he continued, unaccountably changing tack. 'I read somewhere that they dug the clay quite deep here to make crucibles in the local iron works in the 17th and 18th centuries. Any bog or marsh plants would have colonised those bare areas.'

'You're showing off,' I said, and heard a triumphant *Yep!* from Craig who jumped up onto the little sandy track that led to Byrd Cottage. We both seemed to hear the same twig crack towards the cottage, and then another. I knew it was Alice and looked up, but couldn't see her although I understood she wanted me to know that she was there. I looked to Craig but he was staring over towards the lower moor as Hugh was saying there was an earthwork feature there which he thought might be part of the rabbit warren. So the moment passed. We crossed over the main road and found the feature where Hugh said it would be. It was shown as a sunken fence on an early 20th century OS map but it was now a grassed-over bank, roughly six to eight feet wide with filled-in ditches either side, which showed as darker green strips in the finely grazed turf. Rabbit holes pock-marked the top of the bank and just before it disappeared into thick bracken and gorse, the bank split into two and formed a small, roughly round enclosure.

'One of the earthworks for the warren?' I suggested.

Hugh nodded. 'Maybe. Its location is about right. But I don't know why it was called a sunken fence.'

I looked at the ditches. 'Perhaps one of these held a fence at some stage.'

Craig was photographing it.

Hugh shrugged.

'That's part of the mystery of the place,' Craig said. 'And perhaps we don't need to understand everything.'

As I drove them back at the end of the afternoon, I noticed it was only just drawing into evening light – the days were getting longer. I asked something about tomorrow's work, and, getting no answer, looked in the rear view mirror to see them both fast asleep. Hugh's head was on Craig's shoulder and chest and Craig looked the most handsome I'd ever seen him as he slept untroubled, his head falling back slightly.

The next morning I picked Hugh up and, as it was raining, we were back at the Record Office after signing in with Jon Blake.

'I want to apologise about our behaviour yesterday,' Hugh said, staring ahead.

'Pardon?'

'Craig wanted to apologise to you and I said I wanted to too, so here I am, apologising.'

I gave a short laugh. For Hugh it was remarkably garbled. He must have realised it as he too gave a short, embarrassed laugh.

'Craig and I have back problems as a result of being in the book trade – book dealers generally have hernias or slipped discs, or both. It's lifting all those boxes.' Hugh explained. 'Being tall, Craig has more problems than most with discs in his spine, so I grow a bit of weed for our own medicinal use. I know what I'm doing - .'

I thought of the Biological Sciences degree and nodded.

'I grow it so I know where it's come from and we don't get involved with pushers and the drug scene.'

'You don't have to tell me all this,' I said.

'It's all right, I trust you, Kiddo. Anyway, it helps with the back problems, but on this occasion we went on far too long, and we were still rather-'

'It's fine, honestly. Live and let live, I say.'

'It won't happen again.'

I waved him quiet. 'As long as you don't do anything to harm yourselves,' I said, and immediately felt like someone's older, patronising sister.

'That's the last thing I would do, especially where Craig's concerned. I'm very protective of him.'

Turning, I smiled at him. 'Yes, I can see that.'

Alice came to me in my dreams in the early hours of the next morning. We were sitting outside her cottage. Little green buds were starting to show on the hazel twigs, and a blackbird was hunting around in the small vegetable plot that Alice had recently dug over.

'You still ain't found nothing, 'ave you?' she said, and I could sense her disappointment.

'We're getting there. Were any of your relatives warreners?' I asked.

Scratching her midriff, she considered for a moment. 'I knows of one on me father's side was a rope maker and I have heard there was a house for a warrener in the same area. Could've been.'

'So you don't know?'

Alice wrinkled her face up a little. 'No.'

'What was your surname before you married.'

'Jones, I told you that before.'

'So you did.'

'Me great, great grandsire's name was John Jones.'

I looked at her, open-eyed. 'Then we've found him. John Jones was the warrener.'

'Oh.'

'One of me ancestors was called Thomas.'

'That helps,' I said writing it down. 'Thomas took over the lease as warrener from John in about 1725.'

'Me mother's name before she wed was Williams.'

'Thanks.'

'How's the long-haired man?' Alice asked.

'Very well.'

'You might want to take him with you to the place of records.'

I looked at her in question.

'I could see you the other day,' said Alice. 'Tried to get your attention.'

'The two snapping twigs,' I said.

Alice nodded.

The next inclement day I suggested that Craig join us at the Record Office and see what he made of it. Hugh was pleased with the suggestion; Craig appeared not to be.

'What happens if I don't find anything?' he asked. 'Anyway, I don't think your boss would be too happy if I started getting my snout in that trough.'

'Come along as a volunteer,' I said.

Craig considered it. 'I have the book catalogues to print out and get sent off,' he said, and I realised there was a whole different working world he was involved in, of which I knew little, if anything. 'I have to get them sent out on the nail. There's a lot of competition out there. If you're late, people will just go onto the next one.'

'Craig's getting quite a following of die-hard book buyers,' Hugh said.

Craig smiled at that. 'I'll come over on the next day after the catalogues are out,' he said.

Which he did. It was one of those blustery days in early March when the late winter still holds on with its washed-out winter feel.

As we walked into the Record Office I could sense Craig's unfamiliarity and he looked awkward as we signed in. I saw the young man on the reception desk do a double-take when he spotted Craig.

'Wow!' he said, clearly in awe. 'For a moment I thought you were-' and mentioned a guitarist out of a popular heavy metal band.

'Oh Craig's had that look long before *they* were around,' said Hugh, rather ungraciously I thought.

We sat down at our accustomed table. Craig looked too big for the chair and desk, and sat forward with his hands hanging loose between his knees, his hair falling around his face.

'We're going through the archive boxes Hugh told you about,' I said. 'We have to wear cotton gloves to save anything from our skin going onto the documents.' I gave him a pair but even the largest would not go over his hands. The archivist considered, then went round the back to get a pair of XL size.

Out of his jacket pocket, Craig fished out a pair of round glasses.

'And here we have Professor Lyle in his natural environment,' Hugh said. 'Look at those glasses glinting in this, an unusual habitat for -'

'Shut up Hugh,' Craig said in an unusually flat voice. 'I'm feeling like a prat as it is.'

'You don't look one.'

Craig shot him an unpleasant look.

'This could be a bad idea putting me in front of all this,' he said, turning to me. 'I've never done this before and I'm not sure I'm going to be able to work out any of the handwriting.'

'Well, let's just see how it goes,' I said lamely, and wanted to upbraid Hugh for his insensitivity.

It was as though Hugh had guessed what I was thinking, because he said 'I know he can do it. It's down to confidence, a lot of it.'

'Not all,' Craig snapped. 'And stop being so patronising.'

Hugh sat a little further back in his chair and we fell silent. Fortunately, the archive boxes were wheeled out just at that point. Craig tilted his head a little to one side and looked at the boxes. After pausing for a while, he walked across and picked one up, apparently at random. Putting on his reading glasses, he started studying the title of the first document. I explained that the archivists wanted us to give a one sentence title of what each was about, Craig nodded and started writing on a piece of paper. However, as he was next to me, he kept bashing into me as he was so big, so he shuffled up a chair and sat directly opposite Hugh and ignored him. I sighed.

We worked in silence for about fifteen minutes and then Craig looked up.

'This is difficult,' he said.

I looked at the piece of paper he had been writing on and saw he had written far more than either myself or Hugh.

'*Wow*!' I said. 'You're bombing away.'

Craig smiled. 'It's not helped by the handwriting changing all the time. I've just found this,' he said, handing me a parchment. 'Something about John Jones the warrener, buying the house above the bog.'

Chapter Seven

Hermione gathered the ladies around her in the wine bar. It was a fairly unmixed bunch: a few younger women with hard, set expressions and fashionable clothes, but most seemed to be of the fifty to seventy year age bracket. Some of the older women sported stereotypical twin-sets and pearls, while others donned trousers with wide straight legs and elasticated waists, and wore their grey hair in severe haircuts, like steel helmets. Oh well, thought Hermione, the previous bunch were a load of scrubbers and show-offs, let's see what we can do with this lot.

She saw Mrs Little sitting with a couple of the twin-sets. Her incipient jowls were wobbling slightly as she talked. She now wore the air of the emotionally indignant, wounded with pride. Hermione sat down with them.

'I was asked to leave by the sectional boss,' she said. 'The person who should have been fired is Paul Smith from Planning.'

Hermione's expression set to alert.

'Why, did he ask you to say those things?' asked one of the twin-sets.

Mrs Little hesitated. Of course now she would have to work out another story – she had not thought that far ahead. 'Not in so many words,' she replied, and knew that it sounded weak.

'So why should he be sacked instead?' This twin-set was turning out to be the proverbial terrier with a rat.

'Oh, you know,' she replied. The twin-set did not.

'Well, I agree with this lady,' said Hermione, touching Mrs Little on the arm. 'She spoke her mind and is being punished for it.'

Mrs Little raised her face a little, enjoying the sense of being the one who is wronged, the victimhood.. 'Paul Smith is a slimy creature,' she said. 'Goodness knows what pies he has his fingers in.'

'I think he looks like Gollum,' Hermione giggled. One of the few books she remembered being read to her at school was 'The Hobbit' when she was eleven. 'I must ask my husband. He has dealings with Smith.'

Mrs Little turned around in surprise.

'My husband is the property developer – he's in talks about buying that wasteland, Blackman's Moor, to build on.' Hermione loved the reaction she was getting of faces turning to her, in approval, perhaps even in envy. She certainly hoped so. The need to show off was making her careless.

Mrs Little stared at her. 'Your husband knows Paul Smith?' If Hermione had listened carefully, she would have heard the dangerous undertone in the woman's voice.

'Oh yes,' said Hermione. 'They go golfing together.' They did not, but she thought it sounded good, so sod the truth.

Mrs Little's expression closed in. 'Does he indeed?'

Hermione turned to her, opening her perfectly mascaraed eyes wide. 'Oh yes. Row knows lots of influential people. Part of the territory.' The answering *oohhhs* were like lovely personal recommendations.

'Row can talk the hind legs off a donkey, he has such a way with people,' Hermione boasted.

Money, thought Mrs Little.

During the rest of the meeting they discussed how they were going to approach the council. They decided the Stourton Traditional Values Forum sounded professional. As no men had turned up – even though Hermione had put *ALL WELCOME* on the flyers – she decided against putting the word 'ladies' on the posters as she hoped some men, handsome, high-earning men, might still come along and she could play the coquettish chairwoman, perhaps even go as far to joke about spanking them if they misbehaved. She looked over the group and her heart sank, they looked an utterly boring lot, but needs must, she supposed.

She suggested they all draft letters to the chairmen of the parish councils they lived in. Then they should each draft a letter to the county council and in it ask that the council support their move to re-establish the traditional values of the nuclear family (Hermione liked that phrase, which one of the hard-faced younger women had just used). They should be given precedence in council matters, and to please *not* do what London Borough Council had done with promoting homosexual relationships, particularly now that AIDS could also infect the heterosexual population.

'Thought it always could infect heterosexuals,' said one of the younger women. Hermione shot her a look which warned she should shut up.

'What schemes had you in mind?' asked another of the quieter twin-sets.

Hermione had no idea. 'Well, this is why I called a meeting so we could discuss it.'

'Do you have any ideas of your own?' the twin-set persisted.

The Bitch, thought Hermione. 'Positively reinforcing funding-'

'You mean giving more money.'

'Giving more money to projects like after-school activities' Hermione made this up as she was talking. 'So hard-working parents don't have to worry about childcare after school.'

'Do you work?'

'I don't have to,' she said with a little smile. 'Rowland earns a very good salary.' The word 'wages' sounded far too working class to use.

'So you don't have childcare to think about?'

'My children are in prep school.'

'So you really have no idea what you're talking about,' said the mouthy younger woman.

'I am a mother,' Hermione said. 'I think I have every idea.'

The younger woman gave a sharp snort.

'Any other ideas?' Hermione asked, blanking her and looking around the small gathering.

'I think we need to clear up the children's play areas,' said one. 'The playground by the leisure centre is a well-known drugs drop-off area for the town.'

And how would you know? thought Hermione, but instead said 'Let's ask the council to look at that then.'

'There's just too much pandering to the minorities these days,' said a woman in her sixties. 'All this stuff about accepting other people's lifestyles and all that nonsense.'

'Oh yes,' said Hermione. 'We've had gay booksellers and now I see the racial minorities are starting to appear in the town council.'

'So it's a case of no blacks, no foreigners and no homos,' said the mouthy younger women, getting up and donning her coat.

'I wouldn't put it quite like that,' said Hermione, looking startled.

'You sound like a load of pathetic old bags, do you know that?' said the woman. 'I came along just to see how far down the scale you'd go, and you didn't disappoint.' She walked across the room and let herself out, without a backward glance.

'Well,' said Hermione, her hand on her lower neck. '*Well.*'

One of the twin-sets pursed her lips. 'How do we know that she wasn't a plant from a newspaper?'

Oh shit! thought Mrs Little, suddenly alert. What if she had been a plant from the council? What had she said? She felt her stomach knotting. Could she get into more trouble for making out Smith was on the take? Why could she not keep her mouth shut, work out who she was talking to before spreading rumours? But had it not been her 'say it as it is' attitude that made her someone people liked to talk to? In the past maybe, but not now. She had been reduced to seeking work on the checkouts in Stourton supermarket. Fortunately for her, the council had looked over her twenty-five years of work with them which had not been blemished by any other misdemeanour, and said they would not press criminal charges. However, on the checkout last week her clerk – former clerk – had come to her till, by accident from the startled look on her face, and could not get away quick enough – 'tainted by association' was the phrase that came into Mrs Little's mind. The long-haired gink who lived with Winfield had also come to her till with a carton of milk and dog biscuits only a few days ago, did not recognise her, and only spoke to thank her in his flat Stourton accent when she handed him his change at arm's length. She had gone straight to the Ladies and washed her hands over and over. So perhaps this is why she had come along to this meeting – this was a place where she could belong, find friends, some identity perhaps. But now she had blown it by shouting her mouth off about Smith. She had seen Smith in Stourton High Street the previous week and he had held his head in the air and made a point of ignoring her. Perhaps if he had not done that, she would not have said what she had. So it was all his fault.

Cookson was sitting in the morning room with Ferris. He had asked for an interview with him at his earliest convenience. Ferris had kept him waiting for a week, even though Cookson had underlined the importance of what he had to say. The foreboding in the town and the small settlements affected by the enclosure was becoming daily more apparent. The stares after Ferris became angrier and increasingly obvious, the muttering amongst men in the fields and at the taverns was becoming incendiary. The building of the poor houses was not complete, in spite of repeated but vague promises from Ferris that they would be ready to move into by the end of the winter.

Ferris had had several arguments with the builders who had downed tools and left the site. However, the work of pulling down the cottages on the newly-enclosed land had continued in earnest. The place was now a dreadful sea of mud after the heavy winter rains. Cookson was left with the problem of homeless families having to be put up in his outbuildings.

'Lord Ferris,' he was saying. 'While the outbuildings are dry, they are without windows or proper hearths or doors. You can't expect people to live like animals because you have argued with the builders.'

Ferris shrugged.

'I am having to provide bedding and food for these dispossessed folk,' Cookson continued.

'Take it out of the Poor Rate,' Ferris snapped. 'We pay enough into it.'

Cookson was tempted to say 'And you have just thrown dozens more onto it'. Day after day carts had drawn up by his outbuildings and people stepped down with the defeated air of those who have lost everything. Small, thin children were led by the hand by parents whose clothes were shabby and whose faces were pinched by worry and hunger. People carried the world in bundles and did not know what they were going to do next, or where they were going. Cookson and his staff tried to welcome them, made makeshift beds from bales of straw. Searching his own rooms with his servants, he found all the spare blankets he had, and handed them out. The people were cold and asked where they could light fires. Looking around Cookson suggested lighting one or two on the cobbled areas near the doorways, but one got out of hand and was only just stamped out in time, before the straw bales caught. The Poor Rate allowed him money for food, and his own staff worked extra time to cook simple but warming meals which they took over in large pots.

'Get them to work for their bed and board,' Ferris said when Cookson had described what he was doing. 'Let them pay you rent.'

'To live like animals?' Cookson retorted. 'Have you no scruples?'

147

Ferris rolled his eyes. 'These people are too used to having something for nothing,' he explained in what he hoped was a patient voice. 'Now they have to realise they have to pay their way.'

'And what with, Lord Ferris? What?'

'Money,' Ferris said slowly, as though talking to a half-wit.

'These people were getting by -'

'By filching off my land.'

'By exercising their common rights from time immemorial. When people could supplement their lives by what could be had by rights, they could look after themselves-'

'And the lord of the manor was given work in return, remember.'

'Now you have made them into workers who need to work for someone else to survive.'

'And what's wrong with that?' Ferris demanded.

'Can't you see what you've done?' Cookson looked at him, his eyes unusually wide.

'There's work in spade loads creating the new enclosures,' Ferris said. 'Most of the men have work through this process.'

'And the ones you've thrown out of the cottages-'

'My cottages.'

'- are living like cattle.'

'Then they had better find more work, I still have lots more to do.'

'And when you've finished with that? What then?'

'Perhaps if they stopped breeding like rabbits, there would be enough work to go around.'

Cookson narrowed his eyes. For the first time in his life he wanted to strike someone, strike that smug, all too perfect face.

'You really have no shame,' he said.

'I've built the poor houses. What more do they want, blood?'

Probably, thought Cookson. Your blood.

Craig was looking at us as we both stared wide-eyed at him.

'What did you just say?' said Hugh.

Craig pushed the small parchment over to him, and sat back, trying to arch his back to ease the discomfort, I presumed, of sitting in a too small chair.

Hugh was reading the document, perched like a bird of prey.

'What does it say!' I asked. I was virtually bouncing in my seat.

'That John Jones the warrener bought a tenement from the lord of the manor, someone called Timpson-'

'I've seen that name several times today,' I said.

'The tenement called Byrd Cottage and its garden, can't make out the cost, and it's signed by Timpson, and there's a mark made by Jones, with his name written below. And it's sold as freehold.'

'Alice's cottage,' I said. 'She was absolutely right.'

Hugh looked over at Craig and made a twirly motion with his forefinger to his temple. Craig stared at him. I could see from the set of his jaw and the slightly lowered brow that it was not a friendly look.

'I sensed something when I was there,' he said.

'You're an archaeologist by training,' Hugh replied. 'Of course you'd sense something in the ground.'

'It was more than that.'

I'd had a headache hovering all morning which tightened now. This is not how I expected to find such a document. I would have wanted it to be more dramatic, a reveal, a flourish, perhaps even with a lowering of temperature, a sudden unaccountable noise as it was found. Not sitting here on a weekday morning with a headache, and Craig and Hugh sniping at each other.

'Cup of coffee time?' I suggested.

'Let me ask them to copy this first,' Hugh said.

The request was sent through and we went out into the common room. When I walked back with the three coffees, I was pleased to see them talking. Unusually it was Craig who was talking emphatically but I was too far away to catch what he was saying. For a moment I thought he was arguing with Hugh, and then I saw him smiling. I relaxed.

'You don't have to be so two-dimensional,' he said as I sat with them. 'Just because you can't see something doesn't mean it doesn't exist.'

'Yes, you can't see atoms, but we know they're there.' Hugh was trying to be conciliatory.

'Well, if you can accept that, why can't you accept there may be a dimension we don't yet know about?'

Hugh was sitting further back in his chair, his arms crossed and he shrugged. I realised Craig was probably not a person to pick a fight with. He was now unusually animated and was looking hard at Hugh, who was staring back at him stony-faced.

'Hey you two, don't let's start falling out,' I said, putting the coffees down.

'Hugh started it,' Craig protested.

It must have been the 'Just listen to yourself!' look I gave him that made him grin.

Holding up his hands, he turned to Hugh. 'Call it a truce?'

'Truce,' said Hugh, and visibly relaxed.

The next time we were all on the moor, we went to the site of Byrd Cottage which we found was in its present-day, overgrown form. Craig walked around examining the grassed-over foundations.

'I wonder if we should ask if we can excavate this?' he said. 'If the council are going to buy it, it may be a good idea to show what the majority of the population lived in. If there's any detail left, then it would be worth preserving. Small vernacular cottage remains are unusual.'

'I think that's an excellent idea,' I said.

'You'd have to oversee it,' Hugh said. 'We wouldn't know what we were looking at.'

'Do you want to put to your boss?' Craig said.

We nodded and decided Hugh should approach Jon Blake.

Mere got into the passenger seat of Smith's car, his bulk filling the seat. Smith looked at him and his expression soured.

'So getting the plan to get the Manpower people fired was a complete cock-up,' Mere said by way of introduction.

'It wasn't the best thought-out plan, in retrospect,' Smith agreed.

'That's an understatement. So what are you going to do to get these Manpower placements stopped? Have you asked Blake how far advanced they are?'

Smith stared ahead. 'Mr Blake is rather circumspect about telling me things these days.'

'No surprise there...But you must have some idea.'

Smith turned to him, he looked sallow and drawn. 'Of course I have,' he snapped. 'From all accounts they're flying, very *committed*.' The last word was said with disgust.

'Who would have thought such a piece of fucked-up wasteland could be so interesting,' Mere remarked.

'I did hamstring Winfield's car,' Smith said.

'Didn't know you were a mechanic.'

'I didn't do it,' said Smith with disdain. 'I paid a local thug to do something to the engine.'

'What?'

'Didn't ask. Just told him to disable the engine so it wrecked itself. It's a case of what I don't have to know, I don't have to confess.'

'And it worked?'

'When I drove past the next day, the long-haired, hippy-looking creature was out there, with the bonnet up, scratching his head. His hair was tied back. Didn't realise what a-' he was going to say 'what a strong face he has', but that sounded suspiciously queer, so instead he said 'what a yob he looks.'

Mere considered this. 'They had no idea it was you?'

Smith gave a mirthless laugh. 'Have you seen what a scrap heap it is? Was.' Smith was tempted to add, "and thanks to your wife, they can't afford to replace it." 'Thought if he couldn't get into work it would cause problems, but that silly bitch Winfield works with has been ferrying him around, like a taxi service.'

'Do her car as well,' said Mere.

'She has a garage at her house, and she parks the car close to the office at work. I did look. Anyway two cars being destroyed is pushing it.'

'So what are you going to do?' Mere glanced at him, thinking how irritating he looked, with his prominent teeth and pallid, sweaty complexion, and how much he wanted to push him out of the car. But he had given him far too much in bribes to walk away now. Like so many of those with so much money, Mere did not like wasting it, and he was certainly not going to give any away.

'Look, you,' he said, turning in his seat so he almost faced Smith. 'I paid you to get me the sale of Blackman's Moor, and so far you have achieved fuck all. I don't call that a good investment, do you?'

Smith shifted in his seat and carried on staring out of the front window. In truth, he was starting to panic. It was now drifting towards April and word was that the Manpower employees were doing an excellent job. The other one, Lyle, had been seen in the offices with the graphics and printing guys, expensive-looking camera slung over his shoulder. Perhaps he could get that nicked off him, set up a mugging, but they probably had insurance so that wouldn't solve anything. Perhaps he could arrange to get them beaten up? For a moment he considered this, but thought no, the thugs he had approached about the car had been surprisingly hard-headed over business. Money first, otherwise go f--- yourself and we're not doing anything we could get sent down for.

Then he thought of something, and, turning to Mere, said.

'Leave it with me.'

It was in the pre-dawn light that four of Ferris' men crept up to the cottage in which Alice Heath and her three daughters lived. Ferris had been clear: get them out and then pull down the roof. They had brought long poled fire-hooks from the estate and iron bars which might come in useful if the inhabitants gave them any trouble. Positioning themselves either side of the door, the largest of them put his finger to his lips, held up his hand and then, with the biggest kick he could muster, splintered the door off its hinges. Falling into the only room downstairs, he felt dizzy for a moment, then looked around. The room was empty. This was going to be easier than he thought. Then he looked up higher and saw two heads, peering down at him from the sleeping loft above.

'Get out,' the man said. 'And we'll give you no trouble.'

Alice pushed her eldest daughter behind her. Thinking quickly she dragged on her shawl and, turning to her children, motioned them to pull on their boots, pull outer clothes on and stand at the back of the loft.

Crouching back down she looked through the railings at the four upturned male faces. She knew she and her girls were in serious danger. She could feel the roused male energy floating up in the air like some appalling odour.

'We want you out of here, Widow Heath, and your brats.'

'Ferris sent you?'

'Yes' which sounded as 'yeer'.

Thinking of her girls, she decided to get outside with them as quickly as she could. If she had been on her own she would have fought, but her eldest Harriet was going into womanhood and she knew the danger she might be in. So finger to her lips, she led them down. On getting to the ground level, she shielded them from the men and whispered to them to get out and run to Cookson's house. Harriet stared, not daring to move until her mother had finished talking, and then tried to drag her along too. Alice shook her head violently. She pushed them away and Harriet gave her a look that nearly broke her heart: absolute despair, as though Alice was just about to be pushed from the scaffold with a noose tight around her neck.

'*Go! Run!*' Alice yelled. They ran.

At that moment the men crashed up into the sleeping loft and began attacking the roof from inside. Alice stared up in horror.

'You can't do this!' she screamed. 'It's mine. It's not Ferris'. *It's mine!*'

One of the men bundled up her few belongings and lobbed them at her.

'Get out, you evil bitch!' he shouted.

Alice heard the timbers starting to give in the roof. She launched forward and tried to get up the loft ladder but one of the wreckers kicked her savagely in the face and she fell backwards onto the flags, unable to breathe. It was fortunate the men were enjoying the destruction so much as she knew she was in danger of being raped, murdered even. Rolling onto her side, she picked herself up and holding onto the shattered door post, she looked up to see one of the rafters smashing down on her bed as a cloud of dust and grit obliterated the view. There were loud angry voices and the roof started to make a terrible straining noise, wood grating against wood. As it caved in, Alice ran for her life.

Cookson found her collapsed on the path close to his house, She was dust-covered so her hair and face looked deathly grey, and at first he thought she was dead. She was bleeding from the nose and mouth and her left arm was twisted unnaturally behind her. Harriet stepped forward. Sinking down in the mud of the path, she cradled her mother, who was breathing but unconscious.

'We must get her back,' Cookson whispered. Together he and the girl got her up. Surprised at how little she weighed, he carried her while Harriet took the bundle Alice had been carrying. Alice's head fell back. The blood trickling into her mouth made her gag and for a second she stirred.

She came to during the afternoon. Harriet jumped up as soon as she saw her mother's eyelids flutter.

'Mother?' came the terrified word through her confusion. Alice tried to sit up, but could not and stared wildly around her. Her head felt as though it had been cracked open.

'Mother, quiet yourself. You've been attacked, but you're safe now at Mr. Cookson's.'

'The girls,' Alice managed to whisper through her blood-caked mouth. It felt as though someone had sliced her skin away, exposing the rawness and nerves below.

'They're with the cook, helping to make a cake.'

'And you?' the words were barely audible, but Alice clung onto her arm.

'I'm fine Mother.' Harriet was not, but her mother did not need to know this.

Cookson walked over to Byrd Cottage when it was fully light. It was an incongruously bright morning. When he passed the old sandstone post which announced the beginning of the garden plot, he stopped. The air smelled sour with the dust of plaster and mortar which had settled like a strange snow on the lawn and the well-tended vegetable plot, which was just showing the shoots of spring growth. Cookson hardly wanted to look up at the cottage and when he did, he winced. The roof had caved in and the top layers of stone walls had been dragged down. There was no-one around and the place seemed to have died, its soul already departed.

Smith walked into the dark office, a large cupboard in effect, in which Winfield and that silly bitch worked. Not daring to turn on the light, he held a small torch in his sweat-slippery hand - he had remembered to wear disposable latex gloves. Going over to the computer, he held it high in the air and smashed it to the floor, and, just to make sure it was destroyed, he poured a jam jar of water that he had brought for that purpose into its works. Rifling through all of the desk drawers, he emptied the floppy discs on Winfield's desk and forcing them apart, stuffed the filmy middles into a bag slung over his chest. He was wearing a black balaclava and black clothes. When he had dressed up like this, just in case anyone saw him, he had thought how dangerous he looked. Now he was perspiring horribly so the sweat blurred his vision and he kept having to wipe his eyes. Emptying all the box files on the only wall shelf, he scrunched the papers into a hard ball and stuffed them into his bag – he would burn them later in his garden. Looking around he tried to think where else they might have stored their research, but the room was small and he could see he had covered all the possibilities. Knowing he could not leave the destruction in this room only, as people might guess he was involved, he went into several other offices and turned the desk drawers out and stole documents which he would later burn. Destroying two other computers, he found himself thinking what an awful waste it was. Being money-pinching by nature, even though he was living on his own and possessed a large surplus income, he wondered if he should have stolen the machines instead, and then thought that would have meant risking being seen lugging the things out to his car, which was hidden down a back street. So he increased his orgy of destruction, after making it right with his world.

We arrived at the offices the next day to find police milling around in the corridors that led to The Water Closet. We passed three offices with police tape over the doors and, reaching ours at the end of The Resounding Corridor, we were met by a young uniformed policeman.

'Sorry Ma'am,' he said, holding his arm out to stop me. 'No entry. The fingerprint guys are in there.'

'What's going on?' Hugh asked, trying to see around him into The Water Closet.

'Sir. Please,' said the officer, walking us back a little. 'It's no entry. There was a break in last night and some computers were destroyed and documents taken.'

The police officer looked so young and awkward, I immediately backed away, and, tugging at Hugh's windcheater, the expensive one which I liked, moved him on. We went to see Jon Blake, who was on the phone and holding the top of his head. Looking at us, he waved us over and finished the phone call.

'Disaster,' he said. 'There's been a break in, and your office has been badly damaged with three others.' Blake hesitated. 'I am very sorry to say that your computer and files for the Blackman's Moor research have been destroyed.'

Hugh dug into his inner jacket pocket and drew out a floppy disc. 'This is why one should always make back ups.'

Blake sat back in his chair, a big smile appearing on his face. 'Thank goodness! Do you know when I thought all that research had gone I felt desperate...I mean, I was so disappointed.'

'I've also photocopied all our written notes and sources as a back-up too, and Craig has kept the photos with him at home,' Hugh said. 'I may have told you about the sugar in the petrol tank episode, and we know how Smith has been gunning for us, so I decided to stay two steps ahead.'

Blake drew in a long breath, as though he was debating with himself.

'Would you step outside for a moment?' he asked. 'I just want to check something.'

We obediently stood in the corridor, Hugh leaning against the wall like a belligerent teenager waiting to see the year-head at school. Blake's door opened and he called us in.

'You may remember that Mrs Little who was the woman in charge of administration, left quite suddenly.'

We nodded.

'The reason was that she'd falsified your time sheets to suggest neither of you had been in for two weeks.'

'Bloody hell,' Hugh muttered, forgetting himself.

'So we checked for her involvement this time, but this can't have been anything to do with her as she's been in Spain for the last week, so we're casting the net wider. The detectives are saying that the main focus of this attack was your office, and the other offices were probably destroyed to make it look like a random act of vandalism.'

Of course we all knew who was top of the list and who the police should interview, and Paul Smith promptly jumped when two uniformed officers asked if he would accompany them to the police station in Stourton, a 1960s eyesore of a building, all peeling plywood panels and picture windows, diagonally opposite the supermarket in what had once been the beautiful Georgian square.

We were instructed to work in the field if the weather permitted, or at home if not. When we phoned in as arranged, Blake told us that our office should be up and running in a couple of days.

'And by the way,' Blake said. 'You'll be getting a new computer. Whoever did this didn't realise they were doing you a favour. It'll be state of the art.'

The next morning was sunny and warm. I picked Hugh and Craig up from the house with the dogs, who catapulted into the back of the car and looked up alert and dog-smiling. Craig sat in the front while Hugh held court from the back. Craig was wearing a black, heavy metal band t-shirt and I noticed the surprising paleness of the skin on his upper arms.

Sensing I was looking, he said 'I need to get some sun, so I don't look so washed-out. I can burn like hell though, so I have to be careful.'

'It's because you're so fair,' I said.

'It's all that Viking blood,' Hugh said, and snorted with laughter.

'Shut up Hugh,' I mouthed, addressing him through the rear view mirror. I caught his eye and opened mine wide in warning. I don't think Craig had taken much of this in as he was busy talking about where he thought we should photograph, and asking why we had not followed up his suggestion about a small excavation at Byrd Cottage as the weather was set fair. I too wondered why neither Hugh nor I had thought of this so, stopping by the nearest phone box, Hugh rang Blake with the suggestion and a few minutes later he sprang back into the car.

'Blake said that was a brilliant idea, so he's going to ask the vendors if we can go ahead, and he'll also ask the head of the archaeology unit to meet us on site tomorrow if he can arrange it in time, and he'll let us know when we report in at the end of the day.'

'Remember, I've got to go over to my mother's to get the car some time,' Craig addressed Hugh.

'Craig's Mum is giving us her car,' Hugh explained. 'She heard about the sugar episode and offered it to us. The rest of the family were all for it.'

I felt a flash of disappointment as I had grown used to picking them up and dropping them back home. I always felt a curl of pride to be with them, especially Craig. I made some 'Oh that's great!' comment and we parked by the lower part of the common.

'I wish I had more siblings,' I said as we watched Craig photographing an area of lichen. 'There's only me and my brother.'

'Same here,' said Hugh. 'Craig's family are fantastic, really supportive. They're very decent people. They took to the fact of us being a couple with no problem, and that was in the mid-seventies.'

I must have looked puzzled.

'It was technically illegal only eight years before that.'

'*Pardon*?'

Hugh looked at me as though I was daft.

'The Sexual Offences Act 1967. I was seventeen when the bill was passed.'

'Bloody hell, I've never even considered that before!'

'Well, you wouldn't,' said Hugh. 'It didn't apply to most people. But imagine if it had, and you were told when you were in your teens that what you were feeling, what you wanted to do was illegal against the bloody law.'

'Well, can you tell us why your name seems to be linked with several attacks on one of the two people who are working in the Manpower scheme?' said a young woman detective. 'Hugh Winfield.'

'I don't know what you mean.' said Smith, who had waved away the need for a solicitor, against advice. There was nothing on him, he had made sure of that, and if he agreed to a solicitor it would suggest he was hiding something.

'Mrs Little the woman from administration, said you had told her to falsify their time sheets to suggest they were skipping work.'

'I most certainly did not',' Smith protested. That was true – she had suggested it.

'Then the Manpower employees' office was vandalised and their work destroyed.'

'Oh, was it?'

The detective noticed the rise of hope in Smith's voice.

'And we find that Hugh Winfield's car was purposely vandalised and it was rendered undriveable,' said an older, male detective. 'A bit of a coincidence, don't you think?'

Smith sat up straighter, they were handing him the answer, the idiots. 'You do know that the man is a homosexual, that he and his partner have been the victims of a homophobic campaign?' If they could not do their own jobs, he would do it for them. Was it not the standard joke that that policemen were thick, a load of knuckle-dragging plods?

'We are aware of the campaign against them, an illegal campaign organised by the wife of the developer Rowland Mere, who, we are told, has been seen in meetings with you on several occasions.'

Smith inwardly smarted - he had just walked into that one. 'Well, of course people are going to see me in conversation with him, he's the other bidder for Blackman's Moor.'

'Do you think sitting in the leisure centre car park is the appropriate place to hold a meeting?'

'I did not!' Alarm was making him careless. As he saw the female detective open a card file and pick up large colour photographs, he blurted, 'I may have seen him by coincidence on one occasion, by sheer chance.'

'Do you want to reconsider that statement?

'No.' Smith's head was swimming.

'Interesting,' said the woman detective. 'As I have photographs which show four separate locations on four separate occasions – the prints have date-stamps codes on the backs from the developing process.'

'Let me see,' Smith snapped, grabbing the photographs, hoping this was a bluff. They were indeed date-stamped and the photographs had been enlarged and, on each, he could see one or the other were wearing different jackets or coats.

'Then we thought, 'What is the connection here?' 'said the woman detective. 'We thought, 'Ah yes, the potential housing development on Blackman's Moor.' Then we thought: 'Now who are the people who are threatening this development? And, of course, the two who are on the Manpower scheme who are being employed by the very organisation you work for, Mr Smith. Can you see why we started to get interested in you?'

The male detective spoke before Smith could open his mouth. 'The forensics guys said that the centre of the attack on the offices was the little room where the Manpower Commission people work and keep their research. That really was 'done over'. The attacks on the other offices were clearly an afterthought.'

'How on earth can you tell that?' Smith demanded.

The male detective smiled at him. 'Criminals always think they're more intelligent than us plods. Always think they're two steps ahead. But we see things in situations you can't. It's all down to training and experience. Trust me.'

We sat on the bench at the top of the sandy scarp, eating lunch. Hugh had already hoovered his way through two bags of acid-yellow and orange aliens and UFOs, and was now devouring cheese and pickle sandwiches.

'You should eat the junk food after the proper food,' Craig said.

'Like the UFOs and aliens better,' he replied, with his mouth so full so it came out as a muffled murmur. Hugh's eating habits seemed in line with the rest of him. He was always thinking on his toes, precise, heading around an idea laterally, straight through, upside-down even, so maybe eating was a thing to get through as quickly as possible, so he could start on the next project.

It was the first spring-like day and we were in good spirits. The sun was strong, the temperature in the upper-teens or above, and Craig sat on the bench, his arms stretched backwards, face towards the sun.

'You want to be careful, or you'll get sunburnt,' I said.

'I put stuff on to stop me from burning,' he said, squinting into the sun at me.

'You do know the sun's very strong at this time of year,' Hugh said. 'Due to lack of foliage and the air being less humid.

'Thank you Professor Winfield,' Craig leaned forward to see him. 'How many E-numbers have you ingested today?'

Hugh carried on regardless. 'You remember the reference to salt being cut in the lower part of the moor, in the so-called salt holes?' There was no suggestion we would not remember it. 'And I took some soil samples of the most likely areas for cutting to test for sodium levels?'

'*Yes,*' we answered obediently.

'Well, there are suggestions of sodium in a couple of places and we should see if there any halophytes-'

'*Ohhher!*' We chorused with perfect timing.

'They're salt-loving plants-'

'*Aahh.*'

'The sodium would only be at trace levels,' Hugh said, ignoring us. 'But I think it may be a good idea to search the sites for evidence of salt-loving plants.'

'Hugh's halophytes,' announced Craig, jumping up. The dogs, who had been sleeping quietly at his feet, erupted upwards, as one. Catching the leads up, Craig handed one to each of us. I was given Harry who walked, flossy tail and ears up, the feathering flowing in the breeze.

As we walked I filled them in with what I had found in the records. The salt had been brought to the southern boundary of the lower moor in blocks by waggoners. The blocks were then cut into smaller sizes and presumably shipped by river to local and regional markets. This had been occurring until the early 20th century, and there was oral evidence of it occurring as late as the 1920s.

'The salt-loving sea bindweed was found in the vicinity of the salt-cutting area in the very early 1900s,' Hugh continued, seemingly oblivious to Craig who was grinning at me and doing duck bill impressions as we walked towards the bottom of the lowest part of the moor, only two hundred metres from the river. 'That's a very interesting plant usually found on coasts. Of course, there would only be traces of sodium left of the salt in the soil now -

'As the salt is very soluble.' Craig interrupted, and we both looked at him.

'Yes, quite,' Hugh said, as though thrown. 'Halophytes are increasingly found on modern road edges, which are routinely salted during the winter. The salt concentrations, albeit low, are found in these dips here and here,' he pointed to two moderate depressions in the closely-grazed turf areas, close to a track that joined up with the main road. 'So I suggest we have a few good photos of those.'

We both grinned at him stupidly.

Smith left the police station, sweating. The police had let him go but asked him to stay in the area. Loosening his tie, he walked to the taxi rank outside the supermarket and thought about who had been spying on him. Of course it was that woman from the admin department. Shaking his head at his own stupidity, he wondered why he had thought she would go quietly. She was known for her spite and vindictive ways, so why had he not thought she would get her own back?

When he reached home he rang Mere, who answered the phone after a few rings.

'I told you not to ring here in the evening,' Mere said, trying to screen the phone from view, quite why he did not know.

'The police had me in for questioning,' came Smith's whining voice down the phone line.

'And what do you expect me to do?'

'You heard about the break in at the offices?'

'Of course I did. That was you presumably.'

Smith did not answer that but said. 'Apparently the Manpower morons lost all of their work.'

There was pause on the line, and then Mere said with obvious delight. 'Then we might be back on track, my old son!'

Smith winced.

The detectives on the case worked hard and long to find evidence that Smith had vandalised the offices but the only thing they had were his fingerprints. These were to be expected as Smith was known to frequent these offices on a regular basis. There was no security footage and no-one had seen or heard anything, which in itself suggested that it had been an inside job. The perpetrator had known where to go and how to get in without being spotted. They had even smashed a few locks to make it look as though they had been forced, but it had not done it convincingly. The detectives had noted the rise of hope in Smith's voice when he was told that the Manpower employees' research had been destroyed, but, try as they might, they could not find anything to prove his part, and so he eluded them, like a water snake escaping in a fast flowing stream.

Chapter Eight

Cookson stood in the enormous hall of Ferris' house, waiting for him to appear. At length a butler asked him to take a seat in the morning room.

'Lord Richard will be with you shortly, Sir,' he said. In truth Ferris had asked 'What does *he* want?' The butler had repeated Cookson's message that he wanted to see Ferris as a matter of urgency. Ferris knew exactly what it was about.

'This had better be quick,' he said, striding into the morning room.

'I take it you are aware of what happened to Mistress Heath and her daughters?' Cookson said without preamble.

'She was evicted. It's her own fault.'

'She was kicked in the face by one of your henchmen.'

Ferris shrugged. 'She's a vicious creature.'

'She is neither a creature, nor is she vicious. You have just made her homeless and your men are pulling her house down as we speak.'

Ferris glanced at him, his heavily-hooded eyes taking him in. 'I need the land.'

'No, you don't.' Cookson said, and for a moment Ferris had a picture of a wolf circling. 'It was a vindictive attack on a family who have virtually nothing. When will you finish the poor houses?'

Ferris waved his hand dismissively. 'I don't have time for all that,' he said. 'I've far more important things to attend to.'

'Like making money.'

Ferris rounded on him. 'Yes, making money. This enclosure business is punishing, financially.'

'You were the only one who wanted it.'

'It's called progress, Mr Cookson. Progress. If it were left to men like you, we would be scraping around in mud huts and crawling around like animals.'

'A piece of advice for you,' Cookson warned as he turned to leave. 'If you renege on your promise, you will raise the tension in this parish to serious levels.'

'Are you threatening me Sir?'

Cookson shook his head. 'I hear what people are saying and this place is like a tinder box.'

Ferris waved him away.

Jon Blake arranged for the head of archaeology to join us on site at Byrd Cottage. He had written to the vendors who had answered by return and said they would be delighted if an archaeological investigation was carried out. The head of archaeology arrived nearly half an hour late and was clearly irritated by the belief that he was wasting his valuable time having to deal with us. We'd placed measuring tapes to show the dimensions of the cottage and he walked around the small area and shrugged.

'Do you have any experience in excavation?'

'I have,' Craig said, stepping forward a little. 'I studied archaeology at university,'

The man, clean-shaven, of heavy build and in his late forties, wore an immaculate Barbour jacket and spotless, pressed trousers. Looking at Craig, taking in his rock band t-shirt, faded denims, and long hair, he asked wearily. 'And what do you think will be the point of the excavation?'

'To reveal the footings of a small, vernacular cottage which doesn't appear to have been developed since the early modern era,' Craig said.

'And how old do you think it could be?'

'There's a record dating back to 1720 about it being sold, so it could be late or even mid-17th century,' I said.

The man looked at his watch. 'And have you directed any digs?'

'Yes, I helped direct two at university,' Craig said.

The man looked over the site. 'It's a small area,' he said, as though to himself. 'I'll send someone to oversee what you're doing.'

'Me and one other should be enough,' Craig said.

The man looked at him with dislike. 'Well, let's hope your excavation techniques are better than your grammar,' he said, walking away. 'Oh, and don't do anything before they arrive – I can't have amateurs digging wherever and whenever they feel like it.'

We waited until he was out of sight.

'Well, that's put us in our place,' Craig said and I could almost see the anger radiating out of him. 'I helped run a dig ten times bigger than this in the 70s.'

'Probably worried that other people can do his job just as well as he can,' I said. 'Or better – he certainly doesn't have what you'd call the common touch with the public.'

'Probably thinking of his gold-plated pension at the end of it,' Hugh said.

While we waited for our overseer, we focussed on the bog flora which was slowly greening up in the watery depths. Craig called us over and pointed out some strange little rosettes of leaves.

'*Drosera rotundifolia*,' Hugh announced, crouching by him. 'Round-leaved sundew.'

Craig was photographing the leaves close to.

'They have strange, spatula-like leaves which have red, sticky tentacles,' Hugh explained. 'When an insect settles on these tentacles, they close up over it and then the leaf margins curl over. The plant then uses enzymes to dissolve the insects.'

'Sounds rather gruesome the way you describe it.' I said.

'The plant actually *eats* the insect?' Craig asked.

'Dissolves it, yeah,' Hugh said. 'In the Edwardian era the plant was described as plentiful on this moor and there was a big patch close to those houses, right over there,' he continued, pointing to some late red-brick Victorian villas, the gardens of which bordered the boggy area. 'The open areas created by clay cutting here in the bog would have been just right for these plants. Now all we have are these tiny patches.'

'You should be a teacher,' I said.

'Why?' said Hugh peering up.

'Because you never stop lecturing people.'

Hugh's expression contracted.

Craig moved over to the end of the bog and to the remains of the embankment around the putative retting pool. Waving us over, he pointed down to a small violet. The leaves and delicate pale lilac flowers seemed to emerge directly from creepers with no apparent stems.

'Violets,' I said.

'Marsh violet, *viola palustris,*' Hugh said.

'A scentless flower of the violet family found in bogs, marshes and wet heathland,' quoted Craig from a Flora he always carried in a backpack. 'Usually found between altitudes of 1, 200 and 2,500 feet. So this site is much lower than usual.' Putting the book back in the pack, he lay on his stomach to get a close shot of the lovely five-petalled flowers which were just emerging. Kneeling down at his side, I could see the delicate tracery of darker purple lines on each petal, like the finest network of arteries. Beautiful.

Hugh was writing in his notebook, then looked up and seemed to do a double-take. Springing over and onto his knees, he gasped.

'Look!' he shouted, pointing to a small, unremarkable-looking plant with thin, wiry stems and tiny leaves. 'Cranberry!'

We went over and stared down.

'*It's rare!*' squawked Hugh. 'It's only found in bogs that are wet all the time. Photograph it, Craig! - Do you two know how unusual this is?' We shook our heads. 'The nearest site is in North Wales. Oh, eat your hearts out, Smith and Mere!' he shouted, punching the air.

The archaeology overseer was a friendly woman in her late twenties who gave us a big smile.

'I'm Jessica, Jess for short.'

'I'm Hugh, Hugh for short.'

'Ignore him,' said Craig, and shook her hand.

Jess looked momentarily surprised but, as she walked to Byrd Cottage and Craig explained to her what we thought was under the turf, I could see her shoulders relax.

'That was unnecessary,' I said to Hugh who, unusually for him, said nothing.

We removed the fine, thin turf and I stacked it, rolling it outwards so it would not dry out. Craig showed us how to trowel with exemplary patience as Jess watched over us. When we had trowelled to a certain depth, we had to get out of the hole and they stood back, getting an overview of the plot.

'Looking for subtle differences in the colour of the soil,' Craig explained to us as we sat on the grass watching them.

I found the first piece of pottery, a hand-sized sherd of thick, brown-orangey earthenware, glazed generously on one side with yellow slip with wavy cream lines over it.

'Oh, slipware!' said Jess, examining it. Craig went over to look at it.

'Late 17th, do you think?' he asked.

'Yes, possibly even earlier. That's a really good piece Charlotte!' Jess called over. I gave a thumbs up. Hugh found several more sherds of what turned out to be a large plate and handed the pieces up to Craig, who smiled warmly at him.

After every layer, any difference in soil colour was noted and photographed. I could barely see the delicate changes they were describing. Hugh remained uncharacteristically compliant and quiet.

'Born with a trowel in his hand,' I said of Craig.

Hugh nodded. 'Certainly was.'

As we went further down in the hearth area, I could see the darkening in the earth and Jess and Craig photographed it in earnest, setting up ranging poles and smaller measuring tapes.

At the end of the day, we covered it over with a large tarpaulin, weighted down with stones that used to line Alice's vegetable plot.

Jess said she would be back tomorrow at nine, and this time I noticed Hugh gave her a warm smile as she said good-bye.

On reaching the moor the next morning, I was first to round the corner to Byrd Cottage while Hugh and Craig brought the digging equipment up. I had half expected to find the site vandalised, but it was not. I looked up to see Alice waiting for me.

'I want to see you found,' she said. 'Before the others come round.'

I pulled the tarpaulin back and she stood on the side peering down. 'I knows not to jump in,' she said. 'I heard the long-haired man explaining why not.'

'You were here yesterday?'

'I'm always here,' she said. 'The long haired man is much happier,' she added, smiling her broad, gap-toothed smiled. I heard the others coming over and looked back to reply to Alice but she was gone.

Hugh and Craig sat by me.

'What's the matter?' Hugh asked. 'You look like you've seen a ghost.'

I nearly said I have, but stayed quiet. Yet I saw the ghost of a smile on Craig's lips.

Jess arrived about ten minutes later and we got back to work.

The first find of the day was made by Hugh, who held up what looked like a cylinder of rust. Jess came over and examined it with Craig.

'Nice find Hugh,' he called. 'Hand-made nail, probably from the rafters.'

Yes – as they crashed down with their explosion of dust and splinters. And several more would turn up.

'Looks like we're getting to the bottom of the rubble layer,' Craig was saying as we trowelled back. 'When we're through that, we'll be in the occupation layer.'

There was a loud crack of a twig snapping in the copse of hazels. Craig and I looked over simultaneously. I knew we had to carry on.

We worked in silence for the next few minutes. A breeze rustled the hazel bushes and I saw Hugh wiping sweat from his face. The sun was shining right on us.

The original demolition layer had been mostly taken away, usable timbers and stone, so what we found were the sweepings...

... The carts rattled along the wide sweeping driveway towards Ferris' folly. Loads had already been delivered by the ornamental pond. Men were busy building the castle-themed folly, stone by stone from the cottages Ferris had pulled down on the enclosed moor. This moor was now a landscape of brown with a layout of monotonous, rectangular fields, glinting with little suggestions of green as the wheat seeds started to germinate. It was only early March but the temperatures had been mild and the days were lengthening. Ferris sat on his horse and viewed it all.

The night before, Georgiana had gone to her parents, taking the two boys with her. They had argued savagely and both had sensed this was an ending. She had not shouted or cried, but talked to Ferris as though she was speaking to someone of lesser intelligence, as though she found him diseased even. The youngest child was still a babe-in-arms and he had let them go. It was his right to demand they return, but Ferris had not the stomach for it. Nor, if he were truthful, did he want his wife's presence around him – that look of hers which told him she was ashamed of him, that she despised what he had become. That realisation wormed into him and when he felt it, he blamed her for being so critical of him. She was four years older than he, and, when they first met, she had seemed so much more sophisticated. He had felt honoured to be allowed to court her – not that he would have shown even a hairs' breadth of this to his friends or family. He knew that she had been dismissive of previous suitors, that she had exacting standards of behaviour, so he was delighted and secretly surprised when she chose him. At first they had been inseparable, and he felt she was a centre, a sun around which he gladly moved. Her high standards had included her decency to all people she met, and he had loved her for it. So what had gone so completely wrong only after a few years?

Staying up all that night, he stared into the fire. With the blurred edges of drunkenness seeping through him, he found it increasingly easy to blame her for everything. It was so much easier to accept that than the searing sense of loss and humiliation that threatened to break him. As the brandy and wine worked on him, he decided that it was her fault he had had to enclose the moor, her fault because he needed more money, her fault because she had presented him with two sons who needed supporting, her fault because she was so sanctimonious. With that thought he threw the wineglass into the fire and it smashed deliciously, shards twinkling in the flames.

By the next afternoon he was out surveying the work on the folly, watching the carts rattling and banging up the drive dragging the stone from Widow Heath's cottage. His head felt as though it was splitting open, his mind was fogged and tilting, and he was still a little unsteady on his feet, but he sat upright on the horse so no-one would guess. Cookson had asked 'Should he not be finishing the poor houses, instead of constructing the folly, which was of absolutely no value to anyone?' Which was the whole point, Ferris had retorted. Roofless the folly would remain, and, as a final touch, he made sure to employ the cottagers whose houses he had pulled down to build this bit of pointlessness from the very stone from their cottages. The peasants were rather too vocal when he passed them these days, and they needed to get the message. I am in charge here, and you do my bidding.

Rowland Mere looked at the credit card bill, which was liberally splashed with payments to the wine bar in Stourton at which Hermione held her Trad Vamps Club. On one occasion he had used that term, and, on seeing her appalled face, had said 'Cheer up Herm, it may never happen.' She glanced over at him with an undisguised look of disgust.

Hermione's group had indeed written to the chairmen of several parish councils asking that their concerns were raised. They all received the same polite letter, in effect saying nothing, a few weeks later. The same but mildly re-configured letter was sent to their county councillor and they received a round robin letter two weeks later thanking them for their interest and enclosing leaflets on the times of the weekly denture clinic at the health centre, and the new bin-emptying days for Stourton. When Hermione rang up about this, the councillor's secretary said he was away on holiday for the next few weeks.

As a result Hermione and her ladies had quaffed a large number of glasses of cheap wine at the next meeting, discussing what they should do next. While some became giggly and playful with the alcohol, others became obnoxious. Earlier Hermione had taken a few of her 'power pills' and now she popped another two and decided to put up notices saying:

ALL FOREIGNERS TO GO BACK TO WHERE YOU CAME FROM, AND ALL HOMOSEXUALS GO INTO QUARANTINE, NOW!

She thought a direct approach was needed. After all, they had tried the nice approach and look where it had not got them.

When Mere had attempted the usual nightly mauling in bed that night, Hermione told him to 'Fuck Off' and dramatically rose up, turned round and crashed down, so she was facing away from him, dragging the duvet off her husband and over her. When he complained she told him drunkenly to 'Piss off into the spare room, then.'

Looking at the staggering wine bar charges on the credit card statement, Mere stood against the wall, wondering how he was going to bring this up with her. She had been out before him that morning, clutching papers. When he asked what she was doing, she had stared at him, her face wrinkled as though she was smelling something appalling.

It was later that day he found out, when he returned from work and received a message from Stourton police station asking him to come in and pick up his wife.

'Why?' he asked.

'She's been cautioned for defacing buildings,' came the voice on the end of the phone.

'What?'

'Just come and pick her up, will you?' the voice said, and put the phone down.

Mere reached the station about forty five minutes later. Although he could have been there in half the time, he decided to change out of his work clothes into casuals and have a wash. Hermione could bloody well stew, he thought, angry at the credit card bill, and not wanting to find out what the silly cow had gone and done now.

The man on the reception desk in the police station could not wait to tell him. Hermione had been spotted pasting one of her newly-photocopied posters on to the supermarket windows, bearing the sentiments she had decided on at the last meeting. She had not asked permission from the supermarket as the place was fairly festooned with posters, so why should she bother? Although the windows were obliquely opposite the police station, they could still be seen. It was this officer who had noticed her, and he had called over some of his colleagues and they started hooting with laughter at her behaviour. When one of them suggested they ought to go and see what she was posting, they jogged over and, seeing the racist and homophobic content, the good humour vanished. The mood soured even more when Hermione told them to 'Fuck Off! It's a free country!' when they demanded she take the posters down. It worsened when she kicked a young male police officer in the back of the calf as he was trying to peel off the poster she had just pasted up. Another officer promptly arrested her and she was marched off in handcuffs, to the loud amusement of several youths hanging around on BMX bikes.

'You can keep her here,' Mere said when the man on reception had finished. 'Teach her a lesson.'

'We can't – it's Friday, and that means Friday night and drunk yobbos. We'll need all the cells.'

'Rather a gloomy view to take, isn't it, officer?' said Mere trying to be hearty above his anger.

'Happens every week Sir, you could put money on it.'

Hermione was bustled out of the cells. Mere's expression recoiled as he spotted his dishevelled wife, hair awry and smudged mascara, giving her panda eyes. As they reached the car, he had an over-riding urge to push her roughly forward, but Mere had learnt from his father, that a proper man does not raise his hand to a woman. It was perhaps one of Mere's few saving graces.

Hermione refused to talk to him in the car and, when she got home, she rushed up to one of the several bathrooms and barricaded herself in. Then she ran the biggest bubble bath she could. Just sitting on that hard bed in the cell had made her feel diseased.

By the afternoon we had reached the occupation layer of the cottage. Craig gave a shout and waved us over. Embedded at a strange angle in the crumbly soil was a large slipware plate. Craig brushed around the outline with amazing delicate dexterity. Jess joined him. Giving the trowel to her, he jumped out of the trench.

'I didn't mean to take over!" she protested.

Craig grinned and held out his hands. 'One wrong move with these maulers and it might fall to bits. Needs a woman's touch.'

Jess worked, and soon the plate, an 18th-century charger, emerged. It had a hairline crack down the centre but was still intact. It was a dark toffee-brown, and cream slip was applied in wavy lines with a naive picture of a cockerel in the middle, and the words *A & T Jones – therr platte* applied in slip around the edge.

'Nice, ain't it?' I heard Alice say, but, looking around, I could not see her. However, I saw Craig smile, as though to himself and, confusingly, as if in spite of himself.

Jess very carefully eased the charger out of the soil and gave a yip of pleasure when she realised it was complete. Craig was hovering in the background, looking clumsy and big-handed but when Jess passed it to him to place in one of the finds trays, he cradled it like a newborn baby, marvelling at the work, at its completeness. Again we both heard the sharp crack of twigs behind us, and, after he laid the charger down, he turned around, as though expecting to see a person walking up. Looking puzzled, he turned back to the tray.

Hugh was kneeling, peering at the charger, looking at the thick slab of reddish brown clay that had been pressed into shape all in one piece. Touching the glazed front, he looked up at Craig.

'Amazing, isn't it?' he said. 'How did it survive the destruction?'

Craig crouched by him. 'It's an incredible survival. Probably fell under something that protected it. It's almost as though it had to be found.'

Alice was up and walking within a week of the attack, although her broken arm was strapped up and she looked black under the eyes, and her cheeks were even more hollow. As she came back to consciousness, her mind had wrestled with what she should do. How could she find work to feed her family? That would depend on how her broken arm healed. Although slight, she was surprisingly strong and she was able to labour in the fields or at washing longer than most. She had picked up paid work where and when she could find it, secure in knowing that at least the cottage and the little plot was hers, and her rights of common would bolster their basic needs. But that had all gone now because, in one fell swoop, Ferris had taken every last bit of independence from her.

The lower waste was still unenclosed but it was swarmed upon by those who had lost their common rights on the upper area. She had seen the results of that before, when the stinting of cattle had been too lax. Then great sandy expanses had appeared and, in high winds, sand had blown over the fields like dry, light rain. She had seen furze bushes disappear overnight because of the people with cutting rights, and the rabbits swarm into the newly exposed areas to dig burrows and nibble away the smallest returning shoots.

Cookson's kind words promising to make sure she and her family were given one of the poor houses when they were completed had fallen like seed on parched, sun-baked land. Work had stopped abruptly two months ago on this block, and several of the rafters had already twisted after repeated soaking and drying. Cookson had said that she and the girls could stay with him until she was stronger. In fact he had declared that the two eldest girls could start apprenticeships with him in domestic service if that would help her situation. Alice closed her eyes and realised that this was now the only chance they had of having a roof over their heads and a means of employment. As soon as she could walk any distance, she would go to the neighbouring settlements and see if there was any work. In truth she knew her skills mainly set her up for land work or washing clothes, though perhaps she could help in one of Stourton's taverns. But that was exactly where the other dispossessed people from the parish would be heading.

Ferris was on horseback, checking that the hawthorn setts were going in as planned. Men and women worked in lines, digging in the small plants. Several stood up, their hands in the smalls of their backs. From his seat on his favourite chestnut he could see lines and fences where there had once been a tussock-strewn chaos. Now all these people were workers for him, dependent on him for their livelihoods, and that made him feel good about himself.

What Ferris did not realise was that, after dark, men were working, not for him but for themselves. Little by little word went around, and taverns were inhabited by the leaders of men who had a grievance, a grievance about the fences, about the restrictions, about the fact their freedoms had been destroyed. Men sat at tables in the firelight of the taverns, their faces illuminated by the rush lights which streamed small trails of smoking tallow. They talked in huddles and quietly, and no-one tried to listen in, or to stifle them. A man or two might peel off from one huddle and join another. Between the re-filling of mugs and lighting of clay pipes, plans were laid and secrets created.

'So what have you found out?' Mere asked, taking Smith's phone call in his office.

'Apparently that Winfield creature has found a rare plant,' said Smith.

'So?'

'Could put the kibosh on your planning application,' Smith replied, not daring to tell him that he had heard through the grapevine that all the Manpower employees' research had been backed up and nothing was lost. That Winfield was a very astute man, Smith observed when he had heard, not even entertaining the idea that Charlotte may have thought it up.

Smith was of a certain type of old school that thought women were there to be leered at if they were worth looking at, ignored if they were plain and quiet, and put down if they dared to show any intelligence, and most especially if it challenged his. Not surprisingly, none of Smith's relationships with women lasted. Even though he tried to get the best-looking ones by boasting about his income and position, they inevitably drifted off to pastures new when his parsimonious nature seeped out like some rank body odour, after the initial dining and sex in hotel bedrooms.

As he got to middle age, even those ploys did not work, so he tarred all of womankind with the same brush: they were all empty-headed gold-diggers who were only after his money. Women like Hermione Mere only underlined that fact, and he was fairly sure that if he had made a move on her in a trade-off for making sure the planning on Blackman's Moor went through, he would have been in there. Yet it was a transaction he would not dare make because he sensed the hell that woman would raise if she was thwarted. Not worth the aggravation, and he could rent out women who looked as good as her and who were paid to have no opinion, to cause no trouble. Relationships with women - if his form of twisted mating could be called that - were now merely transactional, nothing more.

'Whereabouts is this plant?' Mere was asking.

'It's on the Moor.'

'Er yeah, I rather gathered that, but *where* exactly? You could get rid of it.'

'They're not disclosing the location.' Smith made that up, fairly sure that this plant would not protect the site from development but he still hoped that would be enough to explain why he was pulling out of the deal. Of course, he should have known that Mere was of the smash-it-down and destroy-the-site mentality, as he bragged that several of his property developing acquaintances weed-killed any land they had at least a year before submitting planning applications, just to make sure there was nothing worth saving on the wildlife front, which might otherwise halt their developments.

'Well, you'd better find a way of getting my plans through.' Mere warned. 'And getting my lads building on that moor. I've paid you enough.'

We closed the trench off the following day. A few more sherds of late 17th and 18th century pottery were found, a number of rusted and accretion-coated nails and clouts, and a rather beautifully preserved door latch with hand-drawn scrolling patterns on the main plate and along the latch. However, as I held the door latch, a great sense of loss swept over me, unexpected and worrying. I looked around but there was nothing out of the ordinary: Jess was labelling up the finds bags which she gave to Hugh, and Craig was adjusting something on the lens of his camera. All the items had been cleaned and photographed. I looked for Alice, but she was not there.

The simple stone foundations of a one-bay building had revealed themselves, and where the ladder for the sleeping loft had stood, there were two hard impressions from the ladder's feet. Ranging poles were set out for scale and all the measurements duly recorded by Jess and Hugh. The charger had elated all of us. Rolling back the last bit of turf and carefully treading it in place, I suddenly felt Alice's happiness coming through, in the warmth of that late afternoon sun.

The other place we knew we had to get Craig to photograph was a large pool by the main road, up from and opposite The Warrener pub. Back in the late autumn we had taken pollen cores from this large pool as well as the bog, under the auspices of an archaeobiologist from the nearest university.

When Hugh tried to engage him in conversation about the possible pollen content, the archaeobiologist had talked over him and told him to get on with the coring. Surprisingly, Hugh did not answer back. In fact, apart from ordering us to do this or that, the man barely spoke to us and I had the distinct impression he thought we were on community service orders.

It had been an interesting autumnal day of getting stuck in clay in the bog on several occasions as my wellingtons held fast and Hugh helped me out with many squelching heave-hoes. But when heaving to get a core out, he fell backwards and landed on his back in the odious smelling bog-water, and lay there laughing helplessly. I tried to pull him up, but he was stuck fast. The archaeobiologist merely watched our antics. The more he glared at us, the more hopeless with giggling I became and the less able to summon up the strength to pull him out. Eventually the man sighed ostentatiously and deigned to help, and Hugh came out with a flatulent squelch and a disgusting blast of stagnant water.

'The bog-monster emergeth,' I said as he clambered out of the side of the bog, the water trickling off him. The man looked at us, wrinkling his nose, and said 'I think you'd better go home.'

Hugh stank like a drain all the way back and, by the time I dropped him at his house, he was shivering and looking miserable, but - unusually - thanked me several times for helping him. As he squelched to the front door, it opened and revealed warm lights, dogs jumping up and down madly, and Craig stepping back in surprise, then coming forward to wave a friendly goodbye to me, and the door closing.

Blake gave us a copy of the report from the archaeobiologist when it arrived some months later. The bog had several feet of peat, while the pool we were going to examine that day had at least eight feet and went back to prehistoric times, some 10,000 years. There were two distinct clay layers in the bog shown in the cores, suggesting that, for a time in geological history, the river must have sprawled its way over the lower sandy middle area of the moor, and, sluggishly too at times, as fine sediments settled in depressions during times of slow-moving water. Over millennia, these became the clay layers. The pool had been examined in detail and was found to have a clay layer which had, in effect, sealed it and made it waterproof, making it look incongruous amongst the stretch of dry sand

and heather clumps that surrounded it. The peat deposits revealed tree pollen from prehistoric oak, hazel, elm and pine, and then heather, grasses and plantains, suggesting a time after clearance, but whether this latter was by natural fire or through man could not be determined. An ancient piece of pine branch was found during the coring process and was sent off for radio-carbon dating and was found to be between eight to ten thousand years old.

With this in mind, we decided to spend most of the day studying this odd pool. It was a day of deep blue, crystal clear skies and a warmth which seemed incredible after the recent dreary winter days. The dogs had been kept in this day as we were focussing so much on this prehistoric pool as we called it, and it was next to the lower main road.

When we broke for Thermos-coffees, Craig seemed strangely energised.

'It was the best thing I ever did, going to night school,' he said, looking over the heathy expanse. 'We had these great lecturers who were glad we were there. When I was at school it seemed like you shouldn't get noticed, so I kept my head down and just blundered on, and because I felt I couldn't ask for any help with the things I didn't understand, I came out with very iffy qualifications. At college everyone wanted to do well and help each other. This reminds me of it.'

'How old were you when you started night school?' I asked.

'Twenty. I had to do a foundation course for the first two years, and then A levels over another two with evening classes, while I worked during the day.'

'Bloody hell!' I said. 'How did you manage that?'

Craig shrugged. 'Lots of energy then, I suppose. Anyway the day job was not demanding on the brain, you know. It was a case of all brawn during the day, and the brain came out in the evenings.'

'Craig got two As and a B for A level,' Hugh announced.

'Wow! I managed B, B and C.'

'That's very good,' Craig said. 'There wasn't much of an age difference between the lecturers and us, in fact some of the students were older. We worked together – went on these great field trips. It was a very good time for me. My geography teacher was particularly delighted when I got the university place – the other lecturers too, but she was really chuffed. I think she realised how much work I'd had to put in. I remember going in to pick up the results and she came over and gave me a big hug, said something like "You're on your way now, Craig!"'

'Probably glad to have such an enthusiastic student,' Hugh said. 'Committed too.'

'The college lecturers helped us with our university applications and with the grant application process too. Just as well, as I wouldn't have had the first idea about those either. Imagine,' Craig said, sitting up straighter and addressing Hugh, 'all this with you. Our life together, because I made the decision to go to night school.'

Hugh smiled, and seemingly lost for words, squeezed his shoulder.

Later that day Hugh suddenly crouched, stared into the water of the prehistoric pool and went statue-still, then beckoned for Craig to come over with the camera, putting his finger to his lips. I followed.

'It's a Great Crested Newt,' he whispered. Craig noiselessly stooped beside him and focussed the camera on this strange-looking, dark reptile with yellow toes. It looked like a denizen of primordial creeks with their cretaceous horsetail vegetation. It was about sixteen centimetres long and had a bluntly-rounded head and a large, mostly black tail which was as broad and long as its main body. It was perched on a rock in the pool and its warty skin glistened with water. Craig took several photographs, and it seemed that Hugh was actually holding his breath. The next moment the reptile scampered off into the water and, as it moved, we caught a glimpse of its unexpected orange and black spotted underside. Hugh sat on the bank and drew in a long breath.

'That, my friends, is one of the best things we could find,' he said and there was a quaver in his voice. 'It's been a protected species since 1981 and this will help to save this place. Wait till I tell Blake!'

Craig and I shared a '*Ohher*' expression.

'It 's a male,' Hugh said. 'You can tell because he had a wavy jagged crest along his back which the males produce when it's the breeding season, same with the orange underside, so this is a breeding male. It's sometimes called the Warty Newt.' Hugh was talking as though he could not quite believe what he had seen. 'During courtship the male stands on his front legs and waves his tail around.'

I just about suppressed a snort of laughter, but knew Hugh was being serious. There was an expression on his face like reverence. Craig also stayed quiet and there was a smile on his face, not of amusement, but of deep affection.

'Do you want to look for more?' I asked.

Hugh nodded and we spent some time tip-toeing around. I pointed out another reptile which was standing stock still on a fallen branch. This was smaller, about ten centimetres long, and had a smooth skin of a brownish-greenish colour. I could see it had a spotty orangey underside and it also had a crest, but more rounded and lower than the Great Crested Newt.

'That's a Smooth or Common Newt,' Hugh said. 'And it's a potential breeding male. Good find! They wrap each of their eggs in the leaves of pond plants.' The wonder was still there in his voice. 'Just the habitat you'd expect to see them. This place couldn't be much better!'

Hugh's enthusiasm was infectious and we hunted even harder around the edges of this ancient pond. Then Craig suddenly leaned down to inspect something coming out of the side of the bank, just by the waterline. Giving a sharp intake of breath, he reached forward and gently eased it out of the soil. Standing, he held up the most beautifully crafted flint arrowhead for us to see.

'Tanged and barbed,' he said and stared at it, amazed.

I had never seen a prehistoric flint before, and it was quite incredible. Not much bigger than a man's thumbnail, it was delicately chipped to form the arrow shape. The flint was like grey, opaque glass.

'You can almost see the hunter shooting here, can't you?' I said, examining the dainty flint in Craig's big palm.

'It just goes to show,' he said. 'That our idea of Stone Age man as being some grunting, knuckle-dragging creature isn't true.' Holding the flint up to the light, he added. 'Anyone who could craft this must have had the dexterity of a jeweller. It's amazing. Here, can you take it?' he said, handing the arrowhead to me. 'Need to keep it safe and I'm just too big and clumsy to deal with it.'

I zipped it into my jacket pocket. 'You're not,' I said.

'Can you two go and stand where I found it, and one of you point to the find spot.' There was a nervousness in his voice and I assumed he had not heard my answer. 'I'll put in a marker to show where it was found.'

We posed for the photograph, Hugh playing silly to start with, but when Craig pointed out this was an important find spot, he stood still.

'This pool used to be full of bogbean, *Menyanthes trifoliata*,' Hugh said as we sat on the bank, taking a break. 'It's also called buckbean. There's a record in the 19th century of a man walking twenty miles from a city to collect it to sell on.'

'What for?' Craig asked, opening a bag of crisps and offering us some.

'I think the underground stem was used in the preparation of some tonic for agues and rheumatism – had a very bitter taste apparently. But don't try it,' said Hugh. 'In early 1900s Sweden they used it as a substitute for hops.'

Craig rummaged in his backpack for the flora book. 'Here we go,' he announced. 'Oh – it is odd looking!' he said, showing me the picture. It had a creeping stem and three dark green leaflets on a stalk which were held above the water, and looked like a big clover leaf. On the upright stalk were strange-looking flowers whose buds were rosy pink with the opened flower having five petals that were fringed on the inner surfaces with white filaments, rather like the threads on luxurious towelling.

'It used to be called the *Menyanthes* Pool in the 19th century, in the learned journals,' Hugh said.

'Showing it was once full of it,' I said.

Hugh nodded, he had a found another bag of crisps in the backpack and was shovelling them into his mouth. 'Shows it was worth gathering,' he mumbled with the associated crumb spraying. 'To have walked that far to get it.'

Craig was peering into the pool. 'Found a bit.'

Hugh opened his mouth.

'Spare us!' Craig interjected. 'I'll photograph it.'

We took to the garden of The Warrener pub for our lunch hour. I was driving so they drank pints and became noticeably more carefree over the next hour.

We had the pollen analysis report with us, which revealed that during the last four hundred years the area would have had a lot more shifting sand, as there were some noticeable layers of sand in the upper layers of the cores taken. Alice, I knew, had seen these large areas of sand - I do not know how or why I was so sure.

'I found this the other night, written by Defoe of Bagshot Heath in Surrey,' I said. 'I thought we could include it in the presentation we have to give in the autumn: *For in passing this heath on a windy day I was so far in danger of smothering with the clouds of sand which were raised by the storm that I could neither keep it out of my mouth, nose nor eyes.*' Looking up I saw neither were listening to me. Craig was sunbathing on the grass, hands behind his head, eyes closed and a big contented smile on his face, and Hugh was making notes on the report. I coughed.

Hugh peered up. 'Sorry Kiddo, you were saying?'

'You said something about there being a noticeable layer of sand in the core from the 18th-'

'To 19th century, yes,' he interrupted. 'We should mention that the moor was overgrazed by rabbits and livestock, especially when the top half was enclosed.'

Absolutely, I heard Alice whisper, there were the same number of us, with half the amount of grazing.

'In Eriswell in Suffolk in 1809,' I said. 'A foot of soil was taken by wind erosion from a rabbit warren and dumped on the surrounding fields allegedly.'

'And the evidence from Bagshot Heath?'

'When the wind died down on one occasion, sand was found over the surrounding fields.'

'I was listening,' said Hugh.

'We both were,' said Craig raising his head and squinting my way.

'The evidence for stinting in the mid-15th century suggests overgrazing was a problem here even back then,' I said.

'And now the problem is people using the place as a dumping ground, and property developers,' said Craig.

Only this morning we had to phone in to say someone had off-loaded an old fridge and three piece suite by the road up from The Warrener pub. It was still there. Scarcely a week went by without someone fly-tipping by the side of at least one of the main roads.

Hugh was studying the diagram with the report. 'There's definite evidence of overgrazing in the pollen analysis. From the mid-16th there's more pollen from the heather species, even from sand spurrey and shepherd's cress. Sheep grazing in moderation is good to keep a heathland, but overgrazing ends up with bare patches and then the possibility of wind erosion, which seems to have happened here.'

'The sheep stint changed from 100 sheep in the 1450s to 60 sheep per yardland in the 1500s,' I said, referring to my notebook.

Craig I noticed was lying on his side now, elbow out, supporting his head.

'You two are like a couple of academic computing machines,' he said.

I glanced at Hugh who stuck his tongue out at Craig.

'They've found that bloody reptile,' Smith was saying. Mere was sitting opposite his desk in a hard council chair. 'It's a protected species.'

'What is?'

'Great Crested Newt,' Smith spat the words.

'Lives in water?'

'Yes.'

'Well, let's get some of the boys to have an oil leak into the bog and pond by the road – those are the most obvious places for those things. That'll get rid of them,' Mere said, showing no emotion.

'I don't know who you know, but I wouldn't be able to organise anything like that,' Smith lied.

'You can buy anyone to do anything these days, mate, if you know where to look.'

Smith's left eye twitched. 'It may be too late. That Blake prat has sent a press statement to the local rag. If it suddenly gets polluted, it would be rather obvious, wouldn't it? Seeing you're the only other interested party.'

Mere slouched back and stared at him with a lazy, unconcerned air. 'You know I'll want my sweeteners back if this goes tits-up,' he said.

Smith stared at him. 'This is a business deal, Mere. I've gone out of my way to help you. If you think I've gone through all the trouble I have for nothing, then think again.'

'I don't need to. I want my money back, or I will have words into the ears of your bosses,' Mere said. 'Everyone's dispensable in this game, Smith, and you've turned out to be the biggest bullshitter out. You think about it, and decide how you're going to explain your way out of this one. I hear Mrs Little has more pictures.'

'How do you know?' Smith had visibly gone paler, looked yellow in fact.

'My wife knows her.'

Smith's stomach felt as though it had just done a big nasty flip.

The folly was almost built and the fences were nearly completed around Ferris' newly enclosed land. On this early spring morning Ferris looked out over his fields. The crops were germinating nicely and there were now lines of green instead of odd spots. All the old copses and spinneys and little pockets of scrub and brushwood had been cleared away by men who had stared sullenly at him as he rode by and instructed them what to do. The area was quieter this spring, no birdsong to speak of, and none of the little rustlings from tall grasses and coppices. All that was gone, and replaced with crops and order and bleakness.

Yet Ferris did not feel any order. Georgiana had not returned and he sat up late these nights drinking, occasionally with friends, but even they seemed to be dropping off as he drank more and spoke his mind. There was one place he was welcome, and that was at the gaming tables in the next city. Increasingly he would go up to town and stay over for several days, spending and drinking and fornicating. Women gathered at his arm and he was able to entertain them royally, bedding the most delectable and not caring if they became big with child, for how could any of them prove paternity when they clearly bedded so many men? Leaving more and more to his farm steward, he spent his time learning the intricacies of cards, until that seemed like a business in itself. It was strange how little idea of true time he had, as days, then weeks drifted through curtained and cigar-wreathed halls, and, somewhere outside, day followed night in a rhythm of a world to which he now hardly belonged.

Chapter Nine

It was a still night when the dozens of men, women and children started pouring out from the cottages, small holdings and other tenements in and around Stourton. It was known Ferris was away and, as soon as darkness fell, they began gathering at various points around the newly-enclosed moor. All this had been carefully engineered by the men meeting in taverns during those cold winter evenings, one huddle helping another. They told everyone to bring what they could: iron bars, picks, crow bars, axes and lump hammers, anything that would inflict damage to wood and nail, and help uproot the thorn setts they had spent weeks planting.

Under cover of night family groups moved together, with look-outs posted at vantage points to warn of anyone approaching. If any of the lookouts saw anything, they were to whistle. This would be copied along the rows and everyone would crouch, hiding their faces. It was a thick, black night, so the groups worked steadily, wrenching apart the fencing and laying it flat, for someone else to come up behind and splinter it with pounding blows. The action had been so well organised that in no time the fences bordering the top boundary of the former moor were flattened and shattered. Behind them, people pulled out the hawthorn setts; many did not want to uproot them, but these plants had become symbols of their oppression and they had to be sacrificed.

There was a peculiar energy among the people, jaws set, eyes narrowed. They greeted the other huddles as they crossed paths. In the next hour and a half, the fencing was destroyed on the eastern side and the setts were almost all uprooted. Beer flagons and bread and cheese were produced, this destruction was hungry work. Their futures, with the loss of this land, threatened to be hungrier still.

By day-break all the fences along the boundaries were down, and the dividing fences within the newly enclosed land were broken. The people disappeared into the dawn, silently and without a trace. The alarm sounded by Ferris' land agent eventually reached him as he sat at the gambling tables, a painted lady leaning over his shoulder and feigning interest.

At first Ferris stared ahead, as though he was not really there, as though this was part of some slow-moving nightmare, from which he would wake with a start. Blinking, he opened his eyes wide, and looked again at the messenger.

'What did you just say?' he said, as if asking what time of day it was.

'A message from your land agent, that your fences around and within the new enclosures have been cast down and the thorn setts uprooted.'

'Every one of them?' was all he could say.

'Yes, my lord.'

Ferris sat back in his seat. The painted lady discreetly drifted away and now hung on the arm of another gentleman.

'Your agent asks for you to attend.'

Ferris jumped up, upsetting the numerous cut glasses. 'Does he indeed! The fool should have been guarding my enclosures.'

'It was done during the dark of night, my lord.'

It was later that day when he rode back into the manor of Stourton. There was a deathly quiet, a brooding stillness about the place, with no-one to be seen. Reaching the start of the new enclosure on the connecting turnpike road, he saw a shattered line of the former wooden fences, lying on the ground, like the gigantic carcass of some primordial snake or monster. Thrown randomly were the pathetic hawthorn setts, still budding with new life. If he worked fast, he might save them. But who would he employ to do it? The complete absence of people out and about was testimony to him of their guilt, so it would be bizarre indeed to get them to replant the thorns and re-do the fencing. They might even smash it all down again, to put it all back up again, just to get the money. What if it never stopped? But the setts needed to go in. Riding over to Cookson's he would demand those on the poor rate do the work for free.

Not surprisingly Cookson did not agree. Although he seemed shocked by what had happened, he would not throw any doubt on the people, nor suggest who the ring leaders were. In fact Cookson seemed unusually protective of the parishioners.

After much negotiation, a workforce was assembled, the setts replanted and a watch put over the area at night. What truly grieved Ferris was that the peasants who were not on the Poor Rate demanded twice the day wage to work harder to get the thorn plants back in. Ferris had to consider whether it was cheaper to get new plants and get a completely different workforce, or use what he had and employ the local workers at a much higher rate?

For the first time in his life, Stourton Manor seemed to be slipping from his control. He could see it in little, unspoken ways at first, then in the suppressed anger that seemed to infuse the air, the barely concealed loathing in many of the workers' faces. Of course, no-one had seen or heard anything on the night of the vandalism. Cookson had said so, and it did not matter how Ferris cajoled, bribed or threatened, no names were ever given up as ringleaders or organisers. Ferris even tried bribing the tavern owners to make statements about who was responsible, but he was met with tight-lipped, angry stares and looks of hatred in the eyes that appraised him. Ferris realised his money and his status were not going to get him what he wanted this time, what he thought was his by rights. This was the first time that loyalty to a group had thwarted him in his dealings. Money had easily oiled his life so far and he had assumed that everything, every human emotion, had its price.

As the replanting was done and it appeared the thorn setts had taken root, he realised there was a subtle, but more far-reaching effect. The workers, who now had so little, if anything, to lose, had a scent of control about them. Ferris knew without being told, that if he stepped out of line again, to anyone in the manor, there would be more demolition, and he would have to pay them, the very people who had wrought the destruction, to put it back. Something had shifted in the power balance, and it felt like being blackmailed. Ferris did not like it at all.

Paul Smith had thought about fleeing, but that was not an option. Everything he had was rooted here in Stourton and the surrounding areas. Anyway, Mere had as much to lose as he did. He could go to the council leader or the police and say Mere had been trying to bribe him. Trying, would be the significant word. There was no proof Mere had succeeded. There was no paper trail concerning their transactions – that was why he had insisted on cash. It would be a case of his word against Mere's. Of course there was that Mrs Little woman, but she had been slung out for lying and cheating. Who was going to believe her?

Still, it did feel like a waiting game. He and Mere were watching each other, like two cobras waiting to strike. And who would strike first? Patience was not a word in Smith's vocabulary, but this time he really would have to sit and wait, unless he just caved in and gave Mere his money back. The police had not been able to find anything on him, in spite of more investigations, so might returning the money to Mere be the cleverest thing to do. Be done with it. Not have to look over his shoulder all the time. But the thought of giving several thousand pounds back was too much for his parsimonious nature and he felt a sheen of sweat forming on his forehead. If the police had anything on him they would have struck by now, so it would seem that he was getting away with it...Sod it. He'd keep the money. He had worked for it after all.

Hermione Mere had been given a formal caution about her behaviour and a stiff fine for kicking the police officer, and warned if anything like that happened again, she would probably face a custodial sentence and a hefty fine. And for the first time in her life, Hermione realised that her grip on society was also slipping. Only her power pills seemed to give her any drive these days. She kept them in a zipped up compartment in her handbag, loose so she could take a couple and it would look as though she was merely popping mints.

She had expected Rowland to go to the police station and grease a few palms and get all this to disappear, but that had not happened. She had even been mentioned in the local rag albeit in a two sentence side-report (and on page 14 of a 28 page paper, mark you!) mentioning her offences and fine. The youths on BMX bikes in the square near Stourton supermarket greeted her with hoots and unbecoming ape noises every time they spotted her, even asking 'D'ya get community service, Missus? How long d'ya get? Did the naughty copper spank ya!' All served with whoops of dirty laughter.

Hermione had therefore taken to going to the next town to shop and to make sure she was not recognised, she donned sunglasses, the very best make of course, which she had trouble remembering to wear, as she so wanted to use them as a fashion accessory, the ultra-cool Alice-band. It was during one of those visits that she was surprised to see Winfield and Lyle walking along one of the grocery aisles. You couldn't miss them, especially that blonde one with that hair hanging over his shoulders and down his back, disgusting...Although it was such a good colour of a reddish-tint blonde in this light that she wondered if he dyed it, and what the dye number was. She might use it on – Ughh, Hermione! What are you bloody *thinking*! In her mind they were the symbol of her misery, and the cause of it.

She watched them from a distance, talking to each other, laughing occasionally, an ease about them which she hated. At one point Lyle even put his arm around Winfield's neck and pretended to haul him past the shelves of cakes in a loose head-lock, with Winfield laughing helplessly. They didn't even notice that several people were looking at them. Hermione had never been so relaxed that she could behave like this in public. Merely the idea of having her hair messed up would have been too much. But they really didn't seem to care. You would have thought, after they were so exposed during that AIDS campaign, that they would try not to draw attention to themselves. In her mind she had twisted her hate campaign into being someone else's fault, and she thought of herself as the victim, the messenger who was still being punished. Thinking of the abuse she had to put up with from the BMX yobs, she shuddered. How dare these two flaunt their happiness? How *fucking* dare they!

Ferris stayed in the city after an altercation with Cookson, who was trying to get him to finish the poor houses. Ferris let the place moulder: he had to show these people that they could not dictate every move in his life. But he had been told by Cookson that the families whom he had evicted from the cottages on the enclosed moor, had been agitating for a time when they could move into the finished buildings. Ferris had initially told him to relay the message of 'Go to hell, the lot of you!" but Cookson pointed out that these dispossessed people (he really *liked* that word) were still living like cattle in his outbuildings, and, although he and the Poor Rate had helped them with the essentials, these people needed homes and warmth. Ferris had even suggested that they should go and camp out in his roofless folly, to which Cookson had turned to him and snapped

'You need to stop that!' There was an iciness in his voice and a coldness in his eyes that made Ferris stop short.

'Oh, I'm going to town,' he blurted, waving his hand dismissively.

A few days later he returned and stood in front of his folly and stared. No-one had even been sent to tell him. Daubed in black pitch all over the stones in large, uncompromising letters were those words POX ON YOU FERRIS – MAY YOU ROT. It was repeated many times.

For a second time he felt a flicker of fear, and stepped back. Why had Cookson not told him of this? But what if he had actually done it? Remembering the look of hate in his eyes, Ferris swallowed and looked around, hoping no-one could see him and sense this fear which seemed to rise off him like steam. If he got the folly white-washed, it would acknowledge the hate; if he did not remove the writing, it would show weakness. And all because of some shabby little houses he could get finished and inhabited within a few weeks. But he was in the same quandary: if he finished the building, it would look as though he had caved in. Yet if he did not, then what else would they do? How far would these people go?

At the next meeting of Traditional Values Forum. Hermione sat with the only person present, Mrs Little. Most of the steel-grey haired, older ladies who had previously attended, had sent in garbled words of explanation about why they could not attend any more meetings: holidays booked, grandchildren to look after, gardens to attend to, whist drives that clashed. The others simply did not turn up. So on that evening Hermione sat in the wine bar and plied Mrs Little with expensive but bad quality wine, and worked on her.

Rowland had dropped some comment that Paul Smith from Planning owed him quite a few thousand, but when Hermione pushed for more detail, he became angry and said something about a business deal going wrong. Although she was happy to spend money freely on herself, she did not like the idea of anyone else getting one over on her financially. That was her money. Hers, not theirs.

Mrs Little was getting loose-tongued with drink. Hermione was gleeful. She could tell the old bird could not hold her alcohol. So she started probing about Smith: what was he like? What did she know about his dealings with her husband?

'That Smith is a disgusting creature,' slurred Mrs Little. 'The way he looks at women, you'd think he wants to shag them all.' She giggled at this, surprised at her naughtiness.

Not you dear, unless he goes for the mud-wrestler, thick-ankled look, thought Hermione but smiled sweetly at her. 'Oh, do go on,' she encouraged.

'You know it was him that lost me my job?' Mrs Little said and looked at her like the victim she so clearly was.

'Nooo,' crooned Hermione, her mascaraed eyes opening wide in mock surprise. Of course she knew, why else was she getting the old dear (Mrs Little was in her late 50s – *disgustingly* old, thought Hermione) to neck down so much of this crappy, over-priced wine at her expense?

Mrs Little sat up straight. 'You ask my clerk,' she said swaying a little. 'You ask her.'

No ducky, I'm asking you, and paying for the pleasure.

'Oh, I'm sure you can tell me,' Hermione encouraged. 'Be our little secret.'

Mrs Little looked around, then back.

'Smith asked me to falsify the time sheets of that homo and the Little Miss he works with – the Manpower people, and suggest they had been skipping work.'

'Oh, how awful? Why would he want to do that?'

Mrs Little swayed so much that she nearly fell forwards off the plush-covered seating. Hermione put her arm out to steady her.

'Because Smith wanted them off the Blackman's Moor project and, apparently-' She held her face close to Hermione's. 'Your husband and he are in cahoots, and Smith has been taking backhanders from him.'

'How do you know *that*?'

Mrs Little smirked, looking immensely smug. 'Overheard them one day in the supermarket car park. They were in Smith's car with the windows down, arguing really loudly. There's some bushes next to where they were parked, so I hid in them and listened. I've taken to carrying a dictaphone, as well as the camera,' she added.

In fact stalking Smith had become something of an all-consuming pastime of hers of late. Mrs Little knew the house he lived in (alone, from what she could see), knew the car and registration plate off by heart, knew when he went shopping, and when he met up with various people. In short, she considered herself a bloody good detective.

'When I was in the bushes,' she continued. 'I pushed the recorder button on to record, then shoved the thing out with my umbrella by the back of the driver's door. Didn't think it would pick their voices up, but it got the whole thing: Smith shouting his mouth off about not giving the sweeteners back, your husband shouting he'd better, even gave the amounts!' She laughed. 'I was lucky - the car park was very quiet just then. They were arguing so much they didn't even notice me.'

Hermione sat stock still.

'The dictaphone was from work and it's a superior model – records things other dictaphones don't reach.' Mrs Little shrilled at her allusion to the well-known lager advert. 'I decided not to return it when I found I'd got it.'

Theft, thought Hermione.

'So let's get this straight,' she said. 'You have my husband and Smith on tape talking about backhanders and bribes over Blackman's Moor.'

Mrs Little looked at her with alcohol-fuelled glee. 'Yes!'

Hermione knew she had to act fast. 'How much would you like for it?' She still smiled her most winning smile.

'Pardon?'

'I'm willing to buy it off you. Name your price.'

Mrs Little stared at her. She knew she should be understanding something important here, but the wine had spun her mind, so she felt she was thinking on the edge of a centrifuge.

'You name your price,' Hermione repeated.

'Why?'

'Because I would like to buy it.'

'A thousand,' Mrs Little said, and knew it was a ridiculously high figure.

'Done.'

'*What?*'

'We'll meet here tomorrow, same time. You bring me the tape; I'll give you the money.'

Mrs Little could feel her heart start to bang. 'I have it here, on me.'

Stupid cow, thought Hermione, if we met tomorrow then she could have made herself copies, so she was extra pleased with herself that this would not happen.

'You go and get me the money – the banks are still open – and meet me here in half an hour.'

Hermione paled a little, wondering which account she could mine.

After she had slunk out, Mrs Little ordered herself a pot of overpriced coffee. She was in the money now, she could afford it and she even tipped the waitress when she brought her the coffee things. The girl stared blankly at her, wondering what the matter was. Mrs Little was one of those customers who normally complained about everything: a mark on a saucer, coffee too cold, milk going off, spoon not shiny enough.

Mrs Little became quite jolly as she waited. She knew Hermione would be back. She was an airhead but alert to the dangers of bribery and blackmail.

Twenty minutes later, there she was, holding her handbag crossed over her chest, advertising to the world she was carrying a lot of money.

'Of course before handing this over, I want to hear the tape,' Hermione said, as she sat on the next seat.

'Right you are,' said Mrs Little and pulled out the hand-sized dictaphone and plugging in a pair of small ear phones, she offered it to Hermione and started playing the tape. There they were: the screechy, angry tones of Smith, and the laconic low voice of her husband. The evidence was unequivocal.

There was her husband demanding the return of the 'bungs' as he called them, and the amount made Hermione pop open her eyes. How could they have been so utterly moronic as to start a conversation in a public place with the windows open? she wanted to shout. But instead she nodded, gave her the envelope stuffed with £20 notes and silently took the cassette tape out of the recorder.

'I hope that will be the end of it,' she said, getting up and her face felt tight with all this smiling.

Mrs Little just grinned back, like a triumphant Cheshire cat.

'You bloody *moron!*' Hermione said later that afternoon as Mere returned from the office. 'If it hadn't have been for my quick thinking, your career as a property developer would have been in ruins.'

'What's up Herm?' he said, not really listening to her, just the naw-naw-naw-naw high-pitched tone which he had come to associate with his wife and her endless dissatisfactions.

'This,' Hermione thrust the cassette tape into his face.

Mere backed away and then stared at it. 'What about it?'

'Only that woman from the council admin recorded you and Smith fighting over the bribes you had given him.'

'*What?*' Mere gawped at her, his jaw going slack.

'Oh, don't pretend you weren't giving him backhanders!' Hermione stormed. 'You are such a plod. I knew months ago.'

'Oh,' said Mere.

'What the fuck possessed you to sit in a car with that Smith creature and argue with the bloody windows open?'

'There was no one in sight,' he said.

'Only Mrs F—ing Admin in the bushes, taping you.'

'Who?'

'Mrs Little from the admin department at the County Council.'

'Oh,' said Mere.

'I paid her a thousand for it, luckily she had it with her so she can't make copies.'

'Oh.'

Alice's arm was healing, a little crookedly at the elbow but she would just have to put up with that. Cookson allowed her to stay with her children in the servants' quarters. The youngest child, Hannah, was 'apprenticed' to the cook who had taken a shine to the funny, lively little girl, and was teaching her how to knead bread and roll pastry and letting her chatter and play for as long as she wanted beside her. At the end of each day all three girls would sit with their mother, outside if it was mild, inside if it was inclement. Only her eldest daughter, Harriet, could see the defeat in the back of Alice's eyes, the despair she tried to hide, her arm still in the makeshift sling. The cook would send up extras for Alice, saying that Hannah had made them, which was partly true. Alice ate them quickly, after offering them to her daughters who all refused, wanting their mother to get back to how she had been. But there was a slowness about her now, even after the bruises had faded and the gashes to her face had scabbed over.

On a particularly pleasant evening, Harriet asked her to go for a stroll along the river bank with them. The sun was pleasant. Alice needed to talk in private with them, so she agreed readily, explaining that she was going to the nearest town in the next week and would look for work there, and along the way. That she would be back to see them as often as she could until she was settled, and then, if they wanted to come over to her, of course they must, but she would be happier if they stayed with Mr Cookson, as she knew he would watch out for them. Harriet agreed with all this, happy that her mother seemed to be returning to her indomitable self. As they walked along the river bank, with the pulses of spring in the twigs and sprouting from the myriad spring plants just unfurling beneath the soil, Harriet dared to feel happy.

'Mills today,' said Hugh, leading the way with map, notebook, and trailing Craig and I with the dogs. We ploughed through the soft sand up to the upper moor in the spring sunshine. It was unseasonably hot and Hugh cast off waterproof, then sweatshirt as we walked, tying them round himself so he started to look like a walking mound of clothes.

'Feels the cold,' said Craig. 'Something to do with his heart not being brilliant.' There was a sudden catch in his voice and his expression closed in unexpectedly.

I nodded.

'This is like being on a beach,' I said as we trawled through the loose sand, desperate to say anything.

'Should have brought my bucket and spade,' Craig agreed, and kindly.

'Come on!' Hugh chivvied.

There were records of an old mill immediately to the east of the moor and several of the mill ponds were now part of the land up for sale. Hugh was keen to get over there while the sun was out to get the bird and pond life photographed by Craig, who was striding over the sand in denim cut-offs and a Heavy Metal band t-shirt, looking as though he should be strolling on a sun-soaked beach, not on a moor which today had sprouted an old washing machine and dirty rolled up carpets by the lower main road. Hugh had phoned it in to Blake, and it was recorded. As the fridge and three-piece-suite were still by the side of the same road and, as Hugh pointed out to Blake, dumping begets dumping, it was agreed a bulky-collection council truck would be out some time today. The welfare of this moor was worming its way into each of us, and I sensed Hugh felt the fly tipping as a personal affront, as I did.

We reached the wooded area that bordered the moor and where sweet chestnut trees and oak crept up the slopes back on to the sandy upper terrace. Here it was a different world, with the May sunshine filtering through twigs and stems bright green with new growth. Little plants stared out of the grass: whites, blues, pinks, yellows - nature's palette.

The first pond was bordered with reed mace which still had their velvety dark brown heads that looked like enormous cigars.

'Reed Mace or False Bulrush,' said Hugh. 'The real bulrush is of another species...Would you photograph them?'

Craig jumped up onto a bank and, leaning forward a little, photographed the dark brown heads. I found myself admiring his legs which were toned, so perfectly proportioned.

'Keep your tongue in, Kiddo,' Hugh whispered.

I jumped and glanced at him covertly - he was smirking and staring ahead.

'June onwards is probably the best time for photos,' he said, as though a switch had suddenly been thrown. 'But today's such a good day for photography.

'There's a reference to a tanning mill here in the 17th century,' I said, glad to change the subject,

'And here it is,' Hugh said as we walked out onto the lane. 'One converted mill, which luckily for us is called Tanners Mill and states "former tanning mill" on a plaque. Superb detection on my part.'

Craig feigned tripping him up and then began photographing the mill, taking it from angles that would not have occurred to me. While he photographed, we held his dog Angus, the sprouty-furred, bat-eared character of unflagging good humour. I took Harry, and Hugh walked Bruce, although half the time I am sure he was hardly aware of his companion who walked perfectly, in all his wiry-furred scruffiness, while Hugh held forth on some plant or other. I ended up holding the dog trio as Craig took off his trainers and waded into the pond waist deep.

'Cold in here!' he squawked, and pulled a target-eyed, shocked face.

'Make sure you don't freeze them off!' Hugh called, poking his thumb upwards. 'We'll probably be needing them tonight.'

'*Hugh!*' Craig stared at me, frozen.

'Oh, you don't mind, do you Kiddo?'

I smiled, shaking my head, not exactly sure what they were talking about.

The mill ponds were part of the moor, but apart in their diversity and habitat. Bright yellow marsh marigolds glowed from the sides of the pond, and the riotous yellow and mauve-violet of flag irises blazed among sword-like leaves. It was a perfect scene of clear sky, bright colours and strong sun. Hugh was in his element, encouraged by Craig to take off trainers and socks, roll up his jeans, and wade in to knee-height with *oohhs* and *aahhs* about the cold water, and Hugh commenting that his would be going the same way as Craig's. Craig was in above his knees, taking photo after photo and being directed by Hugh, who was now in a peculiarly bossy mood.

They waded further with Hugh calling 'Oh look, a grebe!' 'There's a moor hen.' 'Did you get the water boatman?' '*Ohh* is that a marsh warbler?' At one point he was jumping up and down as he shouted something about an eel.

I stood with the lurcher trio, trying patiently to work out where all these things were. It did cross my mind that with the amount of disturbance going on, the entire pond fauna was probably trying to flee. But when Hugh came back he was grinning, saying something about finding the inlet channel and following it through to the outflow.

'And there was an eel in there,' he said. 'It snaked around my legs.'

'Bet you enjoyed that,' Craig said.

'No I did not.'

'Amazing what was in there,' Craig said to me. 'Like a world in itself. Would you like to go in?'

I laughed and shook my head.' Your face when you went in said it all.'

We sat in the sun out on the sand for them to dry off. The sun glinted off the fine fair hair on Craig's legs, but, remembering Hugh's taunt, my appreciative glances now felt furtive and somehow unfair to Craig, in a way I could not clearly understand at the time.

'Also saw a few Great Crested Newts,' said Hugh confidentially. 'But didn't want to announce that out loud.'

The next day, I picked up Hugh from their house and he sat down quietly in the passenger seat.

'Craig says I should apologise to you for being coarse yesterday,' he said, staring ahead as he always did when he felt awkward. 'I forget you're a female at times, you know.'

Thank you Hugh, I thought, keep digging that hole.

'I think of you as one of the boys,' he said, and I knew from Hugh that was probably a compliment. 'Anyway, I'm sorry if I was rude.'

I went to wave him away but he continued 'I also wanted to say how much I've enjoyed working on this scheme with you. We both have. When I first started it was because I needed the money, and, yes, it was in line with what I had studied. But my main desire was getting even with Mere and that bloody wife of his. Payback time. But that's changed now, and I can honestly say it's been one of the best things I've been involved with. Most of all though, it's brought Craig back.'

I went to speak.

'Anyway, get driving, it's off to work, Kiddo,' he interrupted, and it was back to the usual ball of energy. The Hugh-Ball as I was then to think of him.

Craig joined us in the record office for the first time for a few weeks. The book catalogues had gone out and he had been very busy with orders. Hugh had asked if it was all right with me that he came along. I don't know why he asked every time: I always said it would be a pleasure having him along and – significantly - I always meant it.

Within minutes of arriving at the Record Office, Craig found a set of leases to the mill and was busy writing down the salient points on a lined A4 pad. I noticed once again he had surprisingly untidy, large handwriting.

'The first mill lease was for a corn mill,' he said, as we drank coffee in the common room at break, and he consulted his notes. 'That was in 1545. That goes on until 1650, when the mill was used for grinding the bark from oaks for the tanning industry. Looks like it was used until the 1750s which links up with the date you thought that tanning stopped further down by The Warreners pub.'

'That fits very nicely,' I said.

'I wonder what sort of effluent was produced by the tanning industry, considering some of its ingredients: tannin, urine and poo,' Hugh said, without any preamble.

'*Hugh*!' I protested and looked at the sandwich I was eating

'Well, think about it, poo has carbon and proteins, and urine has phosphorus and potassium, and also uric acid and urea. If it's been concentrated in watercourses for centuries it might change the surrounding flora. In human settled areas you always get stinging nettles, so I wonder-'

'Do we want to go stamping around either side of the main road by the ditch looking for evidence?' I said.

'Don't you think all that stuff would have leached out by now?' Craig said. 'Been over two centuries.'

'Yeesss..Still worth a look though,' Hugh said.

So on the next day we were out poo-diving as Craig called it, standing around in the litter-strewn ditches looking for indicator species, but we found none, other than the ubiquitous nettles.

'These ditches need to be cleaned out,' Hugh said. 'Disgusting mess,' he added, disentangling a wellington from a mouldering carrier bag.

We spent the rest of the day going over the whole moor, getting Craig to photograph the spring flowers. The moor was starting to look beautiful with colour. The contrasts of sun and shade were striking. There was the slightly misty light of the bog, the stark sunlight over the bare, sandy areas, and then the green, dappled shade of the copses by the old mill pools where dragonflies and damselflies skittered, metallic liquid blues and emerald-greens. On the upper moor occasional ancient oaks, which had somehow survived, were yellow-green with new leaves, and in the sand was an occasional quick movement and quiver of a lizard. It was a world that had been here for centuries, quietly living, and we were just starting to notice it.

Mere walked in unannounced into Paul Smith's plush council office and sat down opposite Smith, who stared at him like a rabbit facing the fox.

'What the hell are you doing here?' he demanded.

Mere smiled. 'You're a council official and I have every right to see you. I've been paying for you twice over – rates, and the other.'

'You know how stupid it is to be seen here with me?' Smith looked around him, a hunted look in his eyes. What did he expect to find? People crouched in the wastepaper basket, or hiding behind doors? It had occurred to him of late, that he must be very careful not to drop himself in it with any further misconduct.

'It's okay,' said Mere. 'I swept the area for bombs. It's called a double-bluff. Everyone thinks I should be keeping a distance from you, so if they saw me in your office, they would think, 'Well, he hasn't got anything to hide'.'

'I still think it's asking for trouble.'

Mere shrugged.

'Anyway, what do you want?' Smith said.

'I want my money back. And you are going to return it.'

'I provided a service and for that you pay.'

'And I should very much think so too,' came a familiar voice as the door opened. Mrs Little walked in. Both men looked at her in amazement.

'How the hell did *you* get in?' Smith demanded.

'Oh, I still have friends in this place,' she answered. 'Who are prepared to turn a little blind eye.'

'What do you want?' Beads of sweat broke out on Smith's upper lip.

'Oh, I think when you hear this, you'll understand,' said Mrs Little putting the dictaphone on the desk and pressing the 'play' button. And there were their voices, thin but unmistakeable, coming out of the machine. Smith and Mere arguing over the spoils, wanting money returned, not giving sweeteners back, all the work Smith had done. Paying for what exactly? Mere's voice. No planning permission through, no deed of sale, just ever more ridiculous schemes from Smith to get rid of the Manpower scheme and destroy their credibility.

'It's all there,' said Mrs Little. 'You went through it in such detail.'

'But Hermione bought that tape off you,' blurted Mere, and immediately knew he had sunk both of them.

'Oh yes, I let her believe you had the only tape. As soon as I realised what I had, I made several copies,' she said. 'Saved them for a rainy day, you might say.'

'What do you want?' Smith repeated.

Alice walked to the nearest town when she could move her arm again. Cookson had pressed money on her which she eventually accepted, after trying to refuse it.

'You knows I'll pay you back when I finds work,' she said.

Cookson nodded.

It took her longer to walk to the next village than she had expected as she was still feeling quite weak, but there was nothing to be found, only people like herself looking for employment. Work would be available during weeding and harvesting, but she needed more than that. She knew Cookson had, in effect, taken her children in. Hannah, the youngest, was nowhere near the age for an apprenticeship but the cook had taken her as her little helper, her pet, and the other two girls were learning skills for service in large houses. That was not what she wanted for them, but what choice did they have?

Walking on to the town in sharp March sunlight, she found herself starting to sweat so she sat down under the nearest tree to cool off. She did not know what work could be found but there had to be something, serving at a tavern, cleaning, taking in washing, but for that she would need her own place. She reached the outskirts of the country town in the late afternoon. She knew she looked like an urchin, for her clothes were dusty and sweat stained her back, her chest and under her arms and she knew she had to clean up before approaching anyone for work. She felt for the coins in her skirts pocket. She had only bought the very basics in food and small beer to keep her walking. However, the money she had would only get her a few days' lodging, and so it was imperative she secured something as soon as she got there.

She found the cheapest lodging over a drover's pub and, asking for water, tried to clean her hair and face and wash out her shift but it was a rough job and she laid the shift out over the window rail to air-dry. It was after she had done all of this that she sank on the little lumpy bed, sitting on the edge with her arms between her knees and her wet hair falling around her thin face, and felt the despair thunder over her like a powerful wave. She had no home, no money and only her daughters kept her from throwing herself out of this window or under the nearest cart. She tried to rally herself, saying to herself that this was the lowest point, that she would get out of it, that she and her family would be back together, they would live in a little cottage somewhere....Somewhere? Where exactly?

She had heard from Cookson and from conversations along the way, that many landowners were enclosing and throwing down cottages on former commons and waste, but as they owned those cottages, they could do as they wished. The evicted did not seem to unsettle their conscience. But Ferris had stolen her property and destroyed it, like a vicious child torturing an animal. She was angry with herself for not knowing how to fight back against him, for feeling so powerless to defend what she knew was hers, and for being unable to react when Ferris rode by on that gleaming chestnut horse and looked down at her and smirked. She had never been treated with much respect by the moneyed classes and had, for the most part, ignored their presence because she was not dependent on them for housing or work. Now Ferris had snatched it all away, and for what? The plot was damp and the house clearly of no use as he had demolished it. Had he really acted solely out of spite? It was incomprehensible to Alice that someone would do that, but then she did not understand people who tormented animals for gratification or beat children for the sake of it. There was a great deal about people she could not fathom, although until the cottage had been snatched from her, she had not had to fully contemplate the damage that mankind could do.

Pulling herself off the bed, she tried to comb her hair with her fingers, but it was still sticky and hung in rope-like hanks even after she washed it. She looked down at her clothes and knew she looked like a beggar. She could not afford to buy new things as the money would run out completely if she so much as bought a new over-skirt. Stepping into the street, she asked the first woman she met if she knew where the nearest washerwoman was. The woman answered her politely, directing her to a back alley.

Alice rapped on the carefully painted door of end-of-terraced house, and at length a short, dumpy young woman answered.

'Yes?'

'I needs me clothes washing,' said Alice. 'How much you charge?'

'You can do them yourself for -' a small amount was given. 'I've got too much on at the moment.'

Alice thought quickly. 'I'm looking for work, washing.'

The young woman considered, then said. 'Have to see what your work's like first.' The first part sounding 'haff ter', in the local dialect.

Alice was led into a small and very clean backyard which had swept flags. It was a sun trap and for a second, Alice's spirits rose.

'Use that tub there,' the woman said, pointing to one in the sun next to some craggy apple trees, which were starting to unfurl fat, light green buds.

Alice looked into the murky depths of the water and shrugging, took off her outer clothes and started kneading them like bread dough. The water turned an embarrassing black very quickly. She was aware of her powerful body odour, drifting up like the smell of old mouse piss. She tied her sticky hair back with her neckerchief and wiped the sweat that was running freely down her face with her hand.

Within half an hour her clothes had been wrung and were dripping from the lines. The young woman came out to inspect her work and Alice could see she was impressed.

'I think your work is good,' she said and gave a small smile. 'You look as though you need to wash. You can use the outhouse. Take the water from the copper.'

Alice stared at her, amazed. She had not expected a crumb of kindness, but now she saw an unlooked-for compassion in the plump face and portly figure of the young woman.

'When you've finished up, you can go to the pie shop for me and get two pies,' she said and pressed a coin into her hand.

Alice frowned at it.

'You look exhausted, if you don't mind me saying. What's happened to you?'

Alice told her and the young woman, called Sarah, shook her head in disgust.

'It's not right,' she muttered. 'Well, mistress, you are welcome to stay with me if you help with the washing, I need a hand and I sense you're a fair person.'

Thus an unlikely friendship arose. Alice vacated her room over the tavern and was given a little back room in Sarah's house. It was a cramped, but scrubbed-clean house and Sarah's husband, a quiet, thoughtful man, an ostler at the town's brewery, was in his early twenties like his wife. They worked from dawn till dusk but the house was hers, Sarah said, left to her by her father, who had built the place back in the early 1700s. Therefore Sarah implicitly understood Alice's rage.

The moneyed classes would get their servants to drop their washing around to this young woman, pushing the basket at her with few words, as they considered themselves rather above such duties and superior to this washer woman. In turn, the moneyed classes thought their servants were, on the whole, little better than animals, and so the class system of England fermented itself in all its twisted tradition. What none of these people could understand was that Sarah was a young woman of unusual sensibility, helped in part by parents who had been poor but exceptionally kind to their only child. When taken around the bustling town with her mother from an early age, Sarah was taught to treat people kindly, not to stare at people who were dishevelled or deformed, to look beneath the surface and try to see a truth.

Of course, the people who pushed washing in her face and dropped bags of coins in her hand, who shouldered past her in streets and averted their eyes in carriages, only saw a dumpy young woman with strong, lye-reddened forearms, and dismissed her as an urban peasant.

Alice's little room was very clean, and the small bed ample for her thin frame. For the first time in weeks she felt warm and comfortable. Day by day, after paying for her board, Alice started to amass enough coin to get to see her children. Sarah had been taught her letters and Alice asked that she write a simple note to Cookson letting him know where she was and what she was doing, and to convey that she hoped to see them one weekend soon when she could spend the day with them. For a moment the heaviness and despair started to recede and Alice's mind started to whirl and consider how she could support herself through taking in washing in and around Stourton, but for the time being, this was enough and she was grateful for it.

Chapter Ten

Mrs Little was pleased that she was now in the position of telling Mere and Smith when she wanted to convene the next meeting. She insisted that it was held at Mere's office at his property development company.

'So it keeps it looking all nice and professional,' she said in the manner of one persuading a truculent child to wear nice, clean socks for school. 'We don't want any eyebrows raised, now do we?' She knew it would make Smith uncomfortable to be seen with Mere like this, which was the object.

Smith and Mere sat mute.

'Now,' said Mrs Little. 'Let's talk terms, shall we?'

Smith looked as though he was sucking lemons, and Mere let out a silent belch and stared at her unblinking.

'What do you want?' Smith snapped at last.

'Oh a little sweetener, little monthly payments of hush money, in cash of course. You can post it through my door. I was thinking of -' she gave a reasonable figure.

Smith snorted. 'Pushing it, aren't you?'

Mrs Little looked at him sweetly. 'I think it's very reasonable, considering.'

'What?' Smith tried to stare her out, but averted his eyes after several seconds. The woman had the eyes of a snake.

'Considering that if I play one of my cassettes to your boss, or to the police, you will be out of a job and in front of the beak in a twinkle.'

Smith worked his mouth but could not form a threatening enough response.

'And what assurance do we have from you that you still won't blab?' Mere asked, slouching back in his chair.

She smiled. 'My good word.'

Smith laughed, cackled rather.

'From you, Mr Mere,' she said, ignoring Smith. 'I want a position in your company as senior secretary, with all perks and allowances.'

Mere only just stopped himself from laughing out loud. Forget it dear, he thought. My secretaries are lookers, and you are most definitely not.

Mrs Little saw the hesitation. 'If I go the local paper with my story and my tapes, I don't think it would be good for you, do you? The public wouldn't buy a new house from a company run by a man who bribes his housing developments through, who uses *fraud.*' She said that last word as though it was among the world's worst perversions. 'I would make it clear what you tried to do. I don't think the police or council would be that happy either.'

Mere thought about it, then, without any emotion, asked. 'How good are your secretarial skills?'

She gave him the resume she had printed in anticipation.

'Well, I suppose we can give you a try,' Mere said. 'See how it works out.' In truth he got through secretaries like assorted chocolates, and this boot-faced lump may in fact be what his firm needed; her secretarial skills were certainly above reproach. 'You can start on Monday at 9am'.'

'I will expect a company car,' she said.

'Forget it, love,' Mere said flatly. 'Remember I've got something on you too. My wife told me all about you falsifying documents. Hermione's got a gob the size of the Mersey tunnel. Important to remember that when you start shooting your mouth off in front of her in future.'

Mrs Little wrinkled her nose. 'I don't like the way you speak to me.'

'Then we're evens,' said Mere, standing up. 'You can start at 9am and you use your own car. Take it or leave it.'

She took it, staring after him with an open-mouthed expression.

Smith watched after him too, thinking, so this is how you do it. Don't back down, or they'll go for the jugular.

'You can forget about me delivering the money to your house-'

'You can fuck off and do what I say,' Mrs Little interrupted, and prepared to leave. 'I've got enough on you to get you locked up for years. My house, envelope, 5.45 pm, the first Friday of every month. Take it or leave it,' she echoed, getting up. 'Or I'll make sure you go down for a *long* time.'

Sarah poked her head out of the back door.

'I'm going up the market. Is there anything you want?'

Alice straightened up from the tub. The lye water was stinging her skin. 'Bit of salve for me skin,' she said, 'if it ain't too much trouble, and would you get a little doll for me youngest?' Alice fished into her skirts pocket and pulled out a couple of coins. 'I'm off to see them this weekend.'

Sarah smiled, waved, and was gone.

Alice carried on beating the clothes in the tub. One perk of this job was that her clothes (the one set of them) looked cleaner than ever. Sarah was generous in letting her use the facilities, was generous all round, in fact. The meals she cooked were well done and large, and the house gleamed clean and bright from her ministrations. If she was on her own, this would not have been a bad life (if somewhat aimless) but with her daughters, she knew she must do better. Get something of her own which they could help her with. A letter written by Cookson had arrived only that week. The girls were doing well and were happy, and often asked about her. It was receiving this letter that made Alice decide to visit them that coming weekend.

Sarah returned from the market and handed her a colourful rag doll and also the coins.

Alice frowned.

'A little gift from me to your daughter,' Sarah said. 'You use the money to help with your journey over there.'

Alice was going to insist she took the money, but the firmness in Sarah's expression quietened any argument.

When they sat in the back yard for a drink of small beer later that morning, Sarah told her about her family. Her father had worked in a brick-making yard on the edge of town and was able to buy bricks cheaply that were not top grade, but still good. Buying a small piece of land, he built his house when the speculator, who owned the brickworks, built this row. It was a simple thing to tie them in as they were erected at the same time. Her father also had to work on the row but would carry on with his build after day's end.

Hugh and I were called in to see Jon Blake as the seasons moved into June, a beautiful riotous month with creamy hawthorn blossoms in rows along the former moor, the same hawthorns indeed that Ferris had paid over the odds to have replanted.

'I've been really very impressed with the findings that have been coming through from your research,' said Blake. 'I know we have agreed on a big presentation in November, but how would you two feel about doing a smaller presentation to the vendors? Just to show them what you've found and what a seriously interesting place it is.' Blake was looking at us, hopeful.

Hugh looked to me and I nodded at him.

'We'd love to,' Hugh said. The phrase 'the royal we' floated stupidly through my mind.

'What length of presentation?' I asked.

'About forty minutes.'

We nodded.

Blake pulled an awkward face. 'Paul Smith has suggested that you also tidy Blackman's Moor, of the litter. Apparently, he looked over there the other day and was complaining about the litter in the ditches and the dumped furniture and so on.'

Hugh rolled his eyes. 'Well, thankfully the white goods and three piece suite were taken away a few days ago.'

Blake hesitated. 'I'm afraid someone's dumped a broken dining room table and chairs on the lower moor this morning.'

'Lend me a chainsaw and I'll cut it up. I can use it in our wood-burner at home.'

'Would you?' Blake asked, and I could see the relief in his face.

'And give us bags, protective gloves and grabbers, and we'll clear the litter,' I said.

Blake smiled at us. 'Thank you both, I hoped you'd be okay about it.'

'I care about that moor,' Hugh said, facing Blake. 'It's become personal.'

'Same here,' I said. 'I take it as an insult when someone dumps stuff.'

'Would you ask Craig if he would like to be involved in making the information boards? The graphic department are very impressed with his work,' Blake said as we were getting up to go.

'Of course,' Hugh said and smiled, the smile reaching his eyes.

As we walked down The Resounding Corridor I honestly did notice a spring in Hugh's step and I thought, so that's one of the aspects of love: being delighted when the person you love is complimented.

As soon as we reached our office, he was on the phone to Craig, relaying the news, and the big smile on Hugh's face as he listened to Craig's replies really did light up the rather gloomy office we worked in.

Just before anyone thinks this project was all about running around doing historical detective work, photographing and recording rare fauna and flora on sunny days, let me describe our day clearing the litter out of the ditches, all with their layers of decomposing or sun-bleached plastic, paper, tin and glass. Craig ploughed into it as he might into a rugby scrum, while I used the grabbers like tweezers to start with and very carefully put the garbage into bin liners held at arm's length, earning me the nickname of Margo from Hugh, who spent most of the time complaining about what he was finding. The stink coming up from these ditches made us gag. It was one of those blustery, rain-laden June days. We put the bags on to the car park near the possible retting pool, from where they were to be gathered by a council truck at the end of the day. We were just depositing our tenth bag, when the publican waved us over.

'You come to the pub and have a drink on us!' he shouted.

We went straight there, choosing hot chocolate and coffee over beer as we were surprisingly cold.

'Been asking the bloody council to clear this place up for years,' he said, placing the mugs down. 'Why people think this moor is a dump is beyond me. I try and pick litter up when we walks the dog, but it's only a drop in the ocean.'

I looked up at the wall as he spoke and, before my eyes, I saw Alice's face materialising in the panel opposite me, the eyes still cast down in great sorrow. I saw Craig rub the back of his neck, and shiver involuntarily. I knew she still had something to tell us.

When Ferris next went back to Stourton, he was surprised at how little had been done to his land. Weeds were starting to appear haphazardly amongst the long lines of green. The farm manager had sent word that his attendance was required, but had not elaborated.

'What the hell's going on here?' Ferris demanded of Cookson after consulting with his land agent, and stopping Cookson as he crossed the square.

'I beg your pardon?' he said, looking up. There was a hard, slightly contemptuous expression on his usually kind face. 'I am not your servant, Sir, and I suggest you do not speak to me in that tone in future.'

Ferris visibly jumped at this, and he could feel the small flares of heat in his cheeks.

'Then I beg your pardon, Sir. But I see that my fields are being left untended. Why are the men on the Poor Rate not out there weeding?'

Cookson stared up at him. 'Those on poor relief have been allocated elsewhere,' he said. 'Half of your day labourers left last week. They've gone to seek better wages in the towns. Didn't your land agent tell you?'

'But they can't have gone!'

'I think you'll find they can. What did you expect them to do, when you reduced their wages?'

'I did that for a few weeks to show them there's a consequence to their acts of vandalism.'

'And they've answered back, in like mind.'

'Go and get them back!' Ferris ordered.

'No,' said Cookson. 'As I have already said, I am not your servant. Nor your agent.' With that he turned his back to Ferris and crossed the road.

Ferris rode over to the stables. The horses had been fed and mucked out, but there was an eerie quiet about the place, when normally the stables were a scene of noise and activity.

'You, boy!' said Ferris to a small shadow lurking behind a pillar. 'Come here.'

The lad, a child of about six years old, peered up under a fringe of brown hair.

'Where have all the grooms gone?' Ferris bent down to the child.

'They gone.'

'*Where?*'

'Away.'

'What did they say?'

The boy stood bolt upright and put his finger to his cheek, deep in thought. 'A man said you were a... haws son,' he recited with great care. 'That he hopes you get the clap, but you probably got it already.'

Ferris froze, then leaning forward swiped the air with his riding crop. '*Get out!*' he roared.

The boy ran.

Peasants! thought Ferris, and realised he would have to demand that men be taken off the Poor Rate and work for him. He would need Cookson to help with that, but the coldness with which Cookson had greeted him made Ferris shiver. He took the saddle and tack from his own horse and fed and watered it, and even brushed it down. The horse nosed him affectionately, and, for a moment, Ferris felt something like an overwhelming despair crash over him.

To begin with, it had been a fairly easy walk in the March spring sun when Alice started out from the town. She rose with the dawn and was out walking on the road as the sun rose, a perfect, deep orange disc. She could not afford to take even the lowest priced seat on a carriage, but had not wanted to say anything to Sarah as she knew the girl would have pressed more money into her hand. No, she would surprise them at Cookson's. She could not wait to see their surprised faces and feel their happiness when she walked in. The birds were singing and on the winter twigs, little suggestions of bright green were appearing. Lovely, pure white skeiny clouds laced the sky.

After a few hours, she hoped that a wagon would offer a lift, even if it was only for a mile or two, but none stopped. Indeed there were unaccountably few on the road. The sun was feeling quite strong now and she eased her kerchief a little looser. By mid-day the back of her heels were being grated raw by her boots. The woollen stockings she wore had finally holed at the back so she sat on a boulder by the road and eased her feet out. They were bleeding on the heels and from around her small toes on each foot. She sighed. This had been a mistake. As in answer to her pleas a large wagon creaked to a stop.

'Jump on the back, Mistress!' called the waggoner. 'If you're going to the next village.'

She hopped up, repeating her thanks. At the next village the waggoner set her down. Alice looked at the curdling, bruise-grey clouds lumping together in the west. Wetting her finger, she held it up to the sky and realised the wind was blowing from that direction. She was still a long way from Stourton, and it must now be early afternoon. At the very next farm or cottage she came across she would ask if she could pay for lodging, and this thought gave her a renewed energy to carry on, which she did, but over the next hour she became slower and slower as her boots grated against her bloody skin and nerves of her heels and toes.

Several times she took the boots off and ripped up parts of her neckerchief and tried to stuff them behind her heels but the cloth slipped away almost immediately. Then the sole of one boot peeled away at the toe end and flapped as she tried to walk. Sitting on the side of the turnpike, she held her face in her hands and wept. The clouds were coming in, big with snow, and had an ominous yellow tinge to them. An icy wind was also picking up. It shouldn't be doing this – it was late March. This was January weather.

The sun had gone some time ago, and now there was a freezing wet feel to the air. She limped on – the sole flapping uselessly and her foot starting to go throb with pain from the cold. The wind was against her and the evening had fallen early because of the lumpen snow clouds that had darkened the day by five thirty. As the snow started to drive at her, no wagons or other traffic came along the turnpike. She felt as though she was burning to death with the intense cold. Her feet now felt frozen solid to the soles of the thin boots and were so painful it made her want to vomit, and her hands in woollen gloves throbbed with the intense cold. She knew she must not stop, must not sit down.

Somewhere along this road a house light would emerge, but all she could see now was black, increasing black, a deepening, deadly dark. Then she remembered she had not eaten all day and found the food she had stuffed in her pockets. If she just sat down for a minute she could eat it and it would give her the strength to reach Cookson's house and her daughters.

Hermione had taken to visiting the wine bar on her own. She went at school closing time, knowing that her few female friends would be picking their children up and it would be several hours before work people stopped by with a friend for a glass or two of chardonnay before going home. She often wondered why she sat in here when she could drink better wine at home and for free. It had started when she set up the latest group which had disappeared like water into desert sand. No-one in authority had taken them seriously, and the places which used to put up her flyers now politely refused them. So she had taken to drinking in the middle of the afternoon, beginning to wonder where it had all gone wrong.

It would be the school holidays soon and her children would be barging back into her life, speaking with those affected little voices and saying 'Oh *Mummy*!' in exasperation and rolling their eyes when it turned out she didn't know where this country was, or what was the capital of that. Who cared anyway?

Just look it up in an encyclopaedia. Her mother had bought the kids a big, expensive set one Christmas between the two of them, and the children had wept with rage. The books had stayed on the shelves in the hallway, unopened, as pristine as the day they arrived. She had thought about opening them once or twice, but there never seemed the time or reason, and she would guarantee that if she read the bloody things from A to Z, they would still ask her something that was not listed. So what was the point?

Mrs Little was getting rather used to the money she found pushed under the door once a month when she returned from her well-paid job at Mere's property development offices. She had not been too greedy in the amount she had requested and it looked as though Smith was going to carry on complying. For how long did one blackmail? A few months, a year, for ever even? It was not as though you could ring up a helpline and ask, was it?

Mr Little was an early-retired man in his sixties who acted like an old person to get out of a host of chores and duties when she was at home; he also knew nothing about this money. When she was out, he would fairly ballroom-dance around the house, doing whatever he liked. And when she returned from work, he would once again became crabbed with age and agues. Fortunately, she preferred working to being with him, so the situation suited both very nicely. The increasing amount of money in her bank account had pleased her, so all-in-all Mrs Little was quite jolly.

The morning after the dramatic snowfall was the first day of spring, and Stourton woke to the unearthly, muffled silence of thick snow cover. The children left in the small town played outside, making snowmen and throwing snowballs at each other. It would have been a perfect Christmas scene, with a deep blue sky and a shining sun which was unusually warm considering the white landscape. Cookson walked out from his house and greeted the children, whom he had known from babyhood, and he looked to them like a favourite grandpapa.

Cookson greeted the ladies sweeping their doorsteps, but did not see Ferris, who had hauled his horse out of sight of the square and now hid in the deep, freezing shadow of a tall house. That was what his life felt like now: one of keeping hidden, staying away, creeping around and not drawing attention. Ferris had hired labour for his weeding through his land agent and they worked with the Poor Rate men, who worked heads down and angry, and stared hard at him as he pranced by on his gleaming horse. Ferris had to get used to ignoring them. In fact he would have to get used to the whispers and the shouts after he rode by. They had taught him what they could do, and he did not know if he could afford to patch the destruction up all over again, especially as he was losing more at the gaming tables, loss chasing loss, as he drank more spirits and woke up next to women he could not even remember fornicating with.

Hermione looked out onto the same location, now the scene of the 1960's brutal architecture. Where Cookson's house had been was now the site of the wine bar with its rexine seats and wipe-clean tables, its false ceilings and plush carpets. But two hundred years earlier it was to the old Georgian house on this site that a message was delivered. Cookson opened the paper up, recognising its child-like handwriting from the previous notes Alice has asked Sarah to send. Then his face fell.

Dear Mr Cookson,
Do please excuse me for writing to you but I am most anxious to know if Mistress Alice Heath is still with you? I was expecting her to arrive back with us on Monday, but now it is several days after and she has not arrived. She decided to visit her daughters last weekend as a surprise and she set off by sunrise Saturday last. The snow storm over here was terrible and I hope it was not the reason for her not returning. Would you let me know if she is with you?'
Your most sincerely,
Sarah Jones.

Cookson felt his heart contract. Alice had not let him know she was arriving; her daughters certainly did not know. The way the weather had swept in late on Saturday afternoon with glacial night when it should have been day had astounded him.

Immediately instructing his man servant to saddle up his horse, he rode out along the turnpike road on the bottom third of the moor. It would be the only sensible way back to Stourton, especially as the weather had changed so violently.

The snow was still on the ground as the cold had remained, and only the roadways were clear from the rumblings of carts and other traffic, but, as the sun was starting to melt the smooth whiteness, the countryside started to appear, little by little. From his vantage point he could see either side of the turnpike.

After going up and down the road for several miles, Cookson found Alice by the side of a small copse, about a mile from Blackman's Moor. In an almost perfect drift of snow, like blown icing, he saw a piece of material appearing from the drift as it began to melt with this renewed sun's vigour. Jumping down and securing his horse to a tree, he scrabbled at the drift as though he was possessed.

When he uncovered her, he brushed the snow from Alice's brow and she looked as though she was only sleeping. Her eyes were shut and she had her arms clamped around her. She lay in a foetal position. It was as though she had just drifted into sleep. Cookson pushed the black hanks of hair that obscured the side of face and her skin was yellow, hard and so cold. Picking her up, he looked around desperately for help, but, as so often for this woman, there was none at hand.

The wintry landscape was empty and it was as though spring had vanished again. He took her to The Royal Oak coaching inn and with the help of the landlady, laid her thin, work-straitened body on the table at which coroner's courts were convened, and at which her inquest would be held. The landlady took off Alice's boots and cleaned her bloodied feet and wept silently, without trying to hide her grief. Before Cookson left Alice, he cradled her head against his and tried to say sorry, but the words stuck in his mouth, and he wept.

Death by accident was recorded later by a stern coroner after Cookson had given evidence. A number of people were there to report that Alice had been forced to seek work away as she had been made homeless by the lord of the manor, who, the coroner noted, had not bothered to attend the hearing.

Death was by freezing. The unexpected nature and timing of the storm could not have been predicted. As the lady was so thin, she would not have had much in the way of reserves to keep warm and she probably froze quickly, and the coroner hoped, knew little about the process.

Alice was buried at Cookson's expense alongside her husband in Stourton churchyard the following day.

The next day Hermione was asked to leave the wine bar by the manager, a beanpole of a youth of early twenties.

'Now I've bought this shit from you,' she sneered. 'I'll bloody well sit here and finish it. *Okay?*' She said the last word into his face, holding the bottle behind her, like Christopher Robin trailing Pooh Bear behind him, the manager thought, incredulous at why he was thinking that.

Hermione had taken two of her power pills earlier and now she took another two, or was it three? She was the Battle Maiden of Stourton, she whooped as an odd rage descended upon her.

As she had only just cracked open the bottle of wine, the manager realised she was going to be there for some time if she had her way. Moving towards the back office, he felt for the phone and its long cord. Dialling the number he whispered into it, requesting that the police attend a drunken customer.

'Do you know who it is?'

'It's Hermione Mere,' the young man said. There was a long-suffering groan on the end of the line,

Through a fog of drunkeness she heard the click of the receiver and bolted down the stairs, the speed of her descent throwing her through the swing doors.

Here she got her balance and saw Winfield, Lyle and that Manpower young woman coming towards her. They were talking and laughing happily. She wondered why they were out of school.

Swaggering, she crossed over the road and, raising the bottle over her shoulder, smashed the thing right at Winfield's face with full force and he fell backwards, hitting his head on a concrete lamppost, and then sprawled sideways. The next thing she knew, she was being held on the ground like an animal, and she kicked and bit the hands and arms trying to restrain her.

The bottle had flown so unexpectedly and so fast there was nothing Craig or I could do to get Hugh away in time, and he flew back as though he had been shot, hitting the back of his head on a lamppost and then fell sideways onto shards of the broken bottle.

We had all been in good humour as we had just given the presentation to the vendors, who were keen to sell the moor to the council as a nature reserve and amenity area for the public.

As Hugh crumpled like a rag doll, Craig fell to his knees, trying to help him, trying to get the glass away from his eyes, stem the blood from the glass cuts in Hugh's face and forearms, but instead the blood oozed over him and through his hair, obscuring his expression.

Several people were screaming and many had rushed back into shops and were phoning 999 on managers' telephones. Hermione Mere was dragged away fighting. People were trying to help Craig, who sat on the ground in Hugh's pooling blood, holding him against his chest to stop him falling on to the pavement. When a policeman crouched in front of him, I thought Craig might not let the officer touch him, but he did. The policeman held his finger to Hugh's jugular pulse and nodded to his companion.

'Pulse and breathing, but out like a light,' he said into his service radio. There was more static and voices, and then an ambulance tore down the road, blue lights streaming and siren deafening as it drew up against us. The paramedics gently disentangled Craig from Hugh, whose blood flowed freely now down the pavement, red, shocking blood that collected in the gutter, then dripped into the drain, pooling for an instant to reflect the late afternoon sun.

The ambulance crew got Hugh on a stretcher. Craig was staring wildly and I explained to the medics and a policeman that he was Hugh's partner, and the police officer seemed to know. They helped him into the back and asked if I wanted to go along to assist him. I nodded at once.

They worked on Hugh with lines, clamps and monitors all wired up. An oxygen mask obscured most of his face.

Craig was sitting, covered in Hugh's blood and shivering, yet also sweating; his face was ghastly whitish-grey. One of the paramedics was trying to talk to him, taking his pulse.

'Needs something for shock here,' she said to her companion. She measured a liquid from a bottle into a syringe and Craig just sat there staring as she injected it into his arm.

'Can you stay with him, love?' the paramedic asked, 'When we get to the hospital?'

'Of course....Will he be all right-' I dissolved into tears, hot embarrassing tears that no-one in this crisis needed, and it was like trying to drag back a bolting horse as I fought to control myself. In answer the paramedic gave a non-committal movement of her hand. It was then that the terror dissolved me.

The next moment the ambulance stopped and the doors were flung open and Hugh was taken out and wheeled quickly into A & E. I stared after it and my bladder nearly gave when I thought we might never see him again.

I reached for Craig. He was being steadied by two nurses who asked me who I was. I told them that I was a good friend of both of them. I gave them their first names and surnames and their address, and Craig was taken to a curtained cubicle.

I told the nurses through the curtains that I was just going to ring my husband and I would be back in a moment. I checked my hands. They were covered in Hugh's blood. Running into the Ladies' toilets, I washed the blood away, wiped my front with paper towels, then ran down the corridor to where there was a range of phones under large plastic hoods. It took me several goes to get our home phone number right, and, when Chris answered, I tried to speak, but broke down. Chris, darling Chris said:

'Are you at the hospital?'

'Yes,' I screeched.

'A&E?'

'Yes.'

'Do you need clothes?'

'Yes.'

I almost fell away from the phone, not caring who saw me crying.

They let us in to see Craig after a while. To my surprise he was on a drip and fast asleep. I knew that was the kindest state for him to be in.

'Is he diabetic?' a nurse asked.

I frowned.

'With type 1 diabetes he would need to inject insulin every day,' she said, trying to help.

'I honestly don't know,' I said.

'We'll check his records, don't worry,' she said, seeing my distress.

'Hugh, how is he?'

'Having a scan.'

'*Why?*'

'To make sure he's not bleeding in the brain.'

The look of horror on my face made her move back a little.

'You saw the attack, didn't you?'

I nodded.

'The police are here. They'll need to speak to you.'

They interviewed me for over an hour. I sat in a small room with a dazzling overhead light and a headache splitting my brain as I tried to tell them what had happened. It was so split second, not even a sound in the air, just a sharp thud, an explosion of glass and then Hugh falling down like a puppet with its strings cut.

But it all seemed to happen in an underwater slow motion too, I remember falling back, with my arms outstretched behind me, Craig on the ground, Hugh's blood seeping through his blonde hair as he held him. The dreadful momentary silence that seemed to go on forever. Then a mad flurry of activity.

I remembered a scream of 'You dirty bastards!' just before the bottle hit and chaos descended with shouts and people running in and out of shops.

I asked the police to go with me to Craig and Hugh's house, so I could get their dogs and take them back with us. A very young police officer agreed to accompany us.

Then I wanted to stay, to sit by Craig's bedside. I begged, but a kind, older nurse explained that he was probably going to stay asleep until next morning as his body needed time to get over the diabetic shock, and the other shock.'

'Hugh?'

'Still having scans. We'll ring if there's any change. Do you know details about next of kin?'

'They are each other's next of kin.' I said.

'I mean parents, brothers and sisters,' she explained.

'*What*?'

'It's a formality, sweetheart,' said the older nurse.

I looked in my address book which I always carried. Hugh had given me his brother's number as a contact when they had had the 'flu. My hand shook so violently when I held out the book, Chris had to steady it.

We got home by eleven thirty that night and Chris sat up with me until dawn, while I shook and sobbed, then eventually sank into sleep at around four in the morning.

Blake let me take the following two days off work. I went to the hospital as soon as I had showered the next morning. Chris asked me to let him know how they both were, to give them his very best regards, and to tell them the dogs were fine.

Almost running to the desk of the ward Craig had been on, I explained who I was and was let in briefly.

I can't put it into words how delighted I was to see them both sitting up and awake, in hospital beds, side by side. I felt a rush of emotion because they were safe, and because the hospital had the humanity to do that when they had so much else to contend with.

I spoke to a nurse at the ward desk.

'Oh, we had to bring Hugh up on the ward, just to keep him quiet,' she confided and gave me an ironic smile, and I could well imagine what she meant.

I beamed at them as I went over, not knowing who to hug first, and, with Hugh, how to hug him as his face and forearms were a bit of a mess with butterfly stitches and bruising. He had two spectacular black eyes forming.

'I broke my nose,' he said in a somewhat muffled voice. 'Hence the black eyes.'

Craig was sitting up in bed. Both were wearing hospital gowns, which made them look oddly vulnerable.

'Hugh came round after about forty minutes,' Craig said. 'Which they tell us is a very good thing for the long term too.'

'The longer you're out, the worse the outlook,' Hugh said, then looked at Craig. 'Have I got that right?'

Craig looked at him, affectionately. 'Yes, that's about it.' Grinning at me, he added 'Hugh was being such an awkward sod in Recovery, that they whipped him up here to get him to shut up.'

'When are you coming out?'

'I'm coming out this afternoon; Hugh will have to stay in for a few more nights for observations.'

'Will you come and stay with Chris and I until Hugh's out?' I asked. 'The dogs are already with us.'

Craig considered for a moment, then said. 'That's very decent of you, and yes I will. Thank you!'

I thought of the ghastly grey of his face in the ambulance and asked. 'Are you diabetic?'

'Yes. Type 1,' he said. 'Injections every day.'

'You turned a very nasty colour in the ambulance.'

'Shock, stress can bring on an attack,' he said. 'But they got me in time. Which is why I was here to give face-ache a welcome.'

'*Craig!*' I squawked.

Craig leaned over and just reached Hugh to pat his arm and said in a daft voice 'Knows I'm only joking.'

Hugh turned sideways and stuck his tongue out at him. I took a closer look. The bruising was coming out strongly, blacks and dark purples, giving him a strange panda look.

'They set my nose when I was under,' he said. 'Luckily only the bridge was broken,'

Only?

'If you break it further down it dislodges the septum and it can mean an operation at a later stage,' Hugh said. 'Hurts like fuck though.'

Nothing much wrong with Hugh's computer memory, I thought.

I was ushered out by the same nurse and arranged to pick Craig up later, after the doctor had seen him.

Cookson could not avoid crossing Ferris' path a few days after Alice's funeral. At first it looked as though Ferris was going to avoid him, but instead he drew up and, unusually, he dismounted.

'I was sorry about Alice Heath,' he said, jiggling the reins in his hands, which Cookson realised were sweating.

Cookson looked at him and was surprised at how ill he looked close to. There was a ghastly pale grey hue to his skin and he had bluish grey bags under his eyes, which looked as though he was wearing round spectacles or had black eyes from a distance.

'The snow must have caught her out,' Ferris stated.

Cookson remained quiet, just looking.

'Does seem a rather foolhardy thing to do,' Ferris continued. 'To walk so far.'

'She had no choice. She had no money.'

Ferris scratched his head. 'But why was she out on the road walking towards Stourton, as I understand it?'

'She had to find work in a town and I apprenticed her daughters. She was walking back to see them. She had a small rag doll she was bringing over for them,' Cookson said. 'She was holding it when she died.'

Ferris looked away. If he could change it all, he would, but he could not. It was all too late. Scratching his head again, he mounted his horse with one expert move.

Hesitating, he looked down at Cookson.

'What is it Ferris?'

'I would be obliged if you would refrain from telling anyone else that I evicted her,' he said, clearing his throat nervously.

Cookson stared up at him. 'I will of course not mention it, but I think you should understand that it has been generally known for several weeks now.' There was no anger in his voice, no contempt, just a world-weariness which made Ferris wince.

Hermione was held in jail for four nights. Her husband refused to sign any bail or cooperate so that she could return home. Mere's life seemed to be imploding quietly all around him. Smith said there was nothing more he could do to help him secure the moor, and his last ploy of getting the Manpower spongers, as he called them, to clear litter from the site, his equivalent of them shovelling shit, had also backfired. Blake and the vendors had been deeply impressed with their commitment and feeling of personal concern for the place, that they cared so much that they had worked on into the evening to get the job done. Smith had heard about the presentation to the vendors that Winfield, the girl and the long-haired yob had given just before the attack, the latter showing slides he had taken, which were of stunning quality.

The sale had been agreed with the council and the vendors had even offered to finance a book written by Winfield and Charlotte and illustrated by Lyle. As Mere pointed out, everything Smith had done had, in effect, strengthened the case for Blackman's Moor becoming a place of interest in terms of its natural history and history. Mere might have just as well have given them a grant to do the work to undermine his bid.

Craig was the perfect house guest, knowing when to give Chris and me time alone, and when to join us watching the television. For the first day I accompanied him walking over Blackman's Moor with the dogs, worried he was going to have another diabetic 'episode' as the hospital put it. The evening before going back to work, I sat with him and asked if he was safe enough to be on his own as I had to return to work. Craig looked at me with unusual seriousness. 'That was a complete one off,' he said. 'I've had diabetes all my life and I know what to do, and what not. So please stop worrying.' The firmness in his voice reassured me. 'Anyway Hugh's coming out tomorrow, so I have to get the place ready.'

Craig invited Chris and me over after work for a 'Welcome Hugh home cup of tea/beer/wine and cake celebration', which was conducted in the back garden of their house. It was a reasonably-sized garden but overlooked, and I understood Hugh's comment from months ago about being constrained and confined, but that evening they seemed completely unaware of the lines of houses set in a terrace up a bank overlooking them, and the clanks and daily chore sounds from next door. It was an interesting garden with a variety of deciduous trees made into hedges, a flower bed with bright summer flowers and a paved area where we sat. The rest was over to lawn.

Hugh was in high spirits but his face was heavily bruised around the eyes and the butterfly stitches down his right cheek were still there and looked painful as did his forearms which had been cut. Every so often he winced and, when asked if he was all right, fobbed it off with 'the stitches are pulling' or 'I'm sure the bridge in my nose just moved.'

'We're taking Hermione Mere to court, in addition to the police prosecution,' said Craig. 'After she ruined our business we were so crushed by her hate campaign that we just hadn't got the fight in us, but now, after this,' he added pointing to Hugh's injuries. 'I realise we have to do something. The woman's crazed and this could have been a bloody sight more serious than it was. Brain damage, or worse.'

I nodded. 'Yes, she's got to be stopped.'

'Our solicitor, the one who dealt with the Cease and Desist case, says we've a rock solid case of libel and the ruination of our business,' Hugh said. 'As well as a case of ABH or even GBH, though the police are dealing with that. She also bit a couple of policemen when she was being arrested, so she's in big trouble.'

Chris shook his head. 'Why does someone act like that? She apparently has everything – big cars, big house, lots of things, doesn't have to work...'

'Empty, vicious mind,' I said.

We sat in the early evening sun, sipping beers and wine, sitting in recliners and looking out over the newly mown lawn and the shrubs and trees and the fat, rounded borders around which the lurcher trio snuffled and rooted. They then erupted into mad bouts of running, sometimes spinning on the spot out of sheer exuberance, the next minute lying upside-down and fast asleep in the sunshine.

I told them about the excellent reception given to our presentation, and that the sale of Blackman's Moor to the council was going through, that it would be safe and used again by the public for recreation, but managed primarily as a nature reserve.

We sat talking about the layout of the forthcoming book, the chapter headings, the balance of illustrations. Fortunately, there was a clear split between us. It was taken as given that Craig would be doing all the illustrations, the layout and design. I suggested that he should write up the archaeology sections too if he wanted.

'Yes. I'd also like to write up what we know about Alice Heath,' he said, as if out of the blue. He looked at me and there, for a moment, was that ghost of Alice's smile on his lips.

Chapter Eleven

On the next rain-soaked day after Hugh had come back to work, we all visited the Record Office, knowing that this might be for the last time in relation to the Blackman's Moor project. While off sick, Hugh had been writing up his research into chapters in the format we had agreed. The bruising to his face had all but gone, but the cuts were still healing and noticeable on his face and forearms even though the stitches had been removed. I noticed he wore long sleeved shirts to cover his arms.

On this day in the archives he was darting from this document to that, checking references, writing down extra notes, checking details with the archivists. The Hugh-Ball was most certainly back.

There were various loose ends I had to tie up and Craig had come along to help. As he opened an archive box he picked up a parchment and began reading it out:

On the morning of - - inst in 1779 the coroner made report of the death of Alice Heath, alias Alys of the Hethe, formerly of Byrd Cottage in Stourton by the lord's waste. She was of the manor of Stourton but recently homeless and searching for work. It is thought she perished in the storm of the 20/21 March when walking back to Stourton to visit her children – her intent in this respect was recorded by Sarah Jones with whom Alice Heath lodged. It is recorded that she was found by the side of the Stourton Turnpike a few days later by Tobias Cookson who, recognising her at once,

*brought her to The Royal Oak Coaching Inn. She died
from freezing. No other hand was recorded and she did
not die by her own hand – death by accident as she did
not mean to die.*

I looked at Hugh and slumped back in my chair; he shook
his head. I could not understand why Alice had not told me
herself, but then I remembered her smile on Craig's lips and
I understood. I made sure we had a good copy of this report.
Craig seemed strangely quiet for the rest of the day, kind as
usual, but without the humour and lightness that usually
surrounded him. Hugh noticed and tried to jolly him up on
several occasions but there was a heaviness we could not shift.
Therefore, we all worked quietly and efficiently, thanking the
staff for their help and promising to let them know when the
presentation was due.

The following day Craig dropped into see us at the office,
putting his head round the door and smiling that broad,
dimpled smile, and I knew he was back.

'Just been to see Blake and the graphics department,' he
said as he sat down. 'They've agreed to do an information
board for Byrd Cottage – I'll use the report Jess the
archaeologist wrote up of the dig. Apologies if I was a bit quiet
yesterday.'

'No need to apologise.'

'Reading the report of that woman dying in the snow really
got to me,' Craig added.

I knew why.

The sale of Blackman's Moor went through within weeks,
with Mere dropping out of the picture completely. Hugh had
been checking facts about the moor's wildlife and flora since
returning to work, but there was a strange detachment about
him during this time, as though wheels were whirring within
wheels, quickly and efficiently but as though he was inhabiting
a lonely but necessary part of himself, which he did not

welcome. When I spoke to him, or asked him a question, he looked as though he had to re-focus for a second or two, and then re-engage.

I knew he and Craig were caught up in their action against Hermione Mere, seeing the solicitor, and also being called to court for hearings to do with the assault case, which the police were bringing and the CPS were prosecuting. I had been called in to give further evidence about the attack. I could see from Hugh's demeanour that it was all constantly on his mind.

I had asked if there was anything Chris and I could do to assist, if talking about what was going on would help. With a kind smile, he momentarily held my shoulder, and said 'Thanks, and I would of course, but this is just one of those ghastly sit and wait ordeals: the law goes at its own unfathomably slow speed. Our solicitor said leave it to him. I just wish I could leave the anxiety with him too.'

'I know how stressful that can be,' I said feeling I had to say something. 'When we were buying our house, I was on the ceiling most of the time.'

'I want you to know what a great support you and Chris have been. How we both really appreciate it.' There was an uncharacteristic wobble in his voice when he said that, and I could sense he really was on a knife's edge.

Thus I was pleased to see Hugh arrive one morning a few weeks later with a perceptible lightness about him, and a relaxed smile on his face.

'Craig and I would like to meet with you and Chris at The Warrener pub this evening if possible, to celebrate,' he said.

'Oh great! Is it...?'

'Rowland Mere is offering to settle his wife's case out of court,' Hugh said. 'Amazingly he's agreed to our solicitor's first suggestion of damages. Wants to keep his name out of the papers as much as possible, apparently. The cheque from Mere, as they say, is already in the bank.'

'Hugh, that's fantastic!' I said. 'Though neither of you should have gone through it in the first place.'

'There's still the assault case, but the police are running that one and I don't feel that involved with it, to be honest.' Hugh gave a short mirthless laugh. 'We weren't even going to proceed with a ruination of business when it first happened – I was far too worried about the effect on Craig at the time - but that stupid woman just wouldn't leave it. There's only so much anyone can take, believe me.'

'Quite right.'

'We'd like to take Chris up on his offer of help to find a smallholding or property in central Wales, close to the coast if possible: Craig loves the sea.' There was the look of child-like happiness on Hugh's face as he said this. I had never seen him look so relaxed since we had met that day in late October the previous year. 'We would also like you and Chris to be regular visitors when we do eventually move.'

I wanted to hug him, but the carapace which he wore like a cloak stopped me, so I just patted his shoulder.

I rang Chris about The Warrener pub visit and he agreed at once. Hugh gave a thumbs-up when I told him, then with his characteristic shift of focus, he announced 'Right, come on Kiddo, back to work – we have a book to write, a presentation to prepare.'

It was a beautifully sunny July evening when we met at The Warrener. It was one of those peach-coloured evenings when motes of tiny insects dance in shafts of sunlight, and the short days and dreary cold of winter seem a distant memory. The lurcher trio came along and we sat at picnic benches as the dogs lay upside-down enjoying the sun. The garden was mostly lawn with dried-out board fencing. Drab, but at least it was a sun trap.

Craig was sitting opposite, looking too big for the bench but with a friendly smile on his face. It was at that moment that the pain of their leaving in the not-too-distant future hit me full-force, and nearly winded me. I pretended to fuss one of the dogs, hiding my face as I forced the emotion down. I could not at that moment think of the time before them, or of a time without them. It seemed impossible, and it hurt.

'So what's the budget you'll be working with?' Chris was asking.

Hugh gave an amount.

Chris nodded. 'That's a good amount. How much of a renovation job?'

'Updating, not a rebuild or big renovation,' said Craig. 'With my back I need to sleep in a bed at night, not roughing it.'

'Yes, that's important,' said Hugh.

Craig had the sort of build that you would expect would find physical work a breeze, but I had been witness to the many times when we were out in the field or in the Record Office, when he had to stand up, or stop and ease his spine, his face sometimes contracted in sudden pain. It was in later years that I was to understand fully, when I too had herniated discs and the sudden pain would leave me cold and nauseous, even take my breath away. Never once during these times was Craig short with anyone, or sarcastic, as I would be with pain, but stoically bore it, giving a 'phew' and an eye-roll when it was all over.

'We'd also like a fair-sized garden, south-facing if possible, outbuildings that can take book stock. A field or two even,' said Hugh.

The landlord came out and, leaning over, shook our hands.

'Me and me wife are so pleased the moor's going to be saved,' he said. 'And you wouldn't believe how many others are too. So the next round's on the house.'

Chris surveyed Hugh and Craig's house and they were pleased with the valuation. They decided to put it up for sale straight away, but knew that the housing market was sluggish in Stourton during the continuing recession. The sight of the For Sale board when I picked Hugh up was like a sharp kick in the stomach. I reasoned with myself to be happy for them, that we would stay in touch, that we would see them regularly, but this pain was visceral and I knew it had to be kept hidden, even from Chris. I longed for the time when it would dull and diminish, but that seemed an impossible amount of time in the future.

Chris found a number of places in Cardiganshire through his colleagues in Wales and we were invited to join them for a weekend stay at a pub in one of the coastal villages to visit the most promising properties. We drove separately as they had the dogs with them.

I have such good memories of driving behind them on the main road through Llangurig to Aberystwyth, with the sun shining and the back window of their car showing the bat-eared and fluffy-eared silhouettes of the dogs as they sat in a row on the back seat. A couple of times we glimpsed an elbow poking out of the passenger window and then Craig's face, with his sun-bleached hair streaming behind him, as he gave us a thumbs-up and a big grin. In response I stuck my head out of the window and poked my tongue out. We then got into a gurning contest, until Hugh must have said something and Craig's head went back in.

'You two are nuts,' Chris said.

This part of west Wales was a place I was yet to discover but, as we wound along the high level main road, I knew instinctively that this was the place for them. Great wide vistas of hills and ancient glacial valleys, of sheep-starred hill pastures. Birds of prey gliding beautifully in the wild skies, and then clouds obscuring the tops of high grazing and threading through conifer plantations like wraiths.

As we turned out onto the coast road, south of Aberystwyth, we caught the first magical glimpse of the sea, and there was the excitement we had felt as children when that smooth horizon of blue stretches out before you suddenly and seemingly forever. I could see Craig turning in the passenger seat and then his head appeared out of the window, so he faced us with a big 'Yeah' expression on his face. I held my thumbs up out of the windows, Chris honking the horn. It was like being teenagers out on our first adventure with friends. Chris and I went down this coast road laughing and talking loudly about the places we were yet to see.

Descending towards Aberaeron, with its harbour stretching out into the sea which was twinkling under the sun, we took a left turn just before the town and were soon driving through a tunnel of ancient oak trees, the branches of which were thick with greyish-green lichen. Here the hills were like swollen downs covered with oak and ash forests, sun-topped and beautiful.

We had picked up the keys along the way from various estate agents. Chris would return them the following week. Confiding that some of the places had been on the market for a year or two, he said there was no rush.

Hugh, being Hugh, found the first property, Ty Coed, with no difficulty. They stopped in a small pull-in at the top of a track and we parked behind them.

'Looking promising,' Craig said as he got out of the car and worked his back. 'Always wanted to live down a track in the middle of nowhere.'

A track it was and it was also a small stream, arched over with grown-out hazel and thorn hedging so it was like walking through a green tunnel. As we picked our way over the stones in the stream with the lurcher-trio on leads we lost our footing as the dogs stopped to snuffle and sniff the undergrowth at unexpected moments. It was then that Hugh realised we had come along an old cart track and the main entrance was a track off a different lane. But I had the feeling we were supposed to come this way.

Craig's sharp intake of breathe made me stop suddenly behind him.

'This is it,' he said, stepping into a meadow at the top of which were old stone buildings running in a range along its length at the back. The meadow was full of wild grasses with an amazing array of seed heads and all sorts of flowers which I had not seen since childhood. The two long sides of the land were higher than the middle where a stream wound at the lowest level (little, if any, chance of flooding the buildings then) and a small tributary met it at forty-five degrees on the furthest side from the house.

The main building had a moss-encrusted stone slate roof and rubble stone walls, which I knew would be many feet thick. The cottage windows needed painting and the paint on the door was flaking, but I could see this was a gem.

Opening the door we were met with a fresh-smelling interior, not the heavy, cloying damp I was expecting. Although the windows were small, it was surprisingly light. Chris and I held the dogs while Craig and Hugh walked around the house. We heard the opening of doors and cupboards overhead, footsteps and muffled talking, occasional laughter, then heavy footsteps coming down the old wooden stairs which Chris said had the original staircase door. They both looked astonishingly happy when they emerged

'Need to see what's outside,' said Hugh, and I had the feeling he was almost not daring to hope.

They were in luck. There were several stone outbuildings with good roofs and dry interiors and cobbled stone floors,

'Perfect for the books,' Craig said as he walked into the second one.

'It looks in good condition,' said Chris, as we walked over the house once again. The dogs were off their leads now and following Craig methodically.

Downstairs there was the big room we had first seen which had a wide, stone inglenook that would easily take a Rayburn or a wood burning stove. There was a small back room with uneven stone walls and old, undulating plaster. Deep grey slate flags were worn smooth with centuries of wear.

'No cracks in any walls,' said Chris, 'That's excellent.'

It had a small window at the back and a larger one at the gable end. It would make a cosy winter room I thought.

There was a big room in front of this, well-lit by several windows. Like the other rooms, it had old unpainted structural beams in the ceilings. Chris examined them, feeling the ancient adze marks and pointing out the carpenters' marks. There was a downstairs bathroom tacked on, as an afterthought by the look of it, in the 1930s.

Upstairs there were three spacious rooms with wide oak floorboards which were smooth and dark brown with age, and the walls seemed to flow and ebb with thick, rounded plaster. Each room had an ancient dormer window. Chris reckoned the building to be at least seventeenth century, possibly even sixteenth century in parts.

The large meadow lawn fronted the house and outbuildings, which were snuggled with their backs against a low bank. Behind, and to one side, were more fields, one thick with thorn and elm saplings.

Craig was bouncing on his toes with enthusiasm and he and Hugh moved off to talk to one side. They were standing sideways to us and facing each other and from the gesticulating and pointing, I could see they were planning in detail what could be done, and how.

As we went back up the stream track, Hugh walked with me.

'We really want this place,' he confided. 'Craig's really excited about it.'

I looked at him directly. 'And you?'

'So much it hurts. I almost don't dare hope.'

We saw the rest of the properties, some of which were suitable, others completely not so, but I could see their hearts were set on the first place, Ty Coed, which I think translated as 'house in the woods'.

We stayed overnight at the pub that Hugh and Craig has chosen because it would accept the dogs. It was a roadside former coaching inn with its back to the sea, green hills billowing above and beyond on the other side of the road. During the night, I could hear Hugh and Craig talking quietly in the next room and then giggling, which reminded me I should be asleep.

Next morning I was the first one down, and I sat outside looking over the beautiful valley, which ranged up to gorse and bracken-covered hills beyond. Hugh joined me carrying a mug of coffee.

'Well, Kiddo,' he said. 'We've decided to put an offer in straight away for the asking price on Ty Coed.'

'Shouldn't you haggle?'

'We want it, and it's very reasonably priced, so why rock the boat? We can buy it outright without needing the sale of the house in Stourton. But we will need that to sell that to cover the updating. Chris will be putting the offer in for us after breakfast.'

I smiled at him and he looked like a little boy just then, almost bursting with excitement. I hugged him, a big hug which, amazingly, he returned, but then he disengaged and turned his face away. When he looked back, I could see his eyes were wet.

'I'm almost too scared to hope,' he whispered.

As we had seen all the properties lined up, and the offer had been put in by Chris and been accepted, we drove down to the long, sandy beach north of Newquay to celebrate. The layered outline of Newquay streets looked like a huge cruise liner docked in the next bay.

It was one of those gorgeous summer days, the type you remember from childhood. As we emerged from the tree-tunnelled path onto Llanina Point, the sea was revealed suddenly with the sun glittering off what seemed to be thousands of wavelets.

As we reached the beach Craig let the dogs off the leads and they exploded over the sand, running frantically in huge circles, dive-bombing each other, and digging wildly, Harry's tail and ears streaming out in the sea breeze. The beach was still fairly quiet and Craig played with the dogs, crouching forwards and running backwards as they yipped and ran in dizzying circles. The next minute he had thrown off his heavy hetal band t-shirt and they were crashing into the water, the dogs running back to the beach but Craig swimming out. Then Hugh pulled off his t-shirt and ran in and they swam and splashed water over each other like teenagers.

When Craig came back in I felt my heart do an unwanted flip. His hair was wet through and was now a reddish fair, and he had a well-toned chest, whispered with light chest hair. I pretended to adjust my shoe as Hugh followed, but glimpsed an equally well-honed body with darker hair. I kept my head down as they dried themselves off with their t-shirts. Thankfully neither Chris nor they seemed to notice my school-girl confusion, and I thought how utterly inept I must appear.

We sat on the sand, enjoying the sun on our skin. Chris had also decided to go in for a dip – he was a strong swimmer; it was only me who could not swim. I saw Hugh and Craig look longingly at the sea again.

'Go on,' I said, and they rushed off towards the waves, throwing their t-shirts in the air like five-year-olds. Retrieving them, I rounded the dogs up, putting them on long leads and they huddled up against me and went to sleep. It is this image of the men in the sea that remains with me down all these years. The splashing, the laughter, the sun catching the myriad drops in the air.

Mrs Little had rather a nice life now. She pootled around Stourton in her new car, bought with the sweeteners from Smith, who had carried on working with the planning department but jumped every time the phone went or the office door opened. Every day he expected to be asked to come in to see the head of department, or to find police officers at his front door, asking him to accompany them to the station and assist them with their enquiries. At 5.30 p.m. on the first Friday of every month he set off for Mrs Little's house and pushed the brown envelope under the door at precisely 5.45 p.m. where it was snatched up immediately. Once she passed Smith in Stourton High Street, driving her shining car and stopped by him, just outside the closed-down bookshop, which was still up for rent.

What a pleasant summer's day it is, Mr Smith,' she said. 'And it's especially nice having such a smart new car with all the mod cons, and all thanks to you!' she added, smiling sweetly. Smith almost ran down the street to get away from her.

Rowland Mere had accepted Mrs Little in his company. She was actually most efficient and ironically his business had increased under her secretarial ministrations, which was just as well as the settlement with Winfield and Lyle had wiped out a big chunk of his capital. Just when he thought that his life might be settling back into some routine, however dull, Mrs Little's head would appear around his office door and say:

'Oh, just a little reminder that I expect another bonus at month's end, just to keep everything nice and tidy, you know.' She would smile that sickly saccharine smile, and he knew, as Paul Smith knew, that wherever he went, Mrs Little would follow, unsettling his days and plaguing his quieter moments. She was the monster you could never vanquish, the stuff of nightmares.

Hermione's father had eventually got her out of custody, and for weeks she pouted and sulked in her own house, appalled that she had been arrested, and angry at Rowland for caving in over the settlement. She regarded her husband as a cowardly moron, along with his numerous other deficiencies. On advice from her solicitor she had pleaded guilty to the lesser charge of actual bodily harm against Hugh Winfield, and was ordered to pay a stiff fine and to do four hundred hours community service at a local charity shop. The judge ordered this high number of hours as he had wanted to jail her for her hate campaigns and assault, but was minded that she was a mother. That she only saw her children for three or four months a year was never mentioned, neither was the fact that they were at boarding school and loving every moment.

She was ordered never to go near to, to write to, or about; never to talk to, or about; or do anything to, or concerning, Hugh Winfield or Craig Lyle – if she flouted any of these restrictions she would go to jail immediately.

Working in the charity shop was the worst experience of Hermione's life. The place smelled, she complained, and the people who came in she viewed as nothing but flea-bitten losers. After a week when the youths on BMX bikes had hooted, whooped and gesticulated at her through the windows with unfailing regularity, and she had served customers with obvious contempt, she was ordered into the back room and told to sort donated clothing, books and bric-a-brac, which she did with obvious bad temper. On returning home each night she rushed up the stairs and ran her daily bubble bath. Thus the weeks passed into late autumn and Hermione Mere stayed trapped in her world of discontented plenty.

Richard Ferris was hardly seen in Stourton now. Half of the newly enclosed land had become untidy with weeds, and each week, more scrub seemed to appear from the sides and spread like a disease, wrote his land agent.

Ferris had been warned by Watts, the surveyor, that areas of the top half of the moor would need extra work if it was to be used for arable. Warned repeatedly, indeed, that it would require a lot of manuring and attention. Of course, the people who knew the land and would have been best suited to working it were the very people Ferris had thrown off when it was enclosed. They had gone to the towns in search of other livelihoods.

At first there were the plants of arable fields that invaded: the pinks of the various willowherbs, and the various yellows of the wild mustards, the hawkweeds and the sow thistles. And then there was the low spread of the thyme-leaved speedwells, and the fumitories with their finely filamented leaves and the dainty, wispy purple-pink flowers, 'earth smoke' someone had called them and they did seem to exhale from the soil, from a different era. Little ash seedlings appeared with the ingress of thorns and a few birch. With the spread of wild grasses it seemed as though the moor was claiming back its own.

At first Ferris had ignored Watts' advice about manuring and building up the soil, and then he could no longer afford to hire an extra workforce to cultivate this area as he was losing more money than he could afford at the gaming tables, largely a consequence of drinking spirits rather than the wines he had once favoured. Day would blur into day, and he would forget about plans for the farm, and forget to reply to his land agent about employing more men to bring the land back to how it had been at the beginning of the season. But none of it mattered much now. The longer he stayed away, the remoter the problems became, and that felt better.

Consequently, over time some of the fences fell and were not repaired, and small animals started to take up residence once again in the thickets and tussocks, and birds began landing on the small twigs of the brush. There was a rustle in the edges and the warble and chatter of birds. The hedge setts were the only aspect of the enclosure that had worked and were now thick and unkempt, home for the birds who returned and stayed, and then thrived and prospered. Birdsong now filled the dawn that had been so strangely quiet after enclosure. Little by little the villagers came back to the land, taking a turf here, cutting a furze there, stealthily at first, and then as if by right. Slowly parts of Blackman's Moor came back to those who remained, and it was as though nothing had changed, except that there in the churchyard lay Alice Heath next to her husband, their headstones commissioned by Cookson, to unsettle those who remembered, and could not say it was as though nothing had happened.

Alice's daughters made loving marriages to kind and attentive husbands, and went on to have happy and long lives, but tinged with sadness for a mother they were not able to save, and a father who had died far too early.

In time Ferris sold up and no-one knew, or cared, where he moved to. Parts of the former moor were later used for enclosed pasture, but the footpaths were saved for those who walked across it, and remembered the old days and the fight there had been for Blackman's Moor.

The poor houses fronting the connecting turnpike were in time taken over by the Poor Rate in Stourton. What had existed of the roof had to be replaced as the inferior timbers had bent out of true. The top three courses of bricks were replaced and all the mortar between the bricks was re-pointed course by course, as the mix had been too weak, and replaced with mortar of the correct type. The interiors of the terraced houses were finished to a comfortable, if basic, standard, and in time some of the displaced families were re-housed and they reclaimed the common rights which were now bestowed on the tenants of each property.

Two hundred and ten years later Rowland Mere got planning permission through with extraordinary speed for the conversion of these six houses to twelve flats. Hoping to attract young, single professionals, Mere had these flats decked out with the latest mod cons and, after marketing them at eye-wateringly high prices, he, at length, took his accountant's advice and flogged them off to those *very* happy, young single professionals for a much lower price, and just about covered his costs.

The sale of Ty Coed went through eventually, after several months, in which Hugh looked saddled with worry and was often remote and uncommunicative. He lost some weight and his face became pinched. It was like witnessing a coiled spring being wound tighter, and not being able to help. Luckily we were busy with the drafts of the book and preparation for the presentation which was to be held in November. Craig had designed the information boards for the talk and helped with the permanent ones that were to be displayed on the moor.

Hugh and I were offered contracts as rangers, to take care of Blackman's Moor and other local amenity areas the council owned. I accepted, and was surprised and pleased when Hugh agreed to his post. As he explained, Ty Coed needed work over a long period, and the house in Stourton was not sold. However, when the council gave us the rangers' uniform of light green shirts, dark green sweat shirts and sorrell-brown cords, the old Hugh re-emerged. Staring in horror at the uniforms, he announced 'We can't wear these! We'll look like the f----ng elves out of Pogle's Wood!'

Craig and he took to spending Friday evening and weekends over at Ty Coed, and each Monday morning Hugh would step into The Water Closet, smiling an all's well with the world. When asked whether they had had a good weekend, he would say 'Brilliant Kiddo, and we want you and Chris over soon.'

The book was launched a week before the talk, and sold out in the local outlets within hours. Hugh and I had to deliver boxes to each shop, and repeat, as every day more were sold. We were given a super write up in the local paper, who gave us a double-page spread with photographs of the most exciting discoveries.

The day of the presentation was a blustery and rainy day. Craig had joined us that morning and asked that we divert to Blackman's Moor with him. I looked at Hugh and he shrugged his shoulders, an 'I don't know either' look on his face.

We walked around to the bog, along the thin, sandy causeway that ran along its western side, past the age-greened sandstone post, past the outgrown hazel coppice, and, just for a moment, I thought I would see Alice and Byrd Cottage, but it was not to be. The footings of the building had been exposed, and in front was an information board with a picture, drawn by Craig, of what the cottage looked like in the 1770s. By the door stood Alice, just as I had seen her. It was eerily accurate. However my eyes were drawn to the final sentence:

In 1777 Alice Heath lived here in Byrd Cottage
with her family.
She loved this place. It was her home.

I felt tears falling down my cheeks, and I knew then that Alice was at peace. We had told her story in the book from the sources we had, and we would reiterate it tonight. I turned to Craig and, embracing him, whispered 'Thank You.'

The presentation was set to start at seven o'clock and we were there at six setting up displays, putting out chairs and displaying the finds which were on loan from the archaeology department. By a few minutes to seven, we had finished.

'We'd like you and Chris to come over to stay for this coming weekend,' Hugh said. 'So we can celebrate the purchase of Ty Coed.'

I nodded at once. 'Love to,' I said as the doors opened and people came in.

The venue was the community centre that Hermione Mere had used in her first hate campaign. But now instead of the hate, we would, we hoped, celebrate; instead of destruction, we would rebuild.

When the chairman of the council introduced us, I felt my heart flip, and suddenly it seemed we were being brought in on a tide.

Hugh presented the findings of the natural history, highlighting the unusual finds, underlining the importance of the so-called ordinary, explaining how all this worked together. Craig operated the slide projector, perfectly timing the pictures with Hugh's words, and his photographs drew intakes of breath at their beauty, clarity and composition.

Hugh explained how we had to create former environments, in the bog, for example, by cutting areas of bare clay, and how scrub had to be removed at times to keep the heather. Then he explained about plant communities and ecological succession in ways that people grasped and nodded their heads in revelatory understanding. I hadn't realised what an excellent speaker he was, how easy he made it seem, when I knew how we had had to strain and work so hard to put this together.

We had checked with Blake that Craig could have the last slot, explaining the archaeology of the place and his findings. So I gave my presentation next. I had dreaded fluffing my words, going blank, or even tripping up when I moved across the platform to point something out on a map, but I didn't. In fact, after a few minutes, when I discussed the wealth of information from the leases of the rabbit warrens, I relaxed into it, felt a little apart, saw myself gesticulating when I explained why the rabbits had been so important to the moor and heathland that we saw today, and how, in many ways, we needed to replicate their work. I told them about the rope-making and tanning industries behind The Warrener public house, and looked up and caught the eye of the landlord and his wife, who beamed at me. I smiled back. I explained about the mill which was involved in the tanning industry, and there was laughter when I tried to explain politely how the tanning process was done. The audience were absorbed with what we said.

Hugh came back and gave another talk about the bog and pool and its prehistoric antecedents and its importance now.

So we continued until it was time to introduce Craig who was given an involuntary applause. Beginning with the prehistoric era, he described the archaeological finds, what they were and what they suggested, and gave a fascinating account of how these things helped us to understand history and the people who lived near or on the moor.

Then he told Alice's story, explained what had happened to her and why she had been evicted. Spoke of the injustice done to this woman and her family, and how we had found the deed which would have saved her house, but which she could not discover in time. There was silence as he talked and described how the plate had emerged in the dig bearing the words 'A & T Jones - therr platte' and the strange feeling of connection he had had when he held the piece. How we all hoped that we had told her story as she would have wanted.

The applause at the end went on and on, and we bowed and joined hands and bowed again, and I saw the happiness light Hugh's face, the smile on Craig's, and I wanted this never to end.

I felt a twitch of Craig's hand in mine and he nodded to the back of the hall. There was Alice, looking peaceful, so happy. Then she looked at us and smiled, and in the next second, she was gone.

The End.